"Do you think it might make her want me back? Doesn't that happen all the time? The one person who's afraid of commitment breaks up and leaves, and then they realize what they've lost, and they beg their ex to get back together!" Willow smiles exultantly. "So, will you help me?" she asks.

When the fog finally clears, I am conflicted. On the one hand, I realize, she's essentially asking me to play a character in a movie she's going to produce for Arden's benefit in order to win her back.

On the other hand, my character would be Willow's Girlfriend. I'd be going on dates with her. I'd be the one who helps her through her heartache. I'd be an accomplice. A trusted ally. And in every rom-com I've ever seen, the fake girlfriend becomes the real girlfriend in the end. Every. Single. Time.

I take a deep breath. "Okay. Let's do it."

Also by Misa Sugiura

It's Not Like It's a Secret
This Time Will Be Different

Love
& OTHER
NATURAL
DISASTERS

Misa Sugiura

HARPER TEEN

An Imprint of HarperCollinsPublishers

HarperTeen is an imprint of HarperCollins Publishers.

Love & Other Natural Disasters
Copyright © 2021 by Misa Sugiura
All rights reserved. Printed in Lithuania.
No part of this book may be used or reproduced in any manner whatsoever
without written permission except in the case of brief quotations embodied
in critical articles and reviews. For information address HarperCollins
Children's Books, a division of HarperCollins Publishers, 195 Broadway,
New York, NY 10007.
www.epicreads.com

Library of Congress Control Number: 2021933331
ISBN 978-0-06-299124-9

Typography by Torborg Davern
22 23 24 25 26 SB 10 9 8 7 6 5 4 3 2 1
❖
First paperback edition, 2022

For my grandmothers,
Mie Sakata, a quick-witted, sharp-tongued
troublemaker who told me stories and made me laugh
and
Sumiko Sugiura, a soft-spoken, brilliant intellect who
taught me to love art and encouraged me to dream

1

IF THERE'S ONE THING I BELIEVE IN, IT'S LOVE.
No matter what the universe throws at you, love will win in
the end—as long as you don't give up. There may be nothing
left of your heart but splinters and cracked cement blocks, but
you have to pick yourself up, dust yourself off, and rebuild. You
can't quit. You can't fall into despair. You have to keep going.

For example: Let's pretend that the girl from your art history elective—we'll call her Helena—she of the short, sleek,
platinum blond hair, hazel eyes, and lips that make your
knees go weak, who's starting Harvard in the fall, and who
has kissed you a thousand times at sunset on an imaginary
windswept moor—shows up at a party you're attending. Let's
say that, fortified by three vodka Jell-O shots and end-of-the-
school-year elation, you walk up to her and tell her that she's

the most beautiful girl you've ever met, and later that night, by some miracle, she finds you under a balcony and kisses you in the shadows until there's nothing left of you but sparkling fairy dust, and in your weakened state, you ask if she wants to hang out next weekend, and her face clouds and she goes, "Ohhh. Um."

And you go, "Oh. Um . . ."

And she says, "Listen, don't get me wrong, okay? You're super sweet. But you're not exactly my type."

And you say, "Oh, right. Of course. I understand," even though you don't. Though, come to think of it, you kind of do. Because she's gorgeous, sophisticated, wildly talented—all the things you're not.

When *that* happens, for example, you can't give up. You have to give yourself credit because hey—you took a risk! You have to say to yourself, "She kissed me, yay!" and swear to remember tonight not as the night you were *rejected* by the girl of your dreams, but as the night you were *kissed* by the girl of your dreams.

And when, even later, you're encouraging yourself under that same balcony and you hear a voice above you saying, "Wait, who?"

And Helena's voice says, "From art history. The mousy Asian one with no sense of style."

"Ohhh, okay. Why, though?" says the first voice.

"Seriously, right? I don't know, I felt sorry for her, I guess.

Whatever. It was fine, actually, but then—get this—she asked me out."

And her friend shrieks and says, "Oh my god, no! She's so . . . blah. It would be like dating wallpaper!"

"*Beige* wallpaper," Helena says, and laughter spills into the night and drips over you like acid.

Even when that happens, you can't give up. You can't go home and crawl into bed and stew in your tears and vow never to leave the house ever again. No. You have to give yourself a mental shake and say, "She's wrong. I am a fun, fascinating human being who does all kinds of fun, fascinating things." You have to ignore that little voice in your head that says, "Am I, though?" and "What's wrong with me?" and "Why am I such a loser?"

Ignore it, I said.

So okay. Maybe it's been a *bit* of a struggle. I may have considered locking myself in my room all summer and burying myself in a queue of movies and a barrel of Red Vines.

But! Then! My uncle Stephen called and asked if my older brother, Max, and I wanted to come live and work with him in San Francisco for a few weeks. Stephen is the director of this private art museum, and he lives in a fabulous house with his husband, Lance, who is an architect and an amazing cook. So instead of rotting under my covers through a summer of isolation in Glenview, Illinois, I'm sitting on a plane on my way to a summer of fun in San Francisco, California. Which goes to show that you should never give up hope.

I gaze down at green hills and rivers, at the endless patchwork of fields punctuated by farmhouses and tiny towns far, far below, and feel a flutter of anticipation. I picture myself strolling on the Embarcadero, or maybe sipping a latte and reading a book in a hip café, or . . . Oh, I know—nibbling on a crusty sourdough roll from some trendy new bakery as I sit on the front stoop of one of those fancy Victorian houses. I'll be with Stephen and Lance, and—no, wait. I'll be with my girlfriend. Yes, that's it. My brand-new, stunning, glamorous . . . I don't care if it's unlikely. It's my fantasy, and I may as well have a girlfriend in it.

I imagine the photos I'll post and the regret that Helena will feel when she sees them. (She doesn't follow me, but you never know. It could happen.) I doze off to pleasant visions of me with a faceless (but gorgeous and glamorous) girlfriend, holding hands and laughing on a trolley at the crest of a hill, the Golden Gate Bridge gleaming in the background—and Helena back in boring Glenview, lamenting through her tears, "Look at her. Why did I let her go? How could I have misjudged her so?"

I wake up with a tiny snort when the plane touches down in San Francisco; Max, thank goodness, is absorbed in conversation with the girl on his other side, and doesn't hear me. I watch as the girl (pale, blond, doe-eyed, named Chloë, probably) giggles and coyly tucks a stray lock of hair behind her ear, then taps her phone as he gives her his phone number. I want to tell her not to waste her time, but I don't. She'll find out soon enough when Max ghosts her.

Max is a junior at University of Michigan. He's tall for an Asian guy, and muscular, with big shoulders and casually messy hair held in place by some über-masculine product that comes in a matte black tube. He spent a lot of time before he left for college trying to convince me that his effortless cool actually came from following some very basic rules that I, too, could learn (running shoes are for nerds; you can do better than jeans and a school-issue hoodie; don't read while you walk), but it seems I was born with an impermeable coating of cool-repellent, and he finally gave up on me as hopeless.

"Why do you keep leading women on like that?" I ask once we're off the plane and out of Chloë's earshot.

"I don't lead them on."

"You gave that girl your phone number. You're leading her to believe you're interested in a relationship when you're not. Hence, leading her on."

"What am I supposed to say? No, you can't have my number, I'm not interested in a relationship? And what makes you think *she's* interested in a relationship?"

"What makes you think she's not? My point is, it's not fair to make her expect something and then not follow through."

"Depends on how you define following through." He leers at me.

"You could be passing up your soul mate is what I mean, you disgusting slimeball."

"Right, whatever, Anne of the Gables."

"Anne of *Green* Gables," I correct him.

"Whatever," he says again. "That show that you always used to make us watch about the nerdy ginger who thought everything was so romantic."

"There's nothing wrong with wanting things to be romantic," I protest.

"Hm." He stares at me appraisingly. Then he shrugs and says, "Figures," and strides ahead.

"Hey! What? What figures? Hey, wait up!" I call after him, hurrying to catch up.

"Your obsession with romance," he answers without breaking stride.

"My what? Why? What's that supposed to mean?"

"It means you're a loser with no life who's never had a girlfriend, so it figures that you'd be obsessed with romance," he says, and I want to kick myself for not seeing this coming. He gives me a condescending smile. "It's okay, though. I still love you."

"Yeah, well, you're an arrogant asshole who will never find true love," I retort, but he only shrugs.

"Oh well."

Ughhhh. "I feel sorry for you, you know that?" I say. "You're going to die sad and alone with no one to mourn your passing."

Max just laughs, like this is the funniest thing anyone has ever said to him. "Okay," he says, and pats me on the head and keeps walking. He's *such* an asshole.

While Max and I have been bickering, my phone has been buzzing nonstop with seventeen thousand delayed texts from Dad. I check them to find a long thread of what he probably thinks are useful tips and reminders, the last of which is *Remember to call when you land!*

"Hey, did Dad text you a million times while we were on the plane?" I ask Max.

"Nope. I'm guessing he texted you?" In response, I hold up my phone, and he lets loose a bark of laughter.

I've always been a daddy's girl, but when Mom moved out this spring, he went from Dad: Warm and Nurturing Ally, to Dad: Maudlin and Overprotective Worrywart. "It's just you and me now, Zozo," he kept saying, I guess since Max was at school. And despite my guilt about leaving Dad alone this summer, I've been looking forward to not having to see him mope around the house, or listen to him telling me how it is important to support each other through this time of emotional crisis, or sit with him and watch *Love Actually* while he weeps silently and says, "It's okay to feel sad, sweetheart," and, "I know it didn't work out with your mom and me, but I don't want you to give up on love."

It's probably not fair of me to be so annoyed with him; he didn't want the divorce, so of course it's wrecked him. Honestly, I was kind of shocked when my parents announced in May that they were getting divorced and Mom was moving out. They had never been what I would have called the ideal couple—but I guess I just assumed that was normal. Or a version of normal. Dad used to come to my room after they fought sometimes and apologize and tell me not to worry, that he and Mom loved each other and that everything would be okay, and I chose to believe him. ("Like a chump," Max said to me when I called him the night they announced their divorce; he'd been predicting it for years, but I'd always dismissed him as hateful, spiteful, and chronically pessimistic. Which, to be fair, he is.) But if Max and I can accept the fact that our family has crumbled into oblivion, you'd think Dad could at least stop acting like the living embodiment of the sad trombone.

Anyway, I'm not the kind of person who looks at my parents' failed marriage and decides that all love is in vain. They're not me, I'm not them. And if you can't believe in love, what can you believe in? What even is the point?

With a sigh, I call Dad. He picks up on the first ring.

"Zozo! How are you? How was your flight?"

"Fine. Crowded. We're on our way to baggage claim."

"Oh, good. And how's Max?"

"Fine."

"I miss you already," he says. "How am I going to make it through the summer without you?" He laughs, but I feel like he might not be completely joking.

"You're flying out in a few weeks, Dad."

"And I can't wait. Mom's here picking up a few things, by the way. Do you want to say hi?"

"Not really." Mom's always been the one who's pushed me

to take risks, spread my wings, all that stuff—she even lob-
bied (unsuccessfully) for Dad to let me fly out in time for Pride
Week. (He refused because he thought Stephen and Lance
would be too busy partying to make sure I stayed safe—as if
I need babysitting.) I know that living with Dad when he was
in worrywart mode was tough for her. On the other hand,
she's the one who left, who refused to go to marriage counseling when Dad asked her to, and who recently started dating
(*shudder*) my tenth-grade English teacher, Mr. Jensen. And
since she left, she's tried to reinvent herself as Fun Single Gal
Pal Mom, which . . . the less said about that, the better. All
things considered, it's been easier for me not to talk to her.

Dad sighs, and I hear him call out to Mom, "Nozomi and
Max say hi!" And then to me again, "You didn't leave anything
behind, right? You remembered to double-check under your
seat before you got off the plane?"

"Uh-huh."

"And you've got Stephen's number in case he's late?"

I see an escalator ahead with a sign above it proclaiming
Baggage Claim. "Hey, Dad, I'm gonna hang up now. I'm almost
at baggage claim," I say.

"Do you see Stephen? Is he there waiting for you?"

"I don't know, Dad, we're not there yet," I say impatiently,
and as I step onto the escalator, I hear Mom in the background
shouting, "Give her some space! She's seventeen, for god's
sake!"

Dad responds with something about *trying to be an engaged parent!* and then they're fighting, which gives me a great excuse to hang up.

I couldn't have designed a more picture-perfect welcome to San Francisco than my dapper, handsome Asian uncles. (Stephen is Japanese American, duh, and Lance is Filipino American.) Stephen is trim and elegantly casual in dark blue pressed jeans and an artfully untucked pink floral-print button-down, his salt-and-pepper hair styled in a sleek undercut and swept away from his face; Lance is shorter, buffer, and more conservative in slim-fitting khakis and a crisp white dress shirt with the sleeves rolled up to reveal strong brown forearms. They're waving and calling, "Nozomi! Max! Over here!" like our own personal fan club.

I forget all about Dad and Mom and walk gratefully into Stephen's outstretched arms. "Welcome to San Francisco, honey," he says. "You're going to have the best summer ever."

Stephen and Lance live in Nob Hill. Their house is sleek and modern, all whites and blacks and muted grays with the occasional pop of color: bright red chairs in the kitchen, a cerulean blue accent wall in the living room. The walls are hung with paintings and photographs that I'm sure cost a fortune, and they have their own lighting like in museums, so you know that you're supposed to admire them. Equally fancy sculptures shine on special tables under their own spotlights. If people were houses, this is the house I would want to be.

I look out my bedroom window, which has a view of the fog sweeping through the cables of the Golden Gate Bridge to the north. It's that time of day when the sun has set but it's still light out, and the air is made of gold and silver. A couple hurries down the sidewalk, a light flicks on in a room across the street . . . It's like watching the opening scene of a movie where you get an aerial view of the city and then close in on the individual stories on the verge of unfolding. I snap a photo and post it with the caption, **SF here I come!**

I throw my clothes into the dresser, shove my suitcase into the closet, and step into Max's room on my way down to the kitchen. He's unpacking in the most Max way possible—shaking out each item of clothing, carefully refolding it, and placing everything neatly in drawers.

"Hey," I say. Something's been weighing on me since the airport, and now that we're really here, now that our summer is really starting, I can't carry it anymore.

"What do you want?" He starts arranging pairs of meticulously rolled up socks in rows.

"Am I a loser?"

"Yes."

Sigh. "No, seriously. Am I?" I hate how much I need to hear him deny it—I'm seventeen years old, after all, and he's just my asshole brother who's been insulting me all my life, so why should I care what he thinks? But I do.

"What?" He straightens, sock arranging momentarily forgotten. "What are you talking about?" Then comprehension

11

dawns on his face and he goes, "Wait a minute. Is this about what I said at the airport? That was a joke, Zo. I was just teasing you. I thought you knew that."

"Yeah, well. It's just that some other people seem to think it for real, so. And now that we're here . . ." I gesture around me. "I don't know if I . . ." Apparently, his assurance that he was joking wasn't enough. What if I *am* a loser? What if everyone I meet this summer sees me the way Helena did? Before I know it, I've told Max the whole sad story.

He groans. "Ughhhh, high school girls. Why do you care what she thinks? Fuck her."

"I know, but . . ." But it still hurts. She's everything I want in a girlfriend (apart from the bitchiness), and if everything I want in a girlfriend doesn't want me back, where does that leave me? I *know* it shouldn't matter, but I can't help how I feel.

"Listen," he says. "Don't go around trying to be something you're not, just because some girl said something shitty about you. Just be who you are."

"Oh, okay. That's not the biggest cliché ever."

"Yeah, you're right. Don't be who you are. Bad idea."

"Ha-ha."

"Whatever. You get my point," he says. He goes back to sorting his socks, clearly over our little sibling bonding moment, so I leave.

I'm halfway down the hallway when he sticks his head out the door and says, "Hey."

"What?" I turn.

"I'm sorry I hurt your feelings earlier. I don't think you're a loser."

"Oh." It's ridiculous how much better that makes me feel. "That's okay. Thanks."

"I mean, let's not kid ourselves, the odds are definitely against you. But there is hope. No one's met you yet, right?"

"Fuck you, Max."

I go down the stairs, pausing at the bottom in front of a mirror to gaze at my reflection. I know Max was joking, but the reality is, he's right. The odds *are* against me. On the other hand, it dawns on me, he's also right about no one having met me. I could be—could become—anyone. Nozomi Nagai, Beige Wallpaper, who fades passively into the background until she blurts out her feelings in a drunken rush, is a thing of the past. This summer, I will take charge of my fate. I will make things happen, live my best life, and—yes, own it, Nozomi!—have the summer romance of my dreams. I will become Nozomi Nagai . . . whatever the opposite of beige wallpaper is. A cerulean blue accent wall? A sculpture with its own spotlight? Anyway. My point is that I can become whatever I want. By the end of the summer, I will be completely transformed.

2

IN THE MORNING, WE ALL GO OUT TO BRUNCH
at the Moonraker, a fancy seafood restaurant tucked into a
cove just south of the city, with tables overlooking the Pacific
Ocean through big picture windows. The last time I was here,
I was just a little girl, and Dad told me that if I watched very
closely, I might spot a mermaid. I spent the entire meal staring
intently out the window. I spotted a lot of kelp and some
driftwood but alas, no mermaid. When I wondered out loud
that night whether I might have seen one if I'd had binoculars,
Max told me I was being stupid and there was no such thing as
mermaids—Dad had only told me that to keep me quiet during
the meal. I hit him, hard, and he hit me back, and I ended up
sleeping in my parents' room, with Dad stroking my hair and
reassuring me that of course there were mermaids out there,

that he'd seen one once, as a child, so he knew they existed, and one day, if I was patient, if I believed hard enough, then I'd see one, too.

While Stephen, Lance, and Max wait inside for the host to call us to our table, I go to the deck to get some time alone with the view. I close my eyes, grip the cold metal railing that separates the deck from the rocky shore, and breathe in lungfuls of bracing ocean air. The wind whips my hair around my face. Ahhhh.

If this is going to be the summer of my transformation, right here is the perfect place for it to start. I lift my face to the sky and fling my arms out, taking in the moment as completely as I can. I can feel myself transforming already. It's like magic. I feel like I can do anything—be anyone—if I just believe hard enough. Inspired, I open my eyes and scan the ocean with my new, magical vision. *Okay, mermaids, I know you're out there. Show yourselves.*

Someone clears their throat next to me, and I realize with horror that I've spoken those last words aloud.

I turn to face a girl so strikingly beautiful it takes my breath away. She has high cheekbones, dark, arched eyebrows, soft, pouty lips, and—ohh, her eyes. Kind and just the tiniest bit sad. Like a teenage Gemma Chan. Her hair is in a braid crown, and her face is framed by a few loose tendrils and drop earrings that sparkle in the sunlight. It's enchanting. Literally, like I can't look away. In my shock, I half wonder if *she's* a mermaid, and I just barely stop myself from looking down to check to make sure she has legs.

"Um. I don't actually believe in mermaids," I mumble.

"Me neither. But you never know, right?" The corner of her perfect mouth edges up and her eyebrow twitches and I think my heart stops beating for a second. "They might exist."

Under the influence of that heart-stopping half smile, a flood of tantalizing possibilities bubbles forth: What if she's queer? And single? What if she became my summer fling? What if *this* is the moment my transformation begins?

My beautiful enchantress's half smile falters, and I realize I have to say something before she flees and takes my transformational moment with her. Focus, Nozomi. What were we talking about? Oh, right—mermaids.

"I read somewhere that Columbus thought manatees were mermaids," I say, which . . . is definitely a sentence about mermaids.

To my utter surprise, she laughs and says, "Well, that tracks."

"Yeah, I guess it does." Buoyed by her bright golden laughter, I manage another sentence. "Though in his defense, I once mistook a sea otter for a mermaid."

"You probably weren't a grown man, though," she says with a little grin.

"No. I was five."

It's at this point of my potentially (please, oh please) life-changing conversation that Max appears at the edge of my field of vision and bellows, "Nozomi! The table's ready!"

I ignore him. I am talking to a fairy queen and things are going far better than I ever could have imagined. The table can wait.

Only I didn't figure on said fairy queen looking down at her phone and saying, "Well, I'm meeting someone in a few minutes, so I'll let you get back to your mermaid search. Good luck!"

"Wait!" I say desperately. I have to get her name. I have to know who she is.

She turns back, her smile a little bemused, but still warm and friendly.

"Um." *Focus! Name!* "I'm Nozomi. I'm visiting San Francisco for the summer."

"Cool!" she says. "I've lived here all my life. You're gonna love it."

So she lives here. The universe is on my side.

"What's your name?" I ask her. Clumsy, yes, awkward, definitely, but there's no time to be clever. She's about to melt back into the void from whence she came.

"Willow."

A beautiful name for a beautiful girl is the sentence that comes into my head. I have the presence of mind, thank goodness, to realize that this is corny-bordering-on-creepy before I say it, but before I can think of an appropriately not-creepy way to get her phone number, I feel a light punch on my arm and Max's voice says, "Hey, Zomi. The table's ready."

"What? Oh, right! Table. Okay! Um, so I guess I should go," I tell Willow.

"Yeah, me too. Have a fun summer." Willow turns to leave again.

"Thanks. Um, actually—"

"Zomi! Let's *go*." Max grabs me by the arm and drags me away before the words *do you want to hang out sometime* leave my mouth.

"I hope we run into each other again!" I call, and almost trip when Max gives my arm another tug, muttering, "Shut up. Shut up. Shut up," under his breath.

"What the hell, Max? Why'd you have to drag me away like that?" I yank my arm back. "I was just about to get her number."

Max rolls his eyes. "I was rescuing you from ignominious defeat, because you were *not* about to get her number."

"I was, too," I say, annoyed.

"She was trying to get rid of you."

"She was not."

"She most definitely was."

"Do you think if I went back there—"

"No."

"But what if—"

"No."

"But—"

"No!" he says, and herds me into the restaurant, and that's the end of that.

Inside, Stephen and Lance wave to us from a table by the window. The Pacific Ocean stretches behind them, and I gaze out at the waves as I take my seat. While Lance and Stephen start talking about the museum's upcoming fund-raising gala, and then about skyrocketing home prices in the city, my thoughts drift back to Willow. What if I'd been a little quicker? What if Max hadn't interrupted us?

We *might* find each other again. She said she lives here. After all, the prince found Cinderella, didn't he? Westley found Buttercup. And I don't know why or how, but when I think of Willow, all the arguments against me—we don't even know each other; she's vanished without a trace; she's a fairy queen and I'm wallpaper (I'm not. I'm *not*.)—quietly fade away, and the only thing left is the shiny possibility of me, Willow, and a thousand fluttering hearts.

3

"SO, A LITTLE HEADS-UP, GUYS. ABOUT BABA," says Stephen. He clears his throat, taps the steering wheel, and glances at me in the rearview mirror, and the tight, prickly feeling that's been hounding me all morning intensifies.

One of the things Max and I are supposed to do in San Francisco this summer is spend quality time with Baba—my grandmother, Stephen and Dad's mom. We haven't seen her in a very long time, and Dad wants us to reconnect.

Calm down, I tell myself. It'll be good to see her. She's my grandmother. She's just a helpless, harmless, little old lady. How bad can it be? But Stephen's obvious anxiety is making me think it could be pretty bad. As is Lance's absence from the car.

The thing is, despite living in the LGBTQIA capital of the

world and Stephen reportedly having been a walking, talking gay stereotype in his teens and twenties, Baba managed to keep her head firmly in the sand about his sexuality until he announced ten years ago that he was in love with Lance, at which point she insisted it was a phase. When he told her a few years later that they were getting married, she cried for days and begged him to "go back" to being straight, and when he said that was impossible, she demanded that he fake being straight so that he could have a "real family." Depending on who you ask, either she refused to attend the wedding, or Stephen told her not to come. Dad took Stephen's side, and since then our visits with Baba have been limited to a short, awkward, stressful lunch date once every two or three years.

It's sad. Tragic, even, because I used to adore Baba when I was little, and here I am dreading seeing her. Because believe it or not, homophobia is not one of this queer girl's Top Ten Favorite Traits in a Grandmother.

Lately, Stephen and Dad have been edging toward a friendlier relationship with Baba, though to be honest, I don't know if it's because she's starting to change her mind, or if it's because her mind is changing. Baba's car has run out of gas three times in the past year. She's forgotten how to work the cable remote and how to do video calls. Stephen, especially, has had to step in and help her manage her life, since he's the one who lives closest to her. I've even heard him and Dad on the phone talking about possibly selling her house and moving her to an elder care facility.

So maybe that's what Stephen's about to tell us. Maybe she's worse off than we've been led to believe, and he's trying to prepare us.

I don't know what to root for: having to talk about Baba's homophobia, or having to talk about her dementia. Both options are decidedly suboptimal.

Stephen pulls cautiously into an intersection and executes a left turn. "Keep an eye out for parking spaces, okay?"

"What's the heads-up?" I prompt him. "About Baba?"

"Well." Stephen clears his throat again, takes a long, fortifying breath, and says, "I just wanted to check in with you. Are you—you're not planning on coming out to Baba, are you?"

Homophobia it is, then.

"Um," I say. "Uh." I really don't know. After hearing about the way she reacted to Stephen and Lance's wedding announcement, I've always done my best not to think about it. Does that make me a bad lesbian, somehow?

"Because . . . well. I'm not sure she's quite ready. It, ah, might make things easier for you—for everyone—if you don't mention it. Oh! Is that a space?" But it's someone's driveway, and he sighs and turns at the next stop sign.

It's not like I had plans to sail through Baba's front door with a burst of trumpet fanfare, my rainbow flag rippling in the wind. But Stephen was the one who encouraged me to come out to Mom and Dad when, on a visit to Chicago a few years ago, he accidentally walked in on me looking up images of girls kissing. He's always talking about how proud he is of me, how inspired he is by the fact that I've been officially out since ninth grade. And now he's suggesting I jump back into the closet like a scared little rabbit because Baba might not be "quite ready" to accept me as I really am?

Helpless, harmless little old lady or not, the idea of "reconnecting" with her is starting to feel a little delusional on Dad's and Stephen's part.

"That's bullshit," Max says. "What's wrong with Zomi being out to her own supposedly loving grandmother? That's not right. Someone needs to tell Baba to get her shit together." Max, defending me! I could hug him right now.

"I know. I'm so sorry, I really am." Stephen makes another turn. "But try to understand. This is your grandmother we're talking about. I want you to have a relationship with her, and she's growing, but it's . . . well, it's a slow process, and coming out to her could be painful. Take it from someone who's been there, Zozo. I just don't want you to get hurt." He meets my eye in the rearview mirror.

I don't want me to get hurt, either. But it's too late for that. Why did Stephen have to bring this up?

I hate that I'm in this situation. My friends all have stronger opinions about pizza toppings than they do about other people's sexual identities. But with the rest of the world, I have to look for rainbow pins and listen for clues about how others might react; I have to decide over and over whether being true to myself is worth risking rejection, or worse. Most of the time, it only takes a second, but those seconds add up. And sometimes, like now, with someone I love, it takes longer and the stakes are so much higher, and all I can do is wish it didn't have to be like this. I wish I didn't have to deal with Baba at all. She's the only thing standing in the way of what could be the best summer of my life.

Stephen makes yet another turn and I'm pretty sure we're back where we started. He sighs, though whether he's sad about this whole thing or about the dearth of parking spaces in the Richmond District, I'm not sure. "I'm not telling you what to do, Zozo," he says. "It's your choice how you want to handle things. Just be aware that she may not react well to you correcting her if she asks you about boyfriends."

"Highly unlikely that question will come up," Max deadpans. "Zomi being the blemish on the face of humanity that she is."

"Ennhh, funny, Max. Better than being a blemish on the ass of humanity like you," I say, sneering, but it's actually kind of nice to be back on familiar territory, and I throw myself into the ensuing squabble with gusto. At least I know what to expect with Max.

Finally, after three more trips around two more blocks, Stephen whoops and pumps his fist in triumph—a space has opened up right in front of Baba's house. "See? It's a message from God: Don't give up hope. Everything will be okay in the end." Once we're out of the car, he kisses my forehead. "Trust me, I know how hard this is, Zozo. I love you."

Baba's house is almost exactly the way I remember it. The paint is peeling on the trim and on the front steps where she taught me to play janken—Rock, Paper, Scissors in Japanese. The winner of each round would get to move up one step, and if I reached the top of the stairs first, I got a quarter from the jar of change she kept on her dresser. The honeysuckle is still climbing up the frame on the front of the house, and the porch is crowded with potted plants: petunias, geraniums, begonias, hydrangeas, and even a miniature rosebush.

The front door opens and Baba emerges. She's shorter than I remember, which I guess makes sense, and her hair is whiter and thinner. She's wearing khaki slacks and a pale pink blouse with pink Crocs, and she looks kind of frail and adorable in her little porch garden. In spite of myself, I feel a wave of affection for her, followed by a wave of nostalgia for the relationship we had when I was little.

"Welcome, Nozomi! Welcome, Max!" she says, hurrying toward us with quick, decisive steps. She reaches Max first and clasps his arms, one with each hand. It's been three years since we've seen her. Her eyes, under peaked eyebrows that make her smiles look impish and her frowns look furious, are as quick and bright as ever—only, are those tears I see?

It must have been lonely, with her husband dead, her two sons barely speaking to her, and her grandchildren almost completely out of her life. Maybe that's why she agreed to let Stephen back in. Dad wouldn't send me into the den of a raging homophobic monster, would he? Maybe Baba *has* learned a lesson about loving and accepting your family. Maybe she'll prove us all wrong.

Maybe not, though, says a voice in my head.

Shut up, I tell it.

Lance wasn't invited to dinner, it persists.

Shut UP.

"Max, you've grown," she says, looking Max up and down and beaming.

Max smiles at Baba and nods. "It's been a long time."

"Yes, it has," she responds, and adds with a proud pat on the shoulder, "You're always so handsome. That is my genes of the family." Stephen rolls his eyes at me. Baba has always maintained that the good looks in our family come from her side. I roll my eyes back, because the last thing that Max needs is someone telling him he's handsome, even if it's his own outrageously biased grandmother.

Baba shifts her attention from Max to me, and I feel myself tense up a little.

"Hi, Baba," I say. Despite the obvious delight in her eyes and my earlier sympathy for her, suddenly all I can think about is whether or not she might have a homophobic meltdown if she ever finds out that I'm queer. Damn Stephen for putting this in the front of my mind.

Or maybe it would have been there, anyway.

Be positive, I tell myself. She's just a lonely old lady who wants to have a relationship with her grandchildren. I step toward Baba and give her the warmest hug I can muster, even though I know she's not much of a hugger. "It's really nice to see you."

Baba hesitates for a flicker of a second and says, "Oh!" before I feel her hands move tentatively around my back, and she gives me a couple of awkward pats: *pat, pat.*

I step back, and she gives me two more pats on the arm before she surveys me and pronounces, "Nozomi, too. You've grown. You're more like your mother, now that you're older."

"Oh. Um. Thanks," I say, out of reflexive politeness—she is my grandmother, after all. Still. Was that supposed to be a compliment or a dig? She can't possibly be happy with Mom, now that Mom's divorcing Dad.

"Don't you wear the makeup yet? Or are you still a tomboy?"

My heart starts thudding. Is this totally random or is she dropping a hint about my sexuality? I mumble vaguely, "Um, not really."

"I wonder if you do remember at all inside the house," Baba says, apparently without having registered my nonanswer, and I breathe a tiny sigh of relief. "It's been so many years." She turns and walks toward the house, and Max and I follow silently, with Stephen behind us.

4

THE INTERIOR OF BABA'S HOUSE IS COOL AND dim, the decor old-fashioned and fussy. She leads us through the foyer, where we stop to take our shoes off. "There's the kitchen," she says, gesturing to the left at a narrow room with a view of the street. I peek in, and without warning, a memory surfaces: making plum jam with Baba. I stood on a chair and stirred the cooking plums as they bubbled on the stove. Baba poured ruby-red spoonfuls into a tiny porcelain bowl and blew on it to cool it before she held it up for me to taste. I wonder if Baba will have her own kitchen wherever she ends up moving to one day.

In the corner of the dining room is a fancy glass-fronted cupboard crammed with framed family photographs. There are tons of photos of Stephen and Dad, from childhood all the way through high school, when Dad was a star tennis player and Stephen was a theater kid. There's a photo of Mom and Dad's wedding, and assorted school photos of me and Max. There are no photos of Stephen and Lance's wedding—no photos of Lance anywhere, in fact. I feel a stab of grief for the two of them, a surge of anger at Baba, and a creeping sense of foreboding for me. Does she think that if she doesn't have to see Lance's face, she can pretend that Stephen never married him? That he doesn't even exist? I can see now why Stephen doesn't think it's safe for me to come out to her.

To distract myself from the photographs, I walk toward the back window, which looks out on a tiny yard, covered with yellow-green grass and surrounded by a fence that leans and sags at surreal angles. The sound of a buzz saw breaks the quiet around me.

"That's Clifford," Baba says. I see an older white guy sawing redwood planks in the corner of the yard. "Stephen hired him to replace the old fence for me."

"He's going to replace some of the decorative elements on the inside as well," says Stephen.

Baba frowns. "Okane mottainai."

"It's not a waste of money, Mom. When Cliff's done, it's going to look gorgeous."

"But no need for looking gorgeous. I am the only one who sees."

Stephen ignores her and explains to me and Max, "Cliff's an artist friend of mine. He does some carpentry on the side to help pay the bills. And I actually meant to tell you, Nozomi—he's building an installation at the museum right now, and his daughter will be coming to help him out. She designed it—and it won a grant contest for young artists. Isn't that fantastic? She's exactly your age *and* she's half Japanese. I think you two would be great friends. I'll introduce you and you can chillax, or kick it, or whatever you young people are calling it these days."

"She's a gay," says Baba in a stage whisper, leaning in dramatically as she delivers this information.

"Ah," I say, and for the second time since we got here, I'm fighting a panicky suspicion that Baba has secret gaydar and she's low-key calling me out. My throat goes dry and my heart starts jackhammering away, as if Baba were standing in front of me wielding a queer-slashing battle-ax in her wrinkly, age-spotted little hands. Which is preposterous. Calm down, Nozomi. Breathe.

"Yes, she is, Mom. And it's fine," says Stephen acidly.

Baba looks offended. "I didn't say anything bad."

Stephen sighs. "Not technically."

"So many young people are gay now. It's a fashion."

It's fine. It's fine. Who cares what she thinks, anyway? She's just an ignorant old lady.

"It's not a fashion, Mom," Stephen says. "It's an identity. It's part of who we are."

"It's a fashion for young people to have the 'gay identity,'" Baba persists. "It's true! My friend says all her granddaughter's friends say they are the bisexual even though boys and girls date each other. Some of them don't even have boyfriend or girlfriend. How can they know they are gay? It's just a fashion to say so."

Now my heart is pounding because I know I'm going to say something. No, not *that* something. But I have to say *something*. Sexual identity may be fluid, but it's not like Rainbow Looms or tennis skirts that everyone tries for a minute before moving on to the next cool thing. And you can know who you like without dating anyone (Exhibit A: me). And being bisexual *literally* means you can be attracted someone who's a different gender than you. Why is it so terrifying to defend my identity in a totally general, not-coming-out way to a frail old lady like Baba? What am I afraid of?

But I know what. I'm afraid that she really *is* a homophobic monster, and she'll say something that will make it impossible for me to love her, or that will make it clear that she'll find it impossible to love *me* if she knows I'm queer.

Why do I even care?

I *don't* care. I don't care. I don't care.

But I do.

And I can't let it go.

"It's *not* just a fashion," I finally blurt out. "It's real. And you can't always tell from the outside who a person is in love with."

There. I said it. Well, I've said something, anyway. My heart is pounding so hard now, I can feel it in my ears.

Baba looks a little startled. I can't tell whether she's

surprised by what I've said, or by the fact that I said it, but anyway, she doesn't argue. "Really. Hm."

I expect to feel my terror replaced with triumphant euphoria, or at least intense relief, and I'm surprised when all I feel is more trepidation. I hope I've done the right thing. I hope she doesn't get angry or suspicious or start pushing me away for some made-up reason.

"Well, that's enough conversation about the controversial topic," Baba says briskly. "Max, do you still like tonkatsu? I have all the ingredients to make."

As Baba slices the pork, pounds it with a wooden mallet, and dredges it in flour, eggs, and panko while the oil heats up, Stephen leafs through a stack of envelopes on the dining room table, muttering, "Where is it, where is it, where is it," until suddenly he goes, "Aha!" and opens one. I lean over to see what it is. "Medical bill," he explains. "I'm handling most of her finances now." He doesn't need to tell me it's because she can't do the handling herself, and I wonder if she really *has* only let him back in her life because he takes care of things like this for her. How depressing for both of them—and yet, weirdly, how lucky. I wonder what Baba would do if it weren't for Stephen. She must appreciate him helping her like this. Assuming she knows how much he's helping her.

"Listen, both of you," he says under his breath. "Your dad and I have put Baba on a bunch of wait lists for some assisted-living places in the area. You know that, right?"

Max and I nod.

"I'm going to bring it up at dinner, just casually, to keep it on her radar. Can you back me up when I do?"

"Is it really that bad?" I ask. "She seems pretty sharp to me."

"We've found ways to help her manage from day to day. But it's not sustainable."

Baba calls me into the kitchen and asks me to set the table, which is when I begin to see what Stephen means. There are labels on every cabinet, every drawer, neatly printed in English, Japanese kanji, and Japanese letters:

```
SILVERWARE    食器    しょっき
PLATES        皿      さら
FRYING PANS   フライパン
SHOYU, SALT, PEPPER   醤油など    しょうゆなど
```

Next to the labels are whimsical drawings of the items—Stephen's work, probably—and I wonder if they're supposed to be cute, or if they're in anticipation of a time when Baba forgets how to read.

Baba spends most of her time at the stove while we gorge ourselves on crisp, succulent pork cutlets. "Sit down, Mom," Stephen entreats her, but she looks at him incredulously.

"Who will make tonkatsu if I sit down?" she asks.

"Just make it all at once and then serve it," says Stephen, and she purses her lips and shakes her head.

"I can't do. If I do, then it won't be hot."

Finally, when all the tonkatsu have been fried, she joins us, smiling happily at how few are left in the serving bowl. She takes two pieces for herself and encourages us to eat the rest.

Stephen tells a rambling story about his coworker's parents, who recently sold their house and moved to a retirement community in San Jose. He paints a rosy picture of an easy, air-conditioned life with movies and lectures and art classes, rides to church and trips to the mall. It actually sounds kind of appealing.

"So." He clears his throat. "Would you ever want to move somewhere like that, Mom? It sounds great, doesn't it?"

Baba doesn't answer right away, so I figure now's when I should chime in and help Stephen. I make my voice bright and enthusiastic. "It sounds amazing. I would totally live there."

Max shoots me a warning look.

"What?" I say. "I would. It sounds like college, but for old people."

Max's jaw drops and Stephen snorts with laughter, but Baba frowns. Crap.

"I'm sorry. I didn't mean—" I start, but she interrupts me.

"I don't like the mall," she says peevishly. "It's a too loud and crowded place."

Of all the reasons not to like a place, she's choosing "trips to the mall?" Oh well. At least "college for old people" didn't upset her.

"You don't have to go to the mall," Stephen reassures her calmly, as if the mall were a perfectly reasonable hill for her to want to die on. "All of these places have lots of activities to choose from."

"But just the play activities. Just a hobby and games."

"That sounds like fun, though," says Max casually, but Baba shakes her head stubbornly.

"I feel useless without a good work," she says. "I need a purpose every day."

"There's volunteer opportunities. And you could still volunteer with your church," says Stephen.

"And gardening! I bet they have gardening," I add, thinking of her flowers.

Stephen nods enthusiastically. "They definitely have gardening. And exercise classes. Mom, I really think you should consider—"

"I am not a child!" Baba bursts out angrily. "I can decide for myself what I want to do."

Which is such a childish thing to say that I feel a little embarrassed for her. On the other hand, I *do* feel like when I was a camp counselor last summer and it was my job every morning to convince this one sad, weepy kid that camp was going to be So! Much! Fun! Am I treating my own grandmother like a five-year-old?

"You can still make those decisions," Stephen is saying. "I just wonder if it would be safer and easier for you if—"

"I don't want to talk about this anymore," Baba snaps. "I am healthy. I don't need old folks' home."

"It's not an old folks' home," says Stephen. "It's an active elder community with continuing care."

"It's a same thing," she says fiercely, and to be fair, she's not wrong.

"Okay, okay, Mom, I got it. We'll stop. But we have to talk about it sometime."

Baba ignores this and starts clearing the dishes from the table. With an apologetic look at Stephen, I get up to help her. One by one I bring the leftover grilled eggplant with miso sauce, salted cucumber slices, and bright yellow triangles of homemade pickled daikon to the counter. It occurs to me that she made this entire dinner on her own. Maybe Baba's right. Maybe we're not giving her enough credit. She's just a little forgetful, really—how many due dates have I forgotten for school? She might need a little help, but she probably doesn't need to *move*.

"Thank you, Nozomi," says Baba brightly, as if nothing has happened. "What a good, helpful girl."

When Stephen comes in and offers to help, though, she turns away from him and pretends not to hear him. He shrugs at me and goes back out to the dining room.

Once the table has been cleared and the dishes washed, Stephen pops into the kitchen again, this time with a lemon-yellow bakery box in his hands. "Would anyone be interested in dessert? I got Beard Papa," he says to no one in particular.

Baba has a deep and abiding love of sweets, and Beard Papa cream puffs, I remember, are her particular favorites. Her mouth is still tight and angry, but her eyes flick to the distinctive yellow box once, twice, three times. She takes her rubber dish gloves off, very slowly, and glances at the box again. This time her gaze lingers a little, and I see Stephen noticing it. He says nothing.

"Nozomi, would you like some cream puff?" asks Baba casually.

"I would love some," I say.

"Do you remember where the dessert plates are?" she responds. "Get four of them. I'll make some tea."

Stephen says lightly, "I'll just bring these out to the table, then, shall I?"

Baba scowls. "No, no! We are not barbarian. Put them on a serving plate. Here." She thrusts a porcelain platter with white, fluted edges at him. "I thought you know better."

I shrink a little at her sharp tone—it's so weird to hear her scolding Stephen like he's a child—but he's grinning broadly, and I realize that he was trolling her, and he's enjoying himself.

"Of course, Mom." He kisses her, but she harrumphs and shoves him away.

"Kashikoi, ne," she says, which kind of means "Aren't you clever." Baba's mouth is still puckered into a disagreeable little frown, but it's less committed than before. And that shove she gave him—it was almost playful. I realize that maybe she's enjoying this, too, that this is a script they've played out a thousand times, that they take comfort in repeating. Parts of their relationship have survived the damage. There's still love underneath, like muscle memory, like a song you know by heart.

At the table, though, I start worrying again, about everything. Baba takes a sip of tea and accuses Stephen of switching the cups; she's sure she put sugar in her tea. Then the talk turns to church. Baba's church has a new junior minister. Stephen raves about him; he's warm and funny, and his last sermon was about building a loving community that accepts all people, regardless of race, sexual or gender identity, or even politics.

"He is a liberal hippie minister," Baba announces. "I like Pastor Joe better."

"It wouldn't hurt to try expanding your horizons," says Stephen, without looking at her.

But Baba is adamant. "No. It doesn't work. I have lived the long life and I know well what I think. The old people don't need to expand the horizon or change their mind before they die."

I listen to them and wonder, how much damage can *our* relationship take? How strong is her love for me, underneath it all? I think back to the way she talked about Cliff's daughter—how Baba treated her being queer more like a juicy piece of gossip than a reason to reject her. It gives me hope that she wouldn't outright reject me if I came out to her; but I don't know if that's enough for me. Should it be?

If I could write a perfect ending to this story, Baba would come around to see me and embrace me for all that I am, and

38

I wouldn't have to sacrifice anything. But even then, I think, looking at the labels on the kitchen cabinets—even if I get the warm, fuzzy coming-out scenario of my dreams and we resurrect our old bond—there's a chance she'll forget it all. If she's going to forget everything, does it even matter whether I tell her or not?

5

I'VE NEVER BEEN GOOD AT DRAWING; NOTHING comes out the way I see it in my head. But my great-great-great-somebody was an apprentice to Hiroshige (one of the most famous artists in the world, so look him up if you've never heard of him), and he ended up making a small name for himself as a woodblock artist in his own right. Baba has a bunch of his original landscape prints hanging on the walls of her house. I used to spend hours making up stories that took place in those pictures, which is how Baba began teaching me to appreciate art, even if I couldn't make it.

"What story do you see?" she used to ask as we flipped through big coffee table books about Michelangelo, or the Impressionists. Later, Stephen taught me how to look at color and space, how to find and follow directional lines, and how artists use those tools to add layers of meaning to their work. I loved all of it, and I got pretty good at understanding how art works, if I do say so myself.

This summer, I get to use everything I've learned in an actual, real job. I'm supposed to update the digital records of all the pieces at Stephen's museum, and write little blurbs about them to help kids understand and appreciate them. I made up a title and put it on my Achievements and Accomplishments list that the school academic counselor makes us keep online:

Digital Archive Intern, The Harrison Collection, San Francisco

It gives me a little thrill every time I say to myself, "I'm Nozomi Nagai. I work at the Harrison Collection in San Francisco in the Digital Archives department." I sound like someone who lives in her own cool apartment in the city and wears cool designer clothes and goes to cool parties with her cool friends. Thank god I'm not Max: *Educational Software Intern* doesn't have the same ring to it.

The only problem is that the Harrison Collection is devoted to contemporary art, most of it very abstract, which is my least favorite kind of art. I like art that suggests a story, and it's hard to find a story in a 36-inch glass cube, which is an actual, literal thing in the collection. But we Digital Archive Interns can't be choosy about what we digitally archive.

I'm wearing a brand-new outfit in honor of my first day: high-waisted jeans, a black mock turtleneck, and an oversized tweed blazer that I stole from Dad's closet. And I flat-ironed my hair and put on some makeup: a touch of eye shadow and a dark red lipstick that Max says makes me look like a clown, but what does he know. Lance did a chef's kiss when he saw me at breakfast, and that was exactly the boost I needed. I feel very hip and artsy.

The Harrison Collection building looks like something you might make out of Legos—a flattish beige box stacked on top of, and overshadowing, a smaller box made of glass, which I find really uninviting. But as dull and boring as the outside looks, once you step through the doors, it's light and airy and attractive, all pale wood floors, white walls, and high ceilings. It makes you want to keep going and see what else is inside.

"Before we get started on your jobs, I want to introduce you to Cliff's daughter," Stephen says to me as we enter. "Remember I told you about her at Baba's? You should come, too, Max, and see what they're working on. You're going to love it. Especially you, Zozo, my contemporary art–hating little philistine. The concept is right up your alley."

Stephen leads us toward the back of the museum, which surrounds a sun-filled courtyard dominated by the beginnings of the wooden frame of a house-like structure. The smell of sawdust fills the air. On the far side of the frame, two people in ratty jeans, work boots, and dirty T-shirts are stacking freshly sawed lumber. One I recognize as Cliff. The other must be his (gossipy whisper voice: *gay*) daughter. Her hair is cropped short, and she's wearing a pair of sunglasses under the baseball cap that shades her face. The sleeves of her dark gray T-shirt are rolled up over her shoulders, and her arms are toned and muscular.

As we approach, they stop their work and turn to face us. Cliff arches his back, hands on his hips. His daughter takes her hat off, wipes her brow with her forearm, and pushes her sunglasses up over her damp brown hair. Stephen introduces us and we all shake hands. Cliff's hands are like giant paws, but Dela's are surprisingly small, with narrow, tapered fingers, though her palms are calloused and her grip is strong. With her hat and sunglasses off, her gaze is intense, and not particularly friendly. The freckles dotting her cheeks do hardly anything to soften her sharp, angular face.

"Dela's an artist in her own right, as I've told you." He smiles at Dela, who smiles back.

"I'm terrible at drawing," I tell Dela with my own friendly smile.

Her smile vanishes and she nods, as if she expected me to say this and she doesn't care.

Unnerved by her rudeness, I start babbling. "Yeah, I'm the worst. Remember, Max, when I went through that horse phase? I loved horses so much. Remember I used to give you all those horse drawings?"

Max rolls his eyes. "How could I forget?"

Dela doesn't laugh, doesn't smile, nothing. Desperate for

a reaction, I continue, "I used to try to copy this one painting, you know that one of Napoleon? On a big white horse? You know which one I mean? I *loved* that horse." Still nothing. "I bet you're good at drawing horses," I finish, in a final, feeble attempt to make her smile.

"My work is mostly in other media," says Dela smilelessly. "It's pretty abstract and conceptual. Not like drawing horses."

I feel my cheeks redden. Cliff looks mortified, and I feel a little sorry for him. It must suck to see your own daughter treating people like this. It's not like I still draw horses and think they're art. I've taken art history classes. I can appreciate good conceptual art. And what's wrong with horses, anyway?

"I *like* horse drawings," says Max, and I feel my heart swell with gratitude.

"Right? Who doesn't love a good horse drawing?" says Stephen smoothly. "Anyway, I've seen Dela's animal studies, kids, and rest assured, she can absolutely draw a horse. But you should see the concept art she did for this installation. It is spectacular. Dela, could we prevail upon you to show Nozomi and Max sometime?"

"Oh," Dela says, "I don't want to make anyone—" at the same time that I say, "No, it's fine, she really doesn't have to," but Cliff cuts us off.

"Come on, Dela," he says. "It'll be fun to make friends with some new people. And you should be proud of your accomplishments."

"I'm plenty proud, Dad. It's more that I like to decide for

myself who I want to be friends with." Her gaze flicks over at me, and I want to disappear. Either that or kick her in the shins.

"Dela!" Cliff looks horrified, as well he should, if you ask me.

"Sorry," says Dela, though she doesn't look like she means it.

"It's fine," I say, and I definitely don't mean it.

"Yeah, it's fine," Max repeats, and I know he doesn't mean it, either.

Dela clears her throat and looks at the ground, and then up at the sky. She puts her hands into her pockets and grinds her toe into a pile of sawdust, clearly eager for this encounter to be over.

"Well. Maybe some other time, then," says Stephen, stretching polite optimism very, very close to its breaking point.

"Yes, maybe," agrees Cliff. He can't be serious. I get that Dela being half Japanese and both of us being gay might have appeared to him and Stephen like a great foundation on which to build a beautiful friendship, but it is clearly not enough, so why push it? Why lie and pretend we're all going to be BFFs when it's obvious that Dela thinks she's better than me? Just because she won some stupid grant. I should have told her I'm the Digital Archive Intern. That would have shown her.

Though probably not. Ugh. Pretentious snob.

"So that was Dela . . ." It's clear from Stephen's tone that he's not being snarky and sarcastic, but after Dela pretty much kicked me in the teeth, I can't help myself.

45

". . . and I will never have to see or talk to her ever again?"
I say.

"Zozo. Be. Nice." When I roll my eyes, he sighs and says, "Look, honey, I know she's not exactly a drop of golden sun, but if you could just try to get to know her—"

"Stephen. She made it pretty clear that *she* didn't want to get to know *me*," I remind him.

"I can't say that I blame her," says Max, and I give him the finger.

"I know, I get it," says Stephen. "But it would mean a lot to me if you'd give her another chance. Cliff tells me she could use a friend. Do you think you could do that? Especially you, my sweet, loving, kindhearted niece?"

I sigh. Before my very eyes, my perfect summer is slowly turning into nothing but a long and thankless effort to be nice to people who I don't want to be nice to. But it's not like I can say no.

"Fine," I grumble. "One chance."

Stephen hugs me. "You darling. I knew you had it in you. You won't regret it, I promise. Once you get to know her, you are absolutely going to fall in love with her." His phone beeps, and he glances at it and says, "Okay, I have to take care of something, but it'll only take a minute. Meet me upstairs and I'll get you started on your jobs."

As soon as he's gone, I return to the subject of Dela, because I, for one, am not done griping. I ask Max that timeless question: "Who the hell does she think she is, anyway?"

Max shakes his head and snickers. "Seriously."

"It wasn't like I was all, 'Ooh, I love horses can you draw me one?' I was just trying to be friendly."

"I know," says Max. "What a bitch."

"I mean, who acts like that?" I put my hand on my hip and say in my snootiest, snottiest voice, "I mostly work in other media," sneering and waving a fake cigarette for effect. "My work is abstract and conceptual, you uncultured swine."

But instead of laughing or telling me that I *am* an uncultured swine, Max goes pale and clears his throat. He's looking over my shoulder at someone behind me.

I freeze.

It's Stephen. Please let it be Stephen.

But if it were Stephen, he'd already be in my face looking disappointed and tragic, and he's not. There's one more beat of silence, during which my shoulders hunch up and my eyes squinch shut, and someone stalks past me, and when I open one eye to check, I see Dela's back rushing away from us, down the hallway toward the back door.

I glance at Max, who looks as guilty as I feel.

"Oops," he says.

"Shit," I say.

I'm not a mean person. I'm really, really not. I want to defend myself to an imaginary audience, to say, *What did she expect? She was loathsome. Aren't I allowed to vent about loathsome people?*

The thing with not being a mean person, though, is that

you feel guilty when you *are* mean. Especially when you get caught. It's a really inconvenient side effect.

"I hate her," I say as we trudge down the hallway to find Dela.

"You're an asshole," Max says, grinning, "and you're going to hell."

"Shut up, Max. *You're* an asshole."

We find Dela sitting on the bumper of a slightly battered van in the alley behind the museum, scowling ferociously into the middle distance as if she can see something vile that's invisible to the rest of us. She's put on a leather jacket and her cap is off, her hair standing up all spiky, and she looks so much like an anime bad boy character that I half expect to see her blow a stream of cigarette smoke up into her bangs and tap some ashes onto the concrete. If she weren't so loathsome and pretentious, I'd actually find it kind of sexy. Minus the cigarette, obviously.

I look at Max. Max looks at me. This is *so* not going to be fun. Max raises his eyebrows and jerks his head at Dela, which I take to mean that I'm the one who has to apologize, which is unfair since technically we're both guilty of being mean. It's not my fault that I'm the one she heard. But I take a deep breath and step forward.

"Hey."

Dela doesn't move.

"Hey, I'm sorry. That, uh. Wasn't very nice of us—of me—to, uh, make fun of you like that. Behind your back."

This time, Dela takes a big breath, then lets it out, s-l-o-w-l-y.

"We're actually very nice people," offers Max, which causes Dela to glance sideways at us for a second before she goes back to murdering the invisible beast with her eyes.

A few more supremely uncomfortable seconds drag by, during which I'm sorely tempted to tell Dela that she was mean first, so it's really her own fault that I made fun of her. But I've read enough self-help articles (courtesy of Dad, who's been forwarding them to me regularly since Mom left) to know that reminding people that they started it isn't the most effective tool if you want to *stop* fighting.

"Just leave me alone, please." Her voice is flat and she's still not looking at us.

Well. If that's what she wants. I look at Max, who shrugs. "Okay. Have a nice day," I say, and I might have let that sentence dip its toe into sarcasm, but really, can you blame me? I have been the very picture of forbearance until now, have I not?

"Bye," says Max, and the two of us go inside, leaving Dela and her invisible demons back in the alley.

6

WE WALK UP THE GENTLY SLOPING RAMP IN THE atrium to the light-filled upper gallery to find Stephen waiting for us. Stephen shows me how to use a tablet to check the information in the database against the actual physical piece, and where to write my little interpretive blurbs. He's just handed me the tablet when we hear someone calling from behind us. "Stephen!"

We turn to see an Asian woman, tall and thin and elegant in white palazzo pants and a silky sleeveless turquoise blouse. Her hair is pulled back into a chignon to showcase a long, slender neck and dangling golden earrings. She embraces Stephen and air-kisses him; he air-kisses her back as if this is the most natural thing in the world. It's all very fancy and chic. "Daphne! You're ravishing, as always."

"Oh, stop it, Stephen." She waves off the compliment, but I can tell she's lapping it up like fancy champagne.

Stephen introduces us and tells us that Mrs. Hsu is chairing the summer fund-raising gala for the museum. The theme: "Fantasia."

"It's pronounced 'Fahn-*tah*-zia,'" she informs us, when Stephen pronounces it to rhyme with "Asia." "I think it sounds so much more sophisticated and magical that way, don't you?"

She's going to have the whole place decorated to match the theme (like prom, I can't help thinking, and I have to swallow a giggle), and she wants Stephen's input on a few logistical details, like whether a fog machine would ruin the artwork.

Stephen introduces me and Max, and tells her why we're here. Mrs. Hsu is very excited.

"Digital interns! What a wonderful experience!" She beams. "I was just telling my husband that we should have pushed our daughter to do more this summer. When I was a teenager in Taiwan, I worked so hard all the time, but all my daughter wants to do is play with makeup. Oh!" She straightens as if shot through with electricity and claps her hands once. "You know what? You should meet her. She's working in the gift shop this summer, as part of her volunteer experience. Come. Come with me. You can get back to your job after I introduce you. And then I need to talk to you about the table arrangement, Stephen. The caterers want to set up low tables in the atrium, can you *imagine*?" She takes Stephen's arm and gestures to me and Max to follow her down to the first floor.

The gift shop is completely open to the central atrium, and you can see most of the inside as you approach. I catch a glimpse of the clerk's profile behind the counter and gasp. Momentarily at a loss for words, I smack Max on the shoulder.

"Ow! What are you *doing*?" he says, and smacks me back.

"It's her," I hiss. "It's Willow! From the Moonraker!"

"What?" He shakes his head violently, as if to clear the debris inside so he can hear me properly. "Who? From the where?"

"It's *Willow*," I repeat between clenched teeth. "From the *Moon. Raker.*"

Stephen glances back at us. "Everything okay?"

"Everything's great!" I reply. Stephen gives me a funny look; I feel slightly out of control, and I'm sure my face shows it. Meanwhile, Max is alternately gaping at me and squinting at the clerk, openmouthed. Oh my god. Nothing like this ever happens to me. This is amazing. This is perfect.

I take a big breath in, and exhale slowly. Think, think, think. What should I do? What should I say? I'm so glad I spent extra time on my hair and makeup today.

Okay, I've got it. What I'll do is, I'll wait till Stephen introduces us, and then I'll say very casually, "I think we already met at the Moonraker," and give her a shy smile. No, a friendly smile. Or maybe a dazzling—

No, wait. I'll never be able to pull that off. Maybe instead I'll peer at her for a moment, then open my eyes wide in sudden recognition and go, "Hey, are you the girl from the Moonraker? Willow, right?"

Yes, that's better. And she'll say, "Why, yes, as a matter of fact, I am!"

No, wait. Scratch that. Maybe I should—

I nearly bump into Max, who's stopped abruptly, and I realize we're standing in front of the counter, and just like that—*click*—my mind goes blank.

But not for the reasons one might think (she's gorgeous, I'm pathetic). Well, not only for those reasons. The main reason is that the girl in front of me is not the girl I met over the weekend.

What I mean is, she's the same girl, but she's giving off a totally different vibe. Her body is curved over her phone in an angry C, her eyes are puffy and bloodshot, and her nose is red, and . . . she's been crying.

Correction: she *is* crying. A tear wells up in each eye and she wipes each one carefully away with a tissue, to keep her makeup from smudging, and then does a secondary sweep with the backs of her thumbs.

Mrs. Hsu clucks her tongue impatiently and says, "Willow. Please pull yourself together and say hello." To us, she says in a stage whisper, "Her girlfriend broke up with her over the weekend, and she hasn't been handling it well."

What. I gawk at Mrs. Hsu. Did she really just say . . . *girl-friend*? And . . . *broke up*? A mob of emotions rise up and begin jostling for space inside me, and they are loud and raucous and screaming, "OH! MY! GODDDD!" I'm being given exactly what I wished for. For a brief moment, I think, *What if I'm magic?* But that's too far-fetched, even for me.

"Mom!" Willow says in a choked voice, her eyes still downcast. "Please. Could you not?"

Mrs. Hsu heaves an exasperated sigh but continues as if she hasn't heard her daughter. "It was their one-year anniversary. Ha! Teenagers. One year is such a long time for them. They have no idea, do they, Stephen?"

Honestly. You'd think she'd have a little more compassion. A year *is* a long time! Willow must feel awful. She was going to meet someone that day at the Moonraker; I wonder if it was her girlfriend—*ex*-girlfriend. I wonder how it happened. Did they break up right after we met? Did she know it was coming? But as I take a closer look at Willow, my curiosity evaporates almost immediately. She looks like she's literally crumpling under the weight of her heartache, and I feel my own heart begin to ache in sympathy.

At last, Willow looks up at us, and a flash of horrified recognition crosses her face before she composes herself and her mouth forms a brittle smile. She's not happy to see me at all. This is not good. But, I remind myself, she's just had her heart broken. Which is . . . well, it's not *good*, but it does increase my chances, doesn't it? Her gaze flits between me, Max, and Stephen, and I can see her trying to figure out how we fit together.

"Willow, this is Nozomi and Max, Stephen's niece and nephew," says Mrs. Hsu.

"Hi," she says stiffly.

"I'm so sorry about your breakup," I say. "But it's great to see you again."

She blinks at me, apparently rendered speechless by my insensitivity; I look at the floor and wish I had invisibility powers. The dreadful, yawning silence is cut mercifully short by Mrs. Hsu, who asks, puzzled, "Do you two know each other?" She looks at Stephen, and he shakes his head, equally puzzled.

"We happened to meet Willow at the Moonraker this past weekend," explains Max. "Totally random."

"What a fascinating coincidence!" exclaims Mrs. Hsu, who must not think it's *that* fascinating, because she follows this immediately with, "Well, I'm sure Max and Nozomi have lots to do, so let's not keep them any longer." She turns to Stephen and says, "And I still need to get your input about the tables."

"Of course," Stephen replies. He offers his arm to Mrs. Hsu and says, "Shall we go to my office?" To us, he says, "Take your time, guys. Max, I'll check in with you in a few minutes."

Mrs. Hsu takes Stephen's arm with exaggerated aplomb, and the two of them swan off, Mrs. Hsu already telling him how the catering company refuses to listen to her about the layout of the atrium. She pauses and addresses Willow over her shoulder: "Willow. Please get that makeup under control. And don't cry in front of the customers," and she and Stephen disappear around the corner.

"Oh my god," Willow mumbles. She takes two deep breaths, exhaling hard, then clenches her jaw and closes her eyes. More tears make their way down her cheeks before she swipes at them with surprising force, this time with the backs of her hands. It makes me want to wrap my arms around her and tell her everything's going to be okay.

Max clears his throat. "We should let you get back to . . . whatever you were doing. Come on, Zomi." He takes a couple of steps toward the door, and when I don't move to follow him, he grabs my elbow and says again, "Come *on*, Zo. Give the girl some privacy."

"Uh-huh," I say. I can't seem to tear myself away. "Are you okay?" I ask Willow, and immediately regret it. Of course she's not okay. "I mean, um . . ." What? What *do* I mean?

"Nozomi, leave her alone. Let's go," says Max even more urgently. He clearly doesn't trust me not to say something cringey and he's trying to get me out of here before I do, just like he did at the Moonraker. I understand and I sympathize. But the way I see it, the universe is giving me an enormous gift right now—a second chance—and I am not letting Max get in the way this time. This was obviously meant to happen, and I'm going to trust the universe to help me say the right thing. I shake Max off and say to Willow, "What I mean is, what can I do for you? Anything?"

See? Perfect.

She draws a shaky breath and looks up, her eyes dark with pain, and she's so beautiful I could swoon. I think I really *would* do nearly anything to make her happy. I start by offering her a pack of tissues from my bag, as she seems to have run out of her own. "What happened?" I ask.

She sniffles and dabs at her eyes with one of my tissues. "You don't want to hear it. It's a lot. Anyway, my mom's right—I can't be crying out here. Sorry about that."

"It's okay. We all need to vent sometimes," Max says in soothing tones, already backing away again. "But you probably need some time alone, and we do have to get to work, so—"

"No, wait!" I say. "We can talk later, if you want. Like after work. Max and Stephen and I are going to Off the Grid, and you could come with us and we could talk then." The words come streaming out in a hopeful rush, and she looks a bit stunned. Oh no. I've gone too far. Why, oh why don't I ever think before I—

"Maybe." She examines her fingernails. "I just . . . I don't know, I feel so down. I just want to go home and crawl into bed and cry."

"Yeah, no, I get it," I backpedal frantically. "Sorry, I didn't mean to—"

"I do love Off the Grid, though," she says, almost to herself, and my heart leaps. "And my parents are doing this all-vegetable diet, so there's literally nothing to eat at home. . . ."

"It might help to process what happened. With, you know, like a neutral third party or whatever," I say. Neutrally. "Or if you don't want to talk, it would take your mind off things for a little while."

She nods. "True." A long pause, during which she runs a hand through her silky hair and I imagine doing the same, and think *say yes, say yes, say yes* at her as hard as I can. Finally, she sighs, looks at me with a faint smile, and announces, "Okay. I'll go with you."

"Great! We'll stop by after work, then," I say, trying to sound like I ask beautiful girls to dinner all the time and this is Not a Big Deal.

But I can't stop the huge grin that spreads across my face once I've left the gift shop.

"Oh my god," Max says. "No. I know what you're thinking, and no."

"Don't be such a wet blanket. A girl can dream, can't she?"

He throws his hands up in disgust. "How am I even related to you?"

I know. I understand. It's madness to think that Willow's going to fall for me when she's so obviously devastated about her ex. But you never know. She just might.

7

ALL EVENING, I'VE BEEN IN WHAT MIGHT BEST be described as a tizzy: heart rate slightly elevated, head a bit light, skin thrumming and sensitive to Willow's presence— literally inches away from me, oh my god. I could probably power the entire city with my crush right now.

Things started off a bit rough; of all the amazing street food that Off the Grid offers, I picked saag paneer kati, a regrettable (though delicious) choice, given its tendency to squidge out of the roti wrap, and even worse, its high potential for Spinach Between the Teeth. It's been difficult to project a sexy, sympathetic listening vibe, what with my body being abuzz with excitement and my brain constantly sending hygiene alerts: *Wipe mouth! Check teeth!*

To make matters worse, when Max and Stephen went on

a quest for giant s'mores, Willow responded with surprising enthusiasm to my subsequent invitation to process her pain— by showing me photos of herself and her ex, Arden Frederick. Arden, naturally, is turn-your-head-for-a-double-take gorgeous. She's Black, with flawless medium-brown skin, tightly curled dark hair, perfect eyebrows, and a radiant smile. She's got the same glamorous It Girl energy as Willow, and she wants to be a filmmaker like Ava DuVernay. As Willow scrolled through photo after photo, I kept having flashbacks to Helena going, "You're just not my type." Willow and Arden are definitely the same type.

But I gritted my teeth and didn't give up, and finally, we're where I want to be: Willow spilling the contents of her heart, and me (mostly forgetting about spinach and) listening.

"We didn't even make it ten minutes before she did it," Willow says. "She was all, 'Willow, I can't do this anymore. I need to date other people.' Just like that! Just . . . boom. Goodbye."

"She didn't give you any warning at all?"

"None! I was totally blindsided." A single tear trickles down her cheek, and she sighs and asks, "Are you sure you don't mind this? I don't want to ruin your evening."

"You're not ruining my evening," is what I say. *You're making my evening*, is what I don't say. "What happened next?"

Willow sighs again and continues. "I told her she was probably freaking out because it's been a whole year, and we could take it down a notch if she wanted, but she wouldn't listen. She was just like, 'You should date other people, too.'"

Here, Willow pauses, and I take the opportunity to suggest, as a purely objective outside observer with no hidden agenda whatsoever, "Well, you *could* try dating other people."

"But I don't want to date other people! I want to date *her*!" Then she winces and says, "Oh my god, listen to me. Just tell me to shut up. Please."

"No. It's okay, really."

She bites her lip and looks at me, unsure, but I nod my head. "Go on."

"Well . . . all right." She leans forward. "So here's the kicker. I'm bawling my eyes out, right, and Arden's sitting there all reasonable, like she's so mature, such a grown-up, and she's all, 'I hope we can still be friends. I hope you'll still come to my birthday party.' I'm like . . . *what*?"

"No!" What a shitty thing to do.

"Right? Like I could possibly show my face there now, after she's dumped me."

"You're not going, are you?"

"No, of course not. It would be too humiliating." Willow pauses to blow her nose, and then adds, "But you want to know something? Part of me *wants* to go, just to see her. To make her take me back." She looks at me with her great, sad eyes, and says in a trembling voice, "I just want to go back to the way we were." Then her face crumples, and she buries her face in her hands and says in a muffled voice, "Oh god. Oh my god, I'm sorry. I'm so pathetic."

"You're not pathetic. You're just sad. You're allowed to be

sad." I'm a bit surprised to hear myself repeating Dad's mantra from the spring. But it's true, I guess.

And it seems to have an effect on Willow, who nods and says, "Yeah. Thanks. I needed to hear that." And then, with a sniffle and wry smile, "You must think I'm a total drama queen."

What I think is . . . well, it's not so much a thought as an endless stream of ginormous heart-eyes emojis. I love everything about her. Her passion. Her sensitive soul. Her willingness to be real, to say exactly what she thinks, even with a stranger like me. I just want to sit here and absorb more and more of her. But obviously I can't say all of that, so I say, "You're just passionate, that's all. And you're not afraid to be vulnerable. And . . ." I take a breath. "And I think that's really cool."

"Ohh." Willow smiles at me. "That's one of the nicest things anyone's ever said to me."

I smile back and try to will her to hug me, but my powers of telepathy are not that strong, apparently.

She adds, "Hey, thanks for listening. My friends are out of town on all these summer programs and vacations, and I haven't had anyone to talk to about this."

"I'm here for you anytime," I say, and I mean it. Honestly, I'd be content to just be her friend. I really would.

Oh, who am I kidding, that's not true. I want to be her girlfriend.

Stephen and Max arrive not long afterward, brandishing four s'mores the size of hamburgers. The marshmallow surfaces are crispy golden brown and white against the graham crackers, with chocolate squares, a generous slathering of Nutella, and pale banana slices peeking out; tucked neatly into sheets of crinkly white parchment paper, they're almost too pretty to eat.

Stephen distributes them and holds his s'more up. "To summer dreams!" he says, and we all raise our s'mores and echo, "To summer dreams!" Stephen hooks elbows with Max, and nods at me and Willow to do the same. So we scoot closer together and link our s'more-holding arms—and as we look into each other's eyes, I realize that she's close enough to kiss, and then it's not just the s'mores that are all warm and melty inside. After a few decadent bites, I recover enough to take a selfie of me and Willow holding our s'mores, and AirDrop it to Willow's phone before posting it on Instagram.

8

BOTH OF MY PARENTS FOLLOW ME ON SOCIAL media, which is not ideal, but it was never a problem until recently. Dad usually restricts himself to the occasional like, but ever since she moved out, Mom has been liking—and commenting on—nearly everything I post. "I just want to stay connected," she says whenever I ask her not to. And I know her life is "in upheaval," as she says practically every other day, but the only other action she's taken to "connect" with me has been to buy an air mattress so I can stay at her apartment three nights a week. So which is it? Does she really want to connect, or does she just want to leave cringey, age-inappropriate comments on my social media?

I should have blocked her as soon as it started happening.

But I didn't, which I see now was a serious lapse in judgment. At the very least, I should have remembered that from the day I set foot in San Francisco, Mom has been stalking me on Instagram with the obsessive commitment and wild-eyed enthusiasm of a K-pop fan. Because when I checked my Off the Grid photo with Willow a minute ago, partly to see who'd liked it and partly to relive the moment, I discovered that Mom had commented:

Gurrrl! Who's the new bae? 😍 😏

So many things wrong on so many levels. I begin by deleting her comment and messaging her: **PLEASE do NOT leave comments on my posts. Especially don't say stuff like gurrl or bae**

She responds right away: **Why not? And what's wrong with saying gurl and bae? Did I use them wrong or something?**

Me: First of all, you're old, and it's weird. But also because gurl and bae are Black Vernacular English and it's not okay to use those words like they're yours. It's like you're pretending to be something you're not.

It's like when people get kanji tattoos when they're not even Chinese or Japanese.

It's just all-around embarrassing and inappropriate.

I know I'm being super lecture-y, but who else is going to tell her? Not her white friends, or her Asian ones.

Mom: I'm just trying to connect with you.

Me: Don't

She doesn't respond, and after a minute I feel bad about how harsh that was, so I add, **Please.**

It only takes a second before a reply pops up: **What if I just DM you?**

Frankly, I'd prefer if she didn't DM me, either. I'd prefer it if she stopped trying to connect with me at all. But I guess that's not fair.

To make myself feel better, I look at the photo again—taken just an hour ago—and bask in the warm glow of the memory, how generous and honest Willow was with her emotions, how great it felt that she trusted me enough to open her heart to me the way she did.

I wonder if Mom really does think Willow might be my . . . no, I'm sure she was joking.

But what if she wasn't? She could just as easily have written, *Who's your new friend?*

I examine the photo more closely. Getting a good selfie requires a lot of close contact, and I was pretty much vibrating with desire when we took it. Is it obvious? Is there something in my body language that gives me away? Or maybe there's something in Willow's body language. I search for clues, but it's no use. My heart—my poor, pitiful heart—is clouding my judgment.

And then another comment appears: **who's THAT?** 😍

Oh my god. "**Who's THAT!**" With heart-eyes! The commenter is Tracey, a girl from the QSA who was in my art history class and whose sister was on the track team with Helena. I feel dual flames of excitement and petty, vindictive hope that Helena will see this. I reply: **wouldn't you like to know?** 😊

On a whim (oh, okay, fine, with a clear purpose), I go to Willow's account.

She's posted the same photo, and it's received lots of likes and several comments. The third one down reads, **gurl who's the new girl lol**

For one blood-curdling moment I think that Mom has somehow found Willow's account and commented on the photo. Then I see that the commenter is not @jennifer_nagai_1972, but someone named @kris_tea_nuh.

Then I look at the replies and almost have a heart attack:

@Cygnet1000: 👆 **what @kris_tea_nuh said!**

@Willow_Shoe: ???????? Idk what you're talking about
😅 😅 😅

@kris_tea_nuh: WAIT WUT srsly WHO IS THIS MYSTERY WOMAN! 👀

@Willow_Shoe: 😂 😂 😂 🤐

She can't possibly—I mean, she's not really—okay. Calm down. She said she didn't know what they were talking about. She posted all those laugh-crying emojis.

But there's that mouth-zipped-shut emoji.

It's a joke. She's joking.

Except . . . if people—that is to say, not my mother, but real, actual, normal people—are saying it, maybe we *do* look like a couple. Maybe there *is* something there. Maybe I have a chance after all.

Seconds later, I get a message from Willow:

hey, have you seen the comments on my post?

I have, and even though it pains me, I text back:

Willow: people are ASKING QUESTIONS, mystery woman
Me: omg lol
We're the talk of the town
Willow: right? it's weirdly empowering lol
Feels way better than crying

A plan begins to form in my head: wispy, vaporous, glimmering. I try to sit with it and wait for it to take shape. But when I begin to consider all the alternatives, all the possible outcomes, I start to doubt myself. I know I wanted this to be the summer that everything changes, the summer I Make Things Happen instead of stumbling around and embarrassing myself, but this . . .

The not-quite-a-plan swirls around, twinkling with tantalizing possibility. *You know what the first step is*, it whispers. *Take it*.

Quickly, before I can succumb to any more second-guessing, I start typing.

Me: wanna do another one?
Willow: . . .
Me: Just for fun, I mean. Like a prank.
Willow: . . .

I try not to pass out while I stare at my phone and wait for her reply. *Breathe, Nozomi. In, out. In, out.*

Willow: omg let's. I'll take you somewhere really cool and tell everyone it's our first date. We'll blow everyone's minds lol

Me: 👍

Willow: this is so much better than moping. The universe sent you to me at just the right time lol

I stare at my phone. *The universe sent you to me at just the right time. I* could have written that sentence to *her.* It has to be a sign. I gaze at it for a while, luxuriate in it. I feel like I could read it forever, over and over, and never get tired of it. Under the golden beams of light emanating from that sentence (Let me read it again: *The universe sent you to me at just the right time.* Yes! Yes! Yes!) my lumpy gray doubt vanishes, and in its place is my plan, blazing and brilliant.

I check Willow's feed again, and she's left a new comment:

Stay tuned for further developments 😉 💕

It takes me forever to fall asleep. My brain starts spinning plans, playing out endless pastel-colored scenarios of Willow and me going on a series of pretend dates that become increasingly romantic and increasingly, perfectly, one hundred percent real.

9

STEPHEN BARELY LOOKS UP FROM HIS PHONE when I go downstairs for breakfast, which is disappointing because I tried a cat eye with my eyeliner this morning and I'm pretty proud of how it turned out. I sit down with a bowl of cereal, and Stephen absently pours us both a cup of tea, sinks into the chair next to me, and sighs heavily. He takes a sip, sets it down, and sighs again, rubbing his hands over his face.

"Is everything okay?" I ask.

He's received an email from Oak Vista, an "active elder community with continuing comprehensive care," according to its signature. The place is in such high demand that there's a wait list to get in, and the email is a reminder that a special auction for spots on the "exclusive wait list" is coming up—which is to say, it's a reminder that the richest wannabe residents can buy their way ahead of the others.

"I think I'm going to do it, Zozo. I could hire someone to take care of her here, but that's just buying time. I wish I knew how to convince her to go."

I blow on my tea, do a test slurp, and put it back down, panting. How does Stephen drink it like this? His mouth must be made of asbestos.

It has to be hard to think about leaving the house you've been in for, what—I do the math—she's been there since before Dad was born, so that makes it over fifty years. On the other hand: "She's a grown-up. I thought grown-ups were reasonable people."

"Ha." Stephen smiles wryly at me and then fondly at Lance, who's just walked into the kitchen. "Hey, love."

"Hey, love," answers Lance. "Good morning, Nozomi. Ooh, that's a new look for you, with the eyes. I love it. Very sophisticated." He putters around, grinding coffee and preparing to scramble some eggs.

"New look?" Stephen looks at me as if he's seeing me for the first time this morning, and his face lights up. "I love it, sweetheart. I'm sorry I didn't notice earlier."

Max walks in, tucking his shirt into his jeans, and yawns mightily, not bothering to cover his hideous gaping maw.

"You're disgusting," I say.

"*You're* disgusting," he responds automatically, and pours some coffee into a thermos. "Hey, Lance, is that a new coffee grinder?"

"As a matter of fact, it is! Nice one, Sherlock." That's Lance's nickname for Max, who notices everything.

"Hey, Max." I poke him with my phone and show him Willow's Instagram. "Read the comments and weep." He scans them and shakes his head, which is not the reaction I was going for. So I escalate. "She said the universe brought me to her at just the right time."

"Wait, what? This sounds like something I want to see. Show me," says Stephen. I turn the phone toward him, a little embarrassed, though I don't know why. There's no need to feel embarrassed. It's just a bunch of silly comments from people who think I could be Willow's new girlfriend. (*does internal shimmy of joy*)

Stephen's eyebrows go down as he reads, and he says, "Wait . . . you and Willow are together?" He transitions to some light side-eye. "Did I miss something?"

Ulp. Now that I think about this from Stephen's point of view, it does feel a bit . . . well, much. "Um. Well, no, it's—"

"What? I need to see this." Lance turns and gestures for the phone with one hand, still stirring the eggs with his other hand.

"Here, sweetheart, let me take over," says Stephen, reaching for the spatula, but Lance waves him off.

"Sorry, hon, but no. I want to be able to *eat* these eggs." Once he has my phone, he looks at it and reads, "'Who's that . . . mystery woman . . . stay tuned for further details?' Zozo! New job, new look, new girlfriend—well done, you!" He takes another look at the screen. "So. When do we get to meet her?"

Ohhhh. This is escalating a little faster than I intended.

"Yes, dear sister. When will you bring your *new girlfriend* home for dinner?" Max gives me a saccharine smile, clearly enjoying my discomfort.

Ergh. I should tell the truth before this gets out of hand. Only I don't want to see the disappointment on Lance's face (or the smug grin on Max's) when I tell everyone what this photo really represents; and if I tell them why Willow commented *Stay tuned*, and what we're planning to do next, they'll say it's petty and dishonest and tell me not to go through with it, which . . . I was really looking forward to going through with it. I try to hedge. "Shut up, Max, it's only been a day. I mean, the emotions are very real. Obviously. But it's not . . . We haven't even had our first official date yet. So back off."

Max rolls his eyes, and Stephen seems to be keeping his face carefully neutral. But I'm not lying, exactly. I didn't actually say that Willow and I were seeing each other, did I?

"Aw, look at you blush. Well, you're smart and beautiful and you deserve a fun romance, so here's hoping it works out." Lance gestures with the spatula, and it slips out of his grasp. "Whoops."

"Sweetheart!" Stephen yelps. "Now there's egg everywhere!"

"It's not *everywhere*. It's just a little bit right here," Lance says. He grabs a rag and kisses a grumbling Stephen. "Don't be such a drama queen."

Max still looks skeptical. "*She* seems like kind of a drama queen."

"Whatever, Max. She's just—" What did I say yesterday? "She's just passionate. And not afraid to be vulnerable."

Max takes another slurp of coffee and says, "No offense, Zo, but I just don't see it. I'd get out now before she comes to her senses and dumps you."

"Shut *up*, Max!" I've so had it with him.

"Max!" says Stephen sternly.

He looks shocked—*shocked*, I tell you! "I was just giving her some friendly advice!"

"Why do you always have to be such a dick?" I gripe.

"Why do you always have to be such a crybaby?"

"Dear sweet children," Stephen says. "Please shut your pretty little pieholes and stop fighting so I can eat my breakfast in peace."

Once we get to the Harrison, I look to see if Willow's in the gift shop, and . . . *yes.* There she is. She looks up and I wave, and she *smiles and waves back*, and suddenly it's as if the world has been dipped in a sparkle filter. I think I'll drop in. Why not? We're almost-girlfriends, after all—at least, that's what Stephen thinks—or that's what I hope he thinks—so really it would be strange if I *didn't* go over.

"Can you take a long lunch?" she asks me as soon as I'm close enough. "I have the perfect location for our first date photo shoot." She shows me pictures of the Fairmont Hotel. "Isn't it gorgeous? Everyone will be so jealous."

I ooh and ahh over the images, agree to meet her at eleven

thirty in the atrium, and rush after Stephen to get his permission to take a long lunch.

"On your second day of work?" he asks.

"Please? It's our first real date!" I say, using my best puppy dog eyes, and he caves immediately. I feel a little guilty about lying, but you could argue that it *is* our first date, kind of—so it's not *exactly* lying.

I don't even get a chance to savor this little victory before Max starts singing quietly in my ear, "Let it go, let it *gooooo* . . ."

"Shut up, asshole." I give him a death stare and quicken my pace.

"Be. Nice," says Stephen to me, which is so unfair. "And no swearing in the museum," he says over his shoulder as he peels off for his office. Which is fair.

When Max and I reach the door to the staff room, he shocks me by saying, "Hey, I'm sorry I was a dick. It's just . . . okay, I'm not trying to be mean, but this has rebound written all over it. And I don't want you to get into another situation with a girl who leads you on and then breaks your heart."

I'm touched that he's being so sweet. I wish I could tell him the whole story, but then he'll try to make me feel bad for lying to people. Anyway, Willow's not Helena.

"It'll be fine," I say.

"I don't think it will."

"Don't worry about me."

"I do. Because you always do this. You tell yourself some wild story about the way you want things to be, and you totally ignore all the signs that point to anything you don't want to see. Like, remember when you convinced yourself that Rosie Demetrius liked you? And I kept telling you she was just using you to do her homework? And you refused to listen? What happened?"

"I didn't listen because you *always* assume the worst of people, so why would I trust your opinion? Anyway, I was younger, and Rosie was . . . she was sneaky."

Max snorts.

"I'm sorry I'm not a grinch like you, Max. But I'm not as naïve as you think, either. I know the risks. I can see the challenges."

He gives me a long look, and sighs. "Fine. Just . . . try to manage your expectations, okay? Try to stay within the realm of reality." He really does seem genuinely concerned. Maybe I *should* tell him about my plan, to prove that I'm not blundering into this with my eyes closed.

I take a big breath and say, "I have a plan."

"A plan? What, to make her fall in love with you?"

"No, stupid." But I realize with sudden clarity that it is, in fact, a plan to make her fall in love with me. I see his face and hear the derision in his voice, and I understand that I can never tell him anything. "It's a plan to . . ." *To what?* "To manage my expectations," I say triumphantly. There. He'll like that.

"Hmm." Max looks somewhat mollified. "Well, be careful. I don't want you getting hurt."

"Aw. My big thtwong ovohpwotective bwutha." I bump

him companionably with my shoulder, but the timing is off and I guess I bump him a little too hard, because it throws him off balance.

"Hey!" He steps back to catch himself before knocking into me accidentally-on-purpose, and we keep bumping each other this way, harder and harder until it's full-on human bumper cars in the staff room and we're bashing into each other and laughing and shouting, "Oh, I'm *so* sorry!" and, "No, pardon *me*!" until finally Max lunges and I lose my footing and fall right into Dela, who (I swear) wasn't there a second ago.

My momentum sends the two of us staggering. I manage to catch myself on the wall, but Dela, after some highly comical windmilling, unfortunately tumbles to the floor.

"Oh my god, I'm so sorry!" I yelp. "Are you okay?" And maybe I'm a bad person, or maybe I'm still giddy from playing bumper cars, but a slightly hysterical giggle rises up and I have to disguise it with a cough. Because of course Dela would walk in just in time for me to bowl her over. Come on, it's kind of funny.

But I can tell that Dela can tell that I'm not really coughing, and that she does *not* think it's funny. Great.

"Here, let me help you up," I say meekly, and extend my hand, but Dela practically slaps it aside, glowering as if I'd knocked her over on purpose, as if I'd thought to myself, *what can I do to make Dela hate me even more?* and crouched behind the door, eagerly waiting for her to walk through so I could pounce on her and embarrass us both.

"I'm fine," she says brusquely, and gets to her feet without looking at me. "Stephen said he'd set aside some space in here for me to store a couple boxes."

"Um." Max and I look at each other in confusion.

"It's fine. I'll figure it out myself," she says, and then, finally, she looks at each of us. "Excuse me. Do you mind?"

We step aside silently.

She opens the door, then pauses and turns halfway around and says, "The stuff inside those boxes I'm bringing in is pretty fragile, and I don't want anything damaged. So seeing as you guys seem to have trouble walking without knocking things over, I'd appreciate it if you could stay away from them."

Max turns so Dela can't see his face, and his mouth makes the shape of the words *what the fuck*, which is the exact feeling that I am having.

Being a mature young adult, however, I look at Dela and say, "Okay, no problem," instead of snickering, or opening my eyes wide at Max and silently mouthing back, *I KNOW*, which is what I really want to do. Though I do make a face at her back when she leaves. Because really. Come. On.

10

GOLD-COLORED MARBLE PILLARS SWIRLING WITH gray and red veins rise all around me in the lobby of the Fairmont to a cream-colored ceiling embellished with elaborate gilded wood scrollwork. A bellhop in a green jacket trimmed with gold braid strides across a gleaming white marble floor, wheeling a cart loaded with Louis Vuitton luggage. It's hard not to feel a little intimidated by all the grandeur, but Willow sweeps through it with an easy nonchalance. "I had my sixteenth birthday party here," she says. "Isn't it great?"

I sit down carefully on a burgundy velvet armchair. "It's like a palace or something."

"I know, right? When I was little, I used to pretend I was a princess and this was *my* palace." As she says this, Willow sinks onto the chair opposite mine and crosses her legs at the ankles, like she is an actual princess. I'm about to cross my ankles so I'll look as casually elegant as she does, but then I notice that the cuffs of my jeans are a little scraggly, so I settle for tucking my feet under the chair.

"I used to pretend I was a princess, too," I say. "And then I said once in kindergarten that I wanted to *marry* the princess, and all my friends said if I was going to marry the princess, I had to be the prince, and I cried. It was the worst. My mom had to have a talk with the teacher."

"Oh my god, same!" Willow exclaims. "Only I told everyone that I wanted to be a princess who married other princesses, and if they didn't like it, they could fuck off." Willow laughs. "My mom got called in because of the swearing."

"No!" That's so badass. "You're my hero," I say, and I'm not even kidding.

"The best part is my mom totally missed the lesbian angle. She literally thought I was just ornery and liked bossing people around. When I came out to her, she was like"—Willow waves her hands frantically—"'But you always wanted to be a princess!'"

I've only met Mrs. Hsu that one time, but Willow does such a spot-on impression that I can't help laughing. "I'm sorry," I say. "I don't mean to laugh at your mom."

"No, it's okay. I laugh at her all the time. She's so smart, right? But she's *so* clueless." Then she rises just as gracefully as she sat down and says, "Okay, let's touch up our makeup and take some pictures."

I follow her to the bathroom, which has a whole entire entry room with a chaise longue, a humongous potted fern in the corner, and a white marble vanity countertop in front of a giant mirror.

Willow reaches into her bag and produces another bag, the contents of which she dumps onto the counter: a couple of eye shadow palettes, several lipsticks, a bag of brushes, and assorted pots and vials. "You want some of these face wipes so you can start over?" She proffers a little pack. "Or do you just want to touch up what you're wearing?"

Oh. Do I look that bad? And I worked so hard on my cat eye this morning. "Uh. I think I'll just do a touch-up." All I have with me is my lipstick—it never occurred to me that I'd need anything else. Why, oh why didn't I think about that? Of course a perfect, beautiful girl like Willow would want to make everything perfect and beautiful for a planned photo op.

Willow must sense my embarrassment because she says quickly, "Don't worry, you look great. I just love playing with makeup, that's all. Can you tell?" She laughs, gesturing at all the products spilled in front of us, and I smile weakly.

"It's kind of my passion," she goes on. "Here, look. I was the makeup artist for a production of *A Midsummer Night's Dream* that we did in this arts program I was in last year. It's where Arden and I met, actually." She pulls her phone out and shows me photos of Puck, Oberon, and Titania. They're fantastic—not just cool-fantastic, but fantasy-fantastic. Wild rainbows for an androgynous Puck, cool blues and silvers for Oberon (played by Arden, who looks stunning), and sparkly gold and green for Titania. They look truly otherworldly and magical.

"You should do this for a career!" I say. "You're so talented."

Willow shrugs modestly as she chooses a lipstick and starts dabbing color on her lips. "Ha! I wish."

"No, for real. You could work in Hollywood and win an Oscar one day."

"Aww, you're so sweet." Willow beams at me. "I *knew* I liked you."

My heart flips over and I say, "I knew I liked you, too," which, once I've said it, sounds like I *like* her–like her, so I walk it back, stammering, "I, uh, I mean, as a friend. Just as a friend," which makes it a thousand times worse, so I laugh: "Ha-ha-ha!" Oh my god.

But Willow seems to think I'm joking and just laughs along with me, thank goodness. I take out my lipstick and try to copy the way she's applied her own. Then I watch as she expertly applies a new shade of eye shadow and fusses with her eyeliner before declaring herself camera-ready. She smiles at my reflection in the mirror and says, "Let's go make some content, girlfriend." Girlfriend. I smile back happily. I know she doesn't mean it for real, but there's something intimate and genuine about the way she says it—that twinkle in her eye, maybe— that gives me goose bumps.

For the next twenty minutes, we wander around the hotel and take a million photos: sitting on the plush chairs and leaning against the marble columns in the lobby; eating tiny sandwiches in the restaurant; standing in front of the fountain on the rooftop garden with the city skyline in the background. We do duckfaces, we do sidelong glances, we do over-the-shoulder smolders. Willow shows me how to hold my arms and hands and how to place my feet so I look like a model; she reminds anyone who takes a photo of the two of us to hold the phone higher—no, a little bit higher. I screw up the courage to suggest we do one where we're kissing, but Willow wrinkles her nose and points out that this is supposed to be a first date, so maybe we shouldn't. Which stings a little, I'll admit. But except for that, and the fact that it's not real (of *course* it's not real), it's everything I could have hoped for. By the time we head back to the museum, I'm buoyant. The photos have been curated and posted (for the record, we look amazing, and Willow's caption, **my new mystery girl**, is genius), and it feels like Willow and I have really clicked. Step One of Operation Make Willow Fall in Love with Me has been a success.

We're just down the street from the museum when Willow stops dead and clutches my arm.

"What? What is it?" I ask, but then I see it.

It's Dela. And . . . is that . . . Arden?

11

I ONLY KNOW HER FROM THE PHOTOS ON WILLOW'S phone, but one look at Willow's horror-struck face confirms my suspicion. Arden and Dela are framed by the front doors of the museum, face-to-face. Arden is smiling down at Dela, who also appears to be . . . smiling? I didn't know that was a thing she did.

"But what . . . but how . . ." I don't even know what questions to ask.

Willow is also struggling to put a sentence together. "What the . . . How could she . . . Already?" Her chest is heaving and her hands, which are now digging into my arm quite painfully, are shaking.

"Maybe they're just friends?" I venture.

Willow gives me A Look. "Seriously?"

They do seem to be standing a *little* too close to be just friends. And there does seem to be a lot of flirty body language going on.

"Will you be my girlfriend?"

WHAT? "Your . . . your . . . ," I stammer. Is she . . . could she be . . . right *now*?

Her grip on my arm tightens even more and she gives it a little shake. "Please? It wouldn't be for real. Just so that Arden—" Right on cue, Arden turns her head, and I see the expressions cross her face one by one as if in slow motion: recognition, surprise, guilt, false cheer. She looks at Dela, and the guilt returns to her face for a second—a barely noticeable grimace—before she flashes a big smile at us. Willow squeezes again. "Please."

My first thought is *Duh. Of course she didn't mean for real, you numbskull.* My second thought is *She has* really *strong hands.*

"Oh, right! Absolutely. Sure!" I say. "I totally knew you didn't mean for real."

Willow sighs and releases her death grip on my arm. "Thank you." Then she lowers her hand to mine and clasps it loosely as we move forward. "Just act natural."

I close my fingers around hers and try to push down the disappointment—and the terror—roiling inside me. Ignore it. Act natural. I can do this. I have to do this. Besides, it's a good thing. We're holding hands, aren't we? I'll focus on that, and on taking care of Willow. I'll pretend she really does want to be my girlfriend. It's fine. I'm fine.

Meanwhile, Dela is openly staring at us as if she can't quite believe her eyes. I bet she doesn't think that Willow and I belong together. Well, I don't care what she thinks. She's rude and pretentious and I'm just going to ignore her.

"Hi there, you!" Willow tosses her hair and takes one of the stances she showed me during our photo shoot, one foot slightly forward, back hip jutted out. "I didn't expect to see you here. Well," she corrects herself, "not after recent events, anyway." Ouch. She may look soft and ethereal, but she has a core of pure, razor-sharp steel. But there's an undercurrent of pain in her voice, too. It makes me feel protective.

"Yeah, I didn't expect to come here, but Dela and I got to talking about her installation, and I just had to see it," says Arden in a voice like warm smoke and honey. She's just as beautiful in person as she is in Willow's photographs: soft and curvy all over, from the mass of tight curls in her side-parted hair, to her round brown face, to her dimpled hands, her strong thighs, and her perfectly pedicured, rounded toenails. She looks at Dela, and then back at Willow and me, her face a portrait of sympathy. "I'm sorry. I hope this isn't too weird." Wow, she is good. If I hadn't seen the guilt on her face a moment ago, I would never guess that she was faking, too.

"No, it's totally fine," says Willow, even though it's clearly not. And then, "Oh! I haven't introduced you to Nozomi. How rude of me. Nozomi, this is Arden, my um . . . well. You know. And Arden, this is Nozomi." She makes a show of smiling at me adoringly and looking down at our intertwined fingers and going, *oh, oops!* and letting go, as if she'd forgotten we were holding hands and suddenly realized that it might make Arden uncomfortable. She's so good, *I* almost believe her.

"Hi," I say. "Nice to meet you." I consider adding, *I've heard a lot about you*, but I don't have the nerve.

"Nice to meet you, too," says Arden, and adds, "I've heard a lot about you," because she evidently *does* have the nerve. She grins at Dela, whose expression changes from brazenly curious to acutely embarrassed; she shifts her feet and refuses to meet my eye, and it's my turn to stare. What has she been saying about me? It can't have been anything good.

"Well! This was fun. But I have to get back to work, so . . ." Willow glides through the space between Dela and Arden, forcing them to step farther apart, and I trail after her, trying to emulate her icy dignity. She pauses at the door and takes my hand in hers again. "Bye, you two!" she trills as we pass through. Once we're inside, she murmurs, "Can you just walk with me to the gift shop?"

I am one hundred percent in favor of walking with Willow to the gift shop. Especially when she takes my hand again. We walk slowly, all the way across the atrium, through the gift shop, and into the tiny office at the back, where she drops my hand and collapses against the closed door.

"She told me there wasn't anyone else. Of *course* there was someone else!" Willow moans. She tells me that Dela and Arden go to the same arts magnet school, where Dela focuses on visual arts and Arden studies drama. The two of them spent hours working together on a collaborative final project for one of their classes. "She *told* me about her! How could I have missed it? How could I have been so stupid?"

She still loves Arden, I think, crestfallen. Although, no kidding.

"And she *works* here! At the museum!" Willow's grief flows seamlessly into outrage as she speaks. "That means I'm going to have to *see* them together. What the fuck! How *dare* she."

"Are we *sure* they're together?" I can't help asking one more time.

"If they aren't together yet, they will be soon. Why else would she have come here?"

"But wouldn't she want to avoid you if she's dating someone new?"

"You don't know Arden," says Willow darkly. "She wants everyone to love her. She wants everyone to be her friend."

"Even the girl she dumped on their one-year anniversary?"

"Especially the girl she dumped on their one-year anniversary. It proves that she's evolved." Willow groans and closes her eyes. "I hate this so much."

"You're going to be okay," I tell her. "You're strong and you're resilient. Look, you ran into your ex and her new . . ." I don't want to say *girlfriend*, since who knows? ". . . and Dela. And you made it through! I was in awe of how smooth you were, really."

"But that was only because you were there with me," she protests.

"And I'll keep being here whenever you need me."

She nods her thanks and we lapse into silence for a while. Then she turns to me, a strange light in her eyes. "How would you feel if we kept pretending to be girlfriends?"

"Kept pretending . . ." I can't finish the sentence. It's not *quite* where I'd hoped our social media romance would lead.

"If we go back to normal tomorrow, they'll know today was an act. Dela would figure it out for sure, since she's here every day."

"Uh-huh."

"It wouldn't have to be for very long." Willow starts pacing back and forth across the cramped space, newly energized. "Just a few weeks. Just long enough to make Arden believe that we're for real."

"For real," I echo.

"Exactly," she says, barely listening to me. "We wouldn't have to go on dates or anything. We could just keep posting pictures . . . Except could you come with me to Arden's birthday party? And the gala! And maybe we could even do a double date at some point!"

"A double date?" I'm scrambling so hard to keep up that it seems I've lost the brain power to do anything but repeat what she says.

"Just enough to make her see what she's missing—" She gasps. "Do you think it might make her want me back? Doesn't that happen all the time? The one person who's afraid of commitment breaks up and leaves, and then they realize what they've lost, and they beg their ex to get back together!"

"Back together?" Stop, Nozomi!

"It happens all the time in movies. And in real life! It happened to my cousin."

"It did?"

"Uh-huh. His girlfriend wanted to get married, and he didn't, so they broke up, and he came to his senses and begged her to take him back, and now they're married!" Willow smiles exultantly. "So, will you help me?" she asks.

When the fog finally clears, I am conflicted. On the one hand, I realize, she's essentially asking me to play a character in a movie she's going to produce for Arden's benefit in order to win her back.

On the other hand, my character would be Willow's Girlfriend. I'd be going on dates with her. I'd be the one who helps her through her heartache. I'd be an accomplice. A trusted ally. And as long as we're talking about movies, in every rom-com I've ever seen, the fake girlfriend becomes the real girlfriend in the end. Every. Single. Time. That's pretty good odds, if you ask me.

I take a deep breath. "Okay. Let's do it."

Willow pumps her fists in triumph. "Yes! Oh, thank you! You're so sweet—I *knew* you'd say yes. I bet you'd make an amazing girlfriend in real life," she says, and she stops and smiles at me, whereupon I promptly melt into a puddle of goo.

"Ha-ha! What are you talking about?" I manage, despite my goofication.

"No, for real, though. I've been such a mess, and you've totally had my back. I'm so grateful," she says. "Truly." She smiles at me again, and for one breathless moment, I forget myself and almost close my eyes for a kiss, but she throws her arms around me and hugs me, whispering, "Thanks for being a friend."

Our first hug. As friends.

I sink into it and breathe in the sweet, citrusy scent of her shampoo. I think I might pass out, though whether it's from hope or disappointment, I can't tell.

12

IN A PERFECT WORLD, I WOULD NEVER HAVE TO deal with Dela again. She'd stay in the courtyard and glare at people and build her art installation with her dad, and I would write about the museum collection and pretend to date Willow (and later, please-oh-please, *actually* date Willow), and our paths would never cross. But Stephen asked me this morning to stay after work and help Dela with her boxes.

"Do I have to?" I whined. "Why can't Max do it?" I rarely get whiny with Stephen, but I was hoping to spend my afternoon savoring the comments on my First Date with Willow at the Fairmont post and maybe going to Sephora to look for eye shadow.

"Please, Zozo."

So now I have to stay late so I can work with a surly

porcupine who hates me and almost certainly doesn't want my help. This should be fun.

I find Dela across the street, wrestling a huge cardboard box out of the back of her van. Being a kind and thoughtful (and okay, conscripted) person, I ask if I can help.

"No, thanks," she says, and grimaces, as if talking to me is causing her actual, physical pain.

"You sure? I really don't mind," I say, but she shakes her head.

"I'm fine."

"I can hold the door for you," I offer, and when she doesn't answer, I finally say, "Look. I'm just trying to help you. This box is obviously too big for you to carry all by yourself, so why don't I just—"

"I said I'm fine." She butts in front of me and pushes the door closed with her hip.

"Did you remember to lock the front doors?" I ask. "I could do that for you."

Dela pauses for a moment and sighs before putting the box down, saying, "Don't touch it." Then she adds as an after-thought, "Please."

"What's inside?"

"Nothing. Just don't touch it, okay?" Cursing and mutter-ing, she walks past me toward the front of the van as if I'm not even there.

How rude.

I look at the box. The flaps at the top are arranged so that each corner is tucked under the flap on the adjoining side—but one of the corners has come loose. Someone was clearly in a hurry, or maybe it got jostled in the van.

Hmm. I hear Dela's voice near the front of the van—from the sound of it, she's on the phone. "I don't *know* where it is, Dad," she's saying. "You're the one who was in charge of loading it."

I call out, "You want to give me the keys so I can lock the back?"

"No! Just stay with the box," she snaps.

I don't know what Arden sees in her.

I listen to Dela argue with her dad. I look at the box. What could be so top secret that she won't tell me what's inside? Human skulls, maybe. Black-market bat wings. I wonder if Arden knows. I bet she does. How come Arden gets to know what's in the box and I don't? I bet Dela thinks I wouldn't understand it. I bet she thinks I'm not smart enough. Well, she's wrong. After all, contrary to what she may think, I've actually *studied* art. And am I the Digital Archive Intern, or am I not? You could even say it's my *job* to know what's inside that box.

There's nothing wrong with pulling on that loose flap and taking one tiny little peek. I'll tuck it right back in afterward. She'll never know.

I have no idea what I thought I'd find, but I am definitely not prepared for the colorful chaos of a thousand origami cranes and butterflies. Intrigued, I pluck out a crane and hold it in my hand. It's perfect. Delicately balanced and precisely folded, it looks ready to take flight. How odd. It feels like the exact antithesis of Dela, with her big black boots and perma-scowl. I lean around the corner of the van to see if I can catch a glimpse of her, trying to find some visual connection between the whimsical contents of the box, and the dour girl sitting in the front seat of the van.

"Yeah," Dela is saying. "Okay, fine, then." Her voice has the sound of someone about to hang up, so I drop the crane back into the box and try to fold the flap back under. But it's trickier than I anticipated, and as I struggle, the other flaps come loose, and then I hear the van door slam, the keys jingle, and Dela's voice saying, "I'll see you in a minute. Bye."

Shit. In a panic, I consider my options: Run away? She'll see me and figure it out. Hide behind the box? What am I, a tod-dler? Under the van? Not enough space, plus—gross. Maybe I can blame someone else? A sneak attack from a notorious box-opening menace prowling the streets?

"Hey!" Dela has rounded the corner of the van. What do I do? What do I say? In the face of her fury, I surrender my last remaining shred of rational thought, pick up the box, and begin walking across the street. *If I can just get this inside the building, everything will be all right,* is what's going through my head. I will have helped her. It will all be fine.

The box is light, but it's huge and awkward and I realize almost immediately that I can't see my feet; a calmer me might reconsider the wisdom of my plan at this point, but panic-mode me is fully committed. I can hear Dela yelling at me, but it does nothing to make me stop. If anything, it makes me walk faster.

I'm about halfway across the street when the box begins to slide out of my grasp. I try to hoick it up to readjust it, but it goes all crooked and tips over slightly, and then the wind picks up, and cranes and butterflies begin spilling out of the top and flying down the street.

I'm dimly aware of Dela still shouting at me, but all that matters is the voice in my head saying *keep going, keep going*, and then my foot catches on something and I'm falling, and there's a screech of tires and for one terrifying moment I'm sure I'm going to feel a car slam into me and hurl me ten feet into the air—but what I feel instead is the box collapsing beneath me as I land on it with a *whump*.

I lie there for a moment, trying to catch my breath as my heart attempts to bang a hole right through my chest. I'm breathing. My heart is going. Which means I'm alive. That's good. I look in the direction of the tire screech, ready to reassure the driver who's probably leaped out to see if I'm okay, but all I see is a garbage truck rounding the corner, and a few pedestrians craning their necks at me from the sidewalk, as if they're trying to decide whether I'm in enough distress for them to come out and help me.

So not a near-death experience, then.

Slowly, I pick myself up and survey the damage, and—oh no. Oh no, oh no, oh no. This is not good.

The box has a me-sized dent mashed into it, and the force

of impact has whooshed most of the origami forms onto the street. I scrabble at them, frantically trying to sweep everything into a pile, but at that moment, the garbage truck groans past and all the cranes and butterflies whirl up and tumble away from me, sucked into its wake. I pick up the ruined box and a few sad, squashed cranes trickle out.

This is very, very bad.

I stand still for a moment, partly because my body seems to have turned to lead, and partly because I'm afraid to turn around and look at Dela. I really don't want to see what this has done to her. She already hates me so much.

Finally, I force myself to face her. She's standing motionless, her face stricken, staring first at the escaping origami forms and then at the crushed box in my hands, as if she can't quite believe what she's seeing. I have this bizarre sensation that the two of us are trapped in this wretched moment while the rest of the world trundles along, blissfully unaware of the drama unfolding here on the street. I wonder hazily if I can rewind my life back to the moment just before I decided to open the box.

And then she starts screaming at me, time lurches forward again, and reality comes crashing back.

Considering the fact that I was making a sincere effort to be nice to Dela and help her with her box, you'd think she would be a little more understanding about the completely accidental accident that happened. But no. She's acting like I came out

97

to the van, tore the box from her grasp, and hurled it into the street, shrieking to the skies in evil triumph as the wind picked up the contents and sent them swirling all over the city.

Even after I apologized a hundred times as I followed her to the recycling dumpster, even after I begged her to let me make amends, all she would say was, "The installation is ruined and there's nothing you can do to fix it." Clang. The lid of the dumpster slammed down.

"What if—what if I helped you fold some more of those things? How many were there? Maybe we could—"

"There were literally a thousand of them in there. It takes three minutes to make each one, and that's if you know what you're doing. Not to mention the time it takes to write on every single one of them. And the time it will take to hang them all up. It's days of work." Her voice is shaking, and if I didn't know better, I'd think she was on the verge of tears.

But I don't back down. "Okay. The installation opens on the night of the gala, which is three weeks away. . . ." I make some estimations and do some calculations. "If we work together two hours a day just on weekdays, we'll be done folding with a few days left for setup. That's not so bad!"

The look she gives me indicates that she thinks it's very bad, indeed.

"Hey," I say, irritated. "I'm not thrilled about it, either, but I'm *trying* to be positive. Maybe you could, too."

There's no other way. I'm the one who ruined her project,

so it's not fair to make her do all the work—and she won't trust me to work on my own.

So now, instead of spending my afternoons and evenings with the future love of my life, trying to turn our fake romance into something real, I'm going to spend them cooped up in the staff room folding a thousand pieces of paper with the most disagreeable girl I've ever had the misfortune to meet. And despite what I said earlier, I do not feel positive about it at all.

13

AS IF MY DREADED ORIGAMI PROJECT WITH DELA wasn't going to be tedious and time-consuming enough, Stephen has decided to put me and Max to work this weekend purging tons of junk from Baba's garage in preparation for her inevitable move elsewhere. We've brought stuff in bit by bit for Baba to identify, and her living room is so full now, you can barely walk. Towering stacks of dusty books and photo albums. Giant plastic bins full of papers, tests, worksheets, and report cards from Stephen and Dad's school days. Big cardboard boxes bursting with old clothes, baby toys, and books.

Naturally, Stephen is still too afraid to mention our real purpose, so he's dressing this project up as a fun family experience wherein Baba goes through all her stuff and tells us stories about her favorite things, and helps us decide what to keep and what to—ahem—not keep.

It doesn't seem fair to Baba to treat her this way, but how else are we supposed to get her to cooperate? As it is, she's steadfastly refused to go through any of the boxes we've brought in, and is currently shut up in her room. I bet she's guessed the real reason we're doing this; she may be losing her memory, but she's not stupid. And even if she doesn't see through the ruse, I'm sure it's tough to have people sweep into your house and dig through everything you've accumulated over fifty years.

Willow has pretty much taken over the corner of my brain labeled Nozomi's Obsessions lately, so I've been able to cram my issues with Baba into a closet—so to speak, ha-ha. But now that we're in her house and going through her stuff, the homophobia keeps surfacing. Literally. Photos of teenage Stephen dressed for Halloween as eighties LGBTQIA icon Boy George in full makeup, braids, and a big, flowy shirt. ("How could anyone miss a sign like that?" I ask, and Stephen shakes his head. "You would not believe how deep in denial people were back then.") A tightly folded rainbow flag and a bag of weed in a shoebox, on which Max promptly calls dibs. An old church pamphlet entitled, "Homosexuals: Hate the Sin, Love the Sinner," which fills me with something gray and heavy.

I don't even want to touch it to throw it out.

"How do you do it? How do you keep being nice to her?" I ask Stephen.

"I don't know sometimes," he says. "I've thought pretty seriously about cutting her out of my life again. But she's trying.

In a perfect world, she'd embrace every part of me. But this isn't a perfect world, and Baba's not a perfect person. And she's poured her entire life into raising me and your dad, and for the most part, I think she's done a pretty good job. I've always felt loved. I've always felt cherished. I know she's proud of me. And if I don't look after her, who will? I owe it to her. I don't know if what I'm doing is right or wrong. But it's what I'm doing."

"What about me, though?"

Stephen looks at me and lets out a shaky breath. "Come here," he whispers, and wraps his arms around me. We stand there quietly for a while. Eventually, though, he says, "Life is long, Zozo. We're all evolving. Try to be patient."

"With life? Or with Baba?"

He chuckles. "With Baba for now. With life in the long run."

Stephen nods in the direction of the stairs and asks me, "Do you think you could go up there and talk her into going for a walk?"

"Do I have to?"

"I bet she'd love it if you asked her to take you to Cinderella Bakery," Stephen says. "Do you remember where it is?"

"Pretty much." Cinderella Bakery is a Russian bakery a few blocks away. Baba used to take me there quite a lot when I was little, and that memory is what persuades me.

"She goes there practically every other day, so it shouldn't be a problem. But make sure you bring your phone. Just in case."

I wince. Stephen had to pick Baba up from the library the other day. "I got tired," she'd explained to him. But she had her little roller basket full of groceries with her, and her house is between the grocery store and the library. Maybe she went straight to the library after grocery shopping—but maybe she accidentally overshot her house and forgot how to get home.

One of my favorite things about Baba has always been how strong she is. Strong body, strong will, strong everything. According to her, she was a tomboy, faster and stronger than all the boys in her class when she was little. Jiji was always working and traveling, so she brought up Stephen and Dad practically all by herself in a country where she barely spoke the language. She fought Stephen's school principal when he got teased by his gym teacher for being "girly" in third grade. She was still climbing up and down the Lyon Street steps in her seventies—something she is very proud of, and I don't blame her.

So it's tough to think about her lost and confused, the way she must have felt when she called Stephen from the library to ask for a ride home. Even if she wouldn't admit it.

I find Baba sitting in a worn leather armchair by the window in her room, looking disconsolately out at the backyard, a knitting project on her lap.

"Hi, Baba," I say, knocking on the doorframe. "I was wondering if you could take me to Cinderella Bakery." Her face lights up.

Ten minutes later, Baba is walking next to me in her

sensible shoes, pointing out the mint plant growing in one of those squares of dirt in the sidewalk with a tree in it. "Don't pick, though," she warns me. "Dogs do pee here sometimes."

We turn the corner onto Balboa, and Baba says, "I think we're close to Cinderella Bakery. Do you remember I used to take you when you were a little girl? Do you want to go?"

"Um, sure," I say, and smile to hide my dismay. It's kind of funny, actually—but also not funny at all.

"You always wanted a napoleon cake. You thought it was a Russian specialty because we always ate it there. You and Max had a big fight about it one time."

I remember that fight. Technically, Max won, since napoleon cake is originally an Italian pastry—but he also lost because it's not French like he thought. And I also won because it turns out that it's so popular in Russia that a lot of Russians consider it a Russian dessert. The best part, though, was that I cried so hard when Max refused to cede victory that Baba bought me two pieces to make up for it.

"I remember we used to tell Dad that we were going to get pelmeni for lunch and we'd just eat pastries instead," I tell her. Baba and I used to be a great team. I miss those days, when she made me plum jam, when she didn't get lost, when I didn't know how problematic she was.

Baba's face crinkles up with laughter, and she says, "I used to do such a thing all the time. I remember we went to Kyōto for a school trip when I was a teenager, and instead of visiting the temple and shrine and listening to the tour guide, I snuck away with Jiji and my friend, Nana-chan, and we spent the afternoon at a café."

This is an old story, one I remember her telling me when I was little. "Did you get caught?" I ask, even though I know the answer.

She shakes her head. "Students had the specific route to go, and the teachers trusted us to follow. But I already knew all about the temples we had to visit, so I made Jiji and Nana-chan . . . what is it that you say? We played hooking."

"You played hooky."

"Yes," she says, nodding. "They were so worried." She laughs: *how silly of them!* "But I told them the answers to our worksheet at the café and we took a taxi to the last temple and no one knew we were gone!" She laughs again at her own audacity, so pleased with her teenage self that I have to smile with her.

"No one? Not a single kid? Not the teachers?"

Baba scoffs. "Teachers didn't pay a close attention—they stayed up late the night before, drinking. I knew, because I snuck out of my room to spy them. And other students didn't care."

We buy a box of napoleons, plus a box of pelmeni for dinner. As we put the napoleons onto plates at home, I ask Baba if she has photos of that class trip to Kyōto.

"They're in a photo album," she says. "Come, I'll show you."

When we walk into the living room, Baba doesn't even

greet Stephen, but says rather shortly, "I want a photo album. I hope you haven't blocked the bookshelf with all of these boxes."

"Why don't you sit on the couch, Mom. I'll grab the albums for you," Stephen says, his voice even. "That'll save you from having to kneel down. I know your knees have been bothering you."

"You don't know which one I want," she complains, but she takes his suggestion and sits down.

He sends me to the kitchen to boil water for tea to drink with the napoleons. It takes me a minute to find the tea; it's not on the shelf labeled *TEA*, but in a drawer full of dish towels. Concern rattles through me like a marble.

A few minutes later, I'm sitting next to Baba with the album open on her lap, and a napoleon and cup of tea for each of us on the coffee table. She's flipped to a page toward the back of the album, to a photograph of a teenage girl with bobbed hair and a dark sailor suit—the quintessential Japanese public school uniform. Her head is tilted slightly away from the camera, and she's smiling coquettishly and holding the skirt of the dress out, totally hamming it up.

Baba points to the guy standing next to her and smiling at her in the photo, wearing dark trousers and a matching military-looking jacket with a mandarin collar and a row of five metal buttons down the front. "Can you guess who this is?"

Even if he didn't have Dad's nose and eyes, I could have

guessed by looking at the goofy, lovestruck expression on his face. "Jiji," I say.

She flips through the album and tells me story after story while I wonder how that rule-breaking, boundary-pushing tomboy whose spirit was too big for her home country grew into the cranky old lady who barely tolerates her gay son's marriage, and who flat-out declares that she's not willing to broaden her horizons. How does that happen? And when? Or maybe she was always this way and I just didn't see it. If I never come out to her, I bet I could get along with Baba the way I used to. But isn't that betraying who I am *now*? Is being myself—my whole self—around Baba worth the risk of damaging what we used to have? I get why Stephen says it's a process, and we have to be patient with her. But I'm less and less sure that we have time for that kind of patience.

14

WILLOW'S REACTION TO THE NEWS OF MY unavailability for after-work socializing wasn't quite what I'd hoped for.

"This is *perfect!*" she exclaimed. She urged me to use my time to learn everything I could about Arden and Dela's relationship, so we could plan our next step in Operation Make Arden Wish She Never Left. "We need to know what we're up against," she said.

She wasn't wrong. And I guess I could also learn useful information for Operation Make Willow Fall in Love with Me. So it's all good. Though a little more sympathy and a little less strategy might have been nice.

After work, I meet Dela and Cliff in the staff room for my first session of origami penance. I have no clue how I'm going to get Dela to even speak to me, much less tell me anything personal. For inspiration, I'm pretending this is a top secret surveillance operation and I am an undercover spy, expert at tricking unsuspecting enemy agents into revealing their secrets. Childish? Perhaps. But I do what it takes to survive.

Cliff presents us with a list of hundreds of wishes downloaded from a website specifically set up for this project. We have to write each and every one on a sheet of origami (I can already feel my poor hand cramping up), and fold them into cranes and butterflies, which will eventually be suspended with silk thread all around the courtyard from bamboo branches and from the rafters of the structure that he and Dela are building.

Wait a second. "This sounds a lot like Tanabata," I say.

Tanabata is one of my favorite Japanese holidays because it's a celebration of true love and magic and wishes coming true, but not in a sappy Hallmark Valentine's Day way. It's based on the legend of Orihime, the daughter of the Tentei, King of the Sky. Orihime was a weaver, and she would sit in the sky next to the River of Heaven, which we know as the Milky Way, and weave the most beautiful silk cloth. But she worked so hard at it that she could never meet anyone to fall in love with. Her father felt sorry for her, so he arranged for her to meet Hikoboshi, a cowherd who lived on the other side of the river.

Naturally, the two fell passionately in love and got married. But once they were married, they were so into each other that they stopped paying attention to their duties. Orihime stopped weaving, and Hikoboshi stopped watching his cows, which crossed the river, wandered all over the sky, and wreaked heavenly havoc. Orihime's father was furious. He sent Hikoboshi and his cows back across the Milky Way and forbade Hikoboshi and Orihime from seeing each other ever again.

Heartbroken, Orihime begged her father to let her be with Hikoboshi. Finally, he relented, and said that for one night each year, he would allow her to cross the Milky Way to meet her husband on the other side. When that night came, Orihime went to the river and found that it was too deep and fast to cross, and she wept with despair. But a flock of magpies took pity on her and formed themselves into a bridge, and she was able to cross over and be reunited with her beloved.

Tanabata is a celebration of that night—the one night every year when heaven listens to our most heartfelt wishes. People write their wishes on paper and hang them on bamboo branches, which is symbolic because bamboo grows fast and straight, so it can carry the wishes to heaven. What more do you need to fall in love with a holiday?

"I guess your mom told you about it?" I ask.

Dela says nothing; she's clenching her jaw shut so hard, I can see the muscles working. I glance nervously at Cliff for an answer, but he's looking at Dela with an unreadable expression on his face. Finally, he says, "Well, yes, but the thing is . . ." He looks at Dela and trails off, then switches to telling me more about the installation.

Whoa. I guess I hit a nerve. I feel like there's a lot to learn here. Maybe not what I came here to learn, but still. I watch Dela carefully.

On the day of the gala, Cliff says, when the Tanabata Pavilion opens, guests will enter the courtyard and write their own wish on a piece of origami "wishing paper." Assistants from the San Francisco Academy of Art University will fold the wishes into a crane or a butterfly, and wishers will choose a wish that's already hanging from a tree, and replace it with their own.

"What happens to the old wishes that come down?" I ask.

"They go in a fire," says Dela, and I can't tell whether or not she's kidding, so I look at Cliff, who nods.

"The fire is symbolic," Cliff explains. "Fire is purifying, so only the purest essence of any wish goes up to heaven. You let go of your wish when you hang it on the branch, and you participate in someone else's wish when you put one in the fire. Because a wish doesn't come true on the power of your desire alone, or even on the actions you take or the plans you make. There are a lot of factors beyond your control. That's the beauty of this piece," he concludes with a tender look at Dela, who looks away. "It's a twist that we developed after Dela won the grant."

"Wow. That's deep," is all I can say.

"That's my girl." Cliff smiles fondly at Dela again, and again she looks away. What is wrong with her? I would be so proud if I'd come up with something like this.

I look at the stack of origami and wonder what I would wish for. Something smart and political, like *Please let the government take real action on climate change?* Or I could wish for something sensible and good, like *Please let Baba agree to move to a retirement home.* Or maybe something ambitious, like *Please let me get into the College of My Choice.* Except those wishes feel like something Dad or Stephen would recommend. Responsible. Practical. They'd be wasted on something as magical as this Tanabata installation. I need something heartfelt. Something with wings, the kind of wish that you can imagine swirling up to the sky, into the stars, for Orihime to pick up and give to her father to grant.

Willow. That's what I would wish for.

Don't judge. It's perfect. It's earnest, full of longing, the kind of wish that would benefit from the extra blessing of a purifying fire and a star princess. And isn't the whole point of the Tanabata story about being with your true love?

I reach out for the list of wishes and leaf through it. "An end to world hunger," I read out loud from the top of page three. Oof. Okay, maybe wishing for a girlfriend was a *bit* frivolous. Dela, however, groans dramatically.

"What?" I say, feeling suddenly defensive.

"Oh, come on. World hunger?" she says. "It's so obvious. Like, of course, world hunger. Who *doesn't* want to end world hunger?"

"Dela," says Cliff, his voice full of reproach, but she ignores him and stares at the table, tracing patterns on the dark wood veneer.

"There's nothing wrong with wishing for an end to world hunger," I protest. "It's a kind, unselfish thing to wish for. Why do you always have to shit on everything?"

Dela looks shocked, and frankly, I'm a little shocked myself. But I'm not taking it back. How can she make fun of wishing for an end to world hunger? I'm glad she doesn't know my wish because she'd *really* shit on that.

"I'm sorry," she says, and she seems sincere. "I didn't mean it that way."

"Didn't you?"

Dela heaves a sigh, and says, "Okay, so here's the thing. Ending hunger? Like, it's a nice sentiment and everything, but we all know it's never going to happen."

"It might. If enough people *cared*. And didn't *make fun of it*." I frown at her pointedly, and she looks a little ashamed—*as well you should*, I think.

But she doesn't back down. "Okay, but what's that person going to do to end world hunger beyond typing their wish into an online form? Probably nothing."

"How do you know? What if they run a food bank? What if it's their life's passion?" I counter hotly. "What if someone reads the wish and decides to volunteer at a soup kitchen?"

Finally, she seems to take it in. She sighs and says, "Fine. You're right."

"How about this one?" I show it to her. It says, *I wish Tamara would be my best friend forever.* "It's so sweet."

"But unlikely."

"You're doing it again! What is *wrong* with you?" I ask, exasperated.

Dela winces, then says with an ironic grin, "It's in my nature?"

"Seriously, though," I persist. "Why?"

Dela shrugs, and for a moment, I think I see something besides hostility, something ineffably sad. But then she looks at me and her face slams shut. "Right now, I think it's that certain people don't know how to mind their own business."

"Well! I guess I'll leave you to it, then," Cliff says—I'd almost forgotten he was here. And I can't believe he's leaving me here with this crabby gorgon like we're getting along beautifully. He ambles out of the room, miraculously surviving the knife-sharp glare that Dela directs at his back, and then she and I are alone in the storeroom. "Here," she says, breaking the awkward silence that's descended on us. She shoves a stack of brightly colored origami at me. "I've already written a bunch of them down."

"Um. I actually don't know how to make these." I gesture at the delicate origami figures that are sitting on the table as models. It hadn't occurred to me until now that Dela would have to help me before I could help her. Oops.

With a groan, Dela takes a sheet off the top and motions for me to do the same. "Fold it in half this way," she begins, and folds the square into a triangle. I copy her.

"No! Not like that," she says, even though I could swear I've done exactly what she just did.

"It's a triangle, isn't it?"

She heaves the sigh of a prisoner who knows the only path

to freedom lies through a long, dark, treacherous tunnel. *You and me both*, I want to say.

"Here," she says finally. "Like this." She shows me how to match the corners ("I said *carefully*! As in, with care!") and hold them down with one finger while I do the creases with my other hand. Then she leads me through about fifteen more steps, and I can feel her not-sighing every time I screw up, which is a lot.

"This is going to take forever," I mutter, disheartened.

"And now you know why I was so upset," she says without lifting her eyes from her work. Ouch. Though it is a fair hit.

"Can't you just buy some prefolded ones? Or skip writing the wishes on some of them? No one's going to read them, right? They can all be fake and no one has to know."

"No."

"Why not?"

"Because that ruins the entire point. People write their sincere wishes down and share them, and other people make an effort to turn those wishes into something that goes up to heaven. If you don't give every person who's shared their wish a real chance to participate, it's not fair."

Dela starts transcribing a wish from the printout onto the wishing paper, leaving me sitting in stunned silence. How is this the same girl who wrote off a child's wish to remain *best frends forever*, who scoffed at a desire to end world hunger? I have so many questions. But it's clear that she is Done Talking, so I have no choice but to go back to folding.

15

ONE EXCRUCIATING, PAINFULLY SILENT HOUR later, I've folded only seventeen cranes. I've also tested and rejected a hundred intel-gathering conversation openers in my head:

So! Tell me about your new girlfriend! (Too gossipy.)

So! Willow tells me you're dating her ex! (Makes Willow look like a jealous stalker. Which maybe she is, but there's no need to let anyone know.)

So! Are you dating anyone? (What if she thinks I'm hitting on her?)

So! I'm totally not hitting on you, but are you dating anyone? (Ugh, even worse.)

And those were the good ones.

I survey my work: a tiny, tiny pile. Only 473 more to go, I

think, and my heart sinks. I've accomplished nothing. My neck and shoulders are already stiff, and I think I might scream from the stress of sitting in this room and not speaking to the only other person in it, except in my head. Dela hasn't looked at her phone even once, and I'm afraid to check mine for fear that she'll bite my head off. I need to take a break.

"Hey, I'm going to the bathroom," I announce.

"Have fun," she says drily.

I roll my eyes, which is lost on her because she doesn't look up, and leave.

Ah, freedom! I pee, wash my hands, and take a few minutes to watch a Willow-recommended YouTube makeup tutorial on how to do a smoky-eye look on Asian eyes. I try out the tip with some new eye shadow, then wash it off so that Dela won't know that I've spent my bathroom break playing with makeup. I try a braid crown like the one Willow had the first day we met, take it out because it's a mess, and try it again.

Okay. So maybe I'm stalling. But think of what I have to go back to! Consider it self-care.

Finally, I run out of things to do. *Come on*, I tell myself. Twenty-three more cranes. If I focus, I can get them done. I'll listen to music or something. I swipe my badge and open the staff room door, steeling myself for another hour of Silent Origami With Dela, and stop cold.

Arden is sitting in my seat—my seat!—and kissing Dela.

"Oh!" The sound escapes my mouth before I can stop it, and Dela practically leaps away from Arden.

Arden recovers immediately and gives me a warm smile and says, "Oh, hi!" but Dela is red-faced and shifty-eyed.

"Uh . . . hiii," I say timidly.

Dammit! I had the element of surprise, but now I'm letting Arden have the upper hand. How did Willow manage to be so icy calm and cutting that last time? What would she say right now? I summon my courage and channel Willow and say, "I'm so sorry, am I interrupting something?"

It was meant to sound cool and ironic, but it comes out solicitous and apologetic, and I cringe inwardly. Come on. Be like Willow.

Arden smirks at me. "I mean. Kind of?" Her voice is low and measured, and it perfectly matches her face, which is one of those faces with heavy lids and long eyelashes that make her look perpetually chill. Or maybe it's her makeup, which is as good as anything I've seen on Willow's face.

The nerve.

Wait. This is *good*. The more Arden likes Dela, the better my chances are with Willow.

The question is, how much *does* Arden like Dela?

"So!" I say. I put on a wide-eyed, innocent smile: I am a secret agent posing as a disinterested third party, exhibiting a casual, friendly, disinterested curiosity in my fellow humans. "Are the two of you like, you know, like, in love, or . . . ?"

Oh shit, I think as Arden's perfectly arched eyebrow twitches. Too far. Quick, course correct. "Curious minds want to know!" I add, and extend a pretend microphone. Oh god.

"I'm feeling pretty good about it so far," Arden says, and it's like she's winking at me with her voice—it's got the self-assured mock-coyness you hear in the voices of movie stars on late-night talk shows when the host asks them about their rumored relationships. Ugh. Does *anything* rattle this girl? "I don't know if I'm ready to call it love, but . . . well. Who knows what the future will bring?" She casts a lovey-dovey gaze at Dela, who looks a bit startled.

Interesting. Though not particularly helpful. And I am kind of enjoying seeing Dela knocked off balance, if you want to know the truth.

"But how about you and Willow? That must be new," I hear Arden saying. "When did you two become a thing?" Crap. *How long have you been a thing* was going to be *my* next question for *her.* Her mouth is still smiling, her tone is still playful, but I detect a sharp glint in her eye, like a cat waiting to pounce, and that undoes me. I forget everything except the fact that Willow and I are supposed to be a couple.

"Right, well, we've been spending a lot of time together lately, Willow and me. A *lot* of time," I gabble. How long have we been *a thing,* though (and what is *a thing,* anyway)? It dawns on me that I haven't ever told this story from start to finish out loud to an actual person. Okay, come on. I can do this. "Maybe you saw on her Instagram that we went to Off the Grid a little while ago?" I can't quite bring myself to say, *Just after you broke up?* like Willow might have. "Anyway, that was my first day working here." I recall the post and the comments, and start warming to my topic. "Yeah, we just totally hit it off. Isn't that wild? It was like magic. We couldn't stop talking. Oh! And we went to the Fairmont for our first date—that's the day we ran into you here, remember? We had the most amazing kiss there—it was in the, uh, in the stairwell, totally unexpected—and she gave me flowers the next day. Roses and lilies. And it's been pretty much nonstop bliss ever since." By the time I finish, I've gotten so carried away with my own story, I almost believe it myself—Willow will be so proud of me. I smile at Arden in triumph.

The glint in her eye has hardened, I notice, from suspicion, or maybe from jealousy.

But it doesn't take long for her to regain her composure. "That's such a sweet story," she says. "Tell Willow I'm happy for her. And tell her I was serious about my birthday party. I'd love for you both to come." The hardness has melted out of her eyes, and as closely as I look, there's nothing there but warmth and sincere goodwill.

"We would love to go!" I chirp, not to be outdone. "And Willow is really happy for you. And so am I. For both of you, in fact. So happy." I catch Dela's incredulous stare—did I overdo it again?

"Thanks." Arden gives me a dazzling smile. "Well, anyway. I should get going. I just stopped in to say hi to Dela and drop off a little treat." She gestures at the table toward a small pink paper bag with little paper handles.

I feel a *plink* of disappointment that Willow didn't bring

me a treat—only, stop it, Nozomi. You're not actually together. (*Yet.* Don't give up.)

"So, hey, Saturday's good, right?" She addresses Dela as she throws on a cable-knit car coat, and my spy antennae go up. An actionable piece of intelligence!

"Saturday's good," Dela says.

"Where are you going?" I ask. Casual. Disinterested.

"The Ice Cream Bar," says Arden. "And maybe we'll do something outside. It's supposed to be sunny and seventy-two this weekend, so."

"Sounds like fun! Maybe Willow and I will do something like that," I say. Not that I'm feeling competitive in any way at all.

"You should totally come with us! Let Dela know if you want to, okay?"

It's clear from Dela's expression that she would rather eat glass than go on a double date with me and Willow, but she's too polite—for once—to say anything.

While Dela walks Arden to the front door, I'm left alone to fold wishes and contemplate what's just gone down. If Arden wants everyone to like her, like Willow said, maybe this whole encounter was an act—but if it is, she sold it like a pro. Already I'm questioning whether I really saw that shrewdness in her eyes when she asked how long Willow and I had been together, and whether the flinty gleam I noticed after I told her my story was just my imagination. I have to remember that under that warm, friendly exterior is a will of iron. Just like Willow, it occurs to me. No wonder Willow is in love with her. She is a force.

What if Willow's plan works and Arden tries to win her back? In the movies, the ex always makes one last attempt to get back together, and the only reason it doesn't work is because the main couple have already fallen in love with each other.

But Willow's nowhere near falling in love with me. And I was not prepared for Arden to be quite so . . . much . . . more. She's more *everything* than me: beautiful, talented, poised, sexy, fashionable . . . How can I possibly compete? Even if they don't get back together, how will I ever measure up?

My ruminations are interrupted by Dela's return. She drops into her chair, shoving aside Arden's pink paper bag, and scans the list of wishes as if she's been sitting there working this entire time.

"What'd she bring you?" I ask, poking the bag. *See? I'm asking because I didn't look inside,* I want to say but don't.

"Cupcakes."

"Ooh." I forget I'm not supposed to be nosy, and peek in to take a look. But the cupcakes are hidden inside a cute pink cardboard box. "Where are they from?"

"She made them."

"What?" Though of course. Why wouldn't she also be a baker?

"You can have them. They've got chocolate frosting, and I hate chocolate."

"Did you tell her that?" (Also: What kind of monster doesn't like chocolate?)

"I didn't have the heart to."

"So you *do* have a heart." Oops. It slipped out before I even knew it was in my head.

Dela lets out a little gust of laughter before she catches herself and clamps her mouth shut. The feeling I get—of making her laugh—reminds me of the first time I skipped a stone on the water. I wonder if I can make it happen again. But I don't get a chance, because she says brusquely, "Let's just get these done, okay?"

Those are the last words she deigns to speak to me for another long, silent hour. When she finally announces it's time to go, we pack up and walk out in silence.

"See you tomorrow," I say, hoping she'll at least say good-bye, but all she does is nod and turn away.

Why does she have to be such a grouch? How can Arden stand her? Or is she only like this with me?

16

ON THE WAY HOME LAST NIGHT, I TEXTED Willow with the intelligence I collected—except for Arden's invitation for us to join her and Dela on Saturday. Even though it would mean a date (of sorts) with Willow, and despite the strange sense of satisfaction I feel at the prospect of pissing Dela off on purpose instead of by accident, deep down, I don't want to do it. It's too much pressure. Too much potential for awkwardness and tension. And what if it works out the way Willow wants, and Arden decides to come back to her?

But Willow never responded. I couldn't understand why until she texted me on the way to the museum this morning:

Omg omg omg

Sorry I didn't get back right away—parents took my phone

(long story)

Anyway holy shit. You have to come by the shop ASAP so we can talk

So I stop in the gift shop right away, and she grabs my hand and pulls me behind the counter.

"Arden was *there* yesterday?" she asks. "Oh my god. I can't believe her."

"Just for a few minutes," I assure her.

"And they're definitely a thing. Definitely a couple? And they're going to the Ice Cream Bar on Saturday?"

"It seems that way."

Willow throws her head back and drops her arms, groaning. "I knew it. I *knew* it. I told you, didn't I?"

"Yeah, you did."

"She has a lot of fucking nerve taking Dela to the Ice Cream Bar. That was one of our favorite spots."

"I'm sorry."

"Yeah, well." She fumes silently for another moment, then gives herself a little shake and straightens up. "It's probably a good thing I didn't find out till this morning. I wouldn't have been able to sleep last night if I'd known."

"What happened with your phone last night, anyway?" I ask.

"I kind of missed a deadline to apply for a research internship for the fall. My parents were livid."

"Oh. So they took your phone? That doesn't seem fair. It was an accident, wasn't it?"

"Welllll." Willow tilts her head and squints at the ceiling.

"I *might* have missed it on purpose. It sounded wretched and I couldn't think of another way to get out of it." She grins at me. "Asian parents, amirite?" But before I can respond, she moves on. "Anyway, whatever. Tell me more. Did they seem good together? What was the vibe?"

She grills me as I give my report: But what did Arden say *exactly*? But her *tone*, what was her *tone*? Together, we break down every gesture, every glance, every possible nuance of word choice. Willow is relieved to hear that Dela didn't seem super into it, but notes grimly, "Arden loves a challenge." We go over Arden's weird reaction to my story of our pretend romance. I hedge a little, because a) I'm less and less sure I *did* see that hard expression in her eyes, and b) Wouldn't it be better for me if Willow thought Arden didn't care and couldn't be won back?

"By the end, I wasn't even sure I saw anything," I say. "She was just so nice, mostly."

"Yeah, that's her. She's not a bad person—well, she's a shitty person for leaving me, obviously." Willow attempts a grin, but it sags almost instantly, and she sighs heavily. "No, she's amazing . . . Ugh, I hate her." She takes another steadying breath and continues, "My point is she's nice, but if you thought you saw something *not* as nice, you were probably right. Which"—her expression lifts a little—"could be good, if it means she was jealous. Do you think she was jealous? Or do you think she was just suspicious?"

"I don't know," I say apologetically.

She waves me off. "Not your fault. Ughhh, I wish I'd been there so I could've seen for myself! Speaking of which, let's talk about Saturday. Do you think we should crash their date?"

"Umm . . ."

"She'd be so pissed. And she'd deserve it, too."

Crap. "It won't feel weird, spending that much time together?" I say.

"That's the whole point, isn't it? To make things feel weird."

It's now pretty clear to me that we'll be going to the Ice Cream Bar no matter what. And the only thing worse than accepting Arden's invitation to double-date would be to crash the date and have Arden go, "But I invited you!"

So I say reluctantly, "Right. Okay. Well. It's just that we don't need to crash it because Arden said it would be fine if we came, too. I just have to tell Dela."

Willow's eyes narrow. "She said what?"

"She said we could come," I repeat. "Like I said, though, we don't have to. In fact, I think maybe—"

"Oh, we do." Willow's expression is thunderous. "She's totally bluffing. She thinks I won't go. So now we *have* to. You weren't sure if she thinks we're really together, right? Well, this is a perfect way to show her that we are!"

The thing is, once I agreed to be pretend girlfriends, I kind of figured it would be all slow dancing at parties, sitting next to each other on the bus, and sharing a bed or a hotel room—the kind of faking you can do without having to actually interact with your audience. Like our social media posts. But we're not at school where the gossip mill could do the work for us, or on a road trip where kindly old B&B owners we've never met will hilariously mistake us for a married couple. Willow's right. The success of our fake romance hinges on lots of quality time with Arden and Dela.

Sigh.

"Good point," I say. "Okay. So then I guess I'll talk to Dela."

"Okay, awesome. Oh, hey—what if I come to your house beforehand, so we can plan your outfit? I'll bring some of my clothes, and you can borrow whatever you want. And I can help you with your makeup."

"That . . . would be great!" I say. That is to say, Willow in my room, lending me clothes and maybe even touching my face—definitely great. The fact that she seems to think her help is necessary? A tad demoralizing. And there's the matter of Stephen, Lance, and Max. "Um. You should know that my uncles and my brother might kind of . . . sort of . . . think we're dating for real."

I hold my breath, ready to apologize for spreading a lie, but Willow is delighted. "Oh my god, that's perfect! The more people who believe we're dating, the more convincing it is. I'll make sure to tell my mom tonight."

Okay. That's cool. Very cool. Everything's cool.

"So, cool," Willow says. "Find out what time we need to be there, and I'll come over like an hour or two before. Okay?"

"Got it," I say with a quailing heart. Can I really pull this off? Dela and Arden, okay. Stressful and awkward, but necessary.

Stephen and Lance shouldn't be *too* hard to fool, but I feel like a jerk, escalating the lie. Lying to a social media audience is one thing. Lying to your family is something else. And Max—I don't even want to think about Max. I have no issue lying to him, but he's already a Willow skeptic. And as I've mentioned, he's Sherlock Holmes–level observant.

Willow gives me a hug, which lifts my spirits and helps me focus. The plan is working. The plan, in fact, is the only reason I have her in my arms right now. If it means surviving the fuss my uncles are sure to make over her, Max's scrutiny, and one uncomfortable lunch with Dela and Arden, so be it. I just need to focus on making sure that it's all so great that she'll want to make it real.

17

WHEN I GET HOME FROM THE MUSEUM, MAX IS IN his room. Stephen and Lance have gone out, but there's a plate of Lola's lumpia—a secret family recipe handed down from Lance's grandmother—and a note from Stephen that says,

> Z,
> *Talked to your dad earlier! He misses you and he's*
> *dying to see you. Be a good girl and chat with him tonight.*
> xo,
> S

I finish off the plate and dutifully FaceTime Dad, hoping he'll already have gone to bed, but he's up.

"You've been holding out on me, Zozo," is the first thing

he says. "Stephen tells me you're dating that girl I keep seeing on your Instagram."

Dad, too? "It's only been a couple of weeks. It's really not worth talking about." I try to move on. "How've *you* been?"

"Oh, so you're deflecting, huh?" he says, all jokey-jokey. "Yeah, I see how it is. A couple of weeks in San Francisco and you're too cool to share things like your very first girlfriend with your dear old dad." I can hear the reproach under the joke, and now in addition to being nervous about what to say, I feel guilty for leaving him alone in Chicago and irritated with him for being so needy and making me have to lie to him.

"There's really nothing to tell, Dad."

"All right, I'll give you your space. As much as it kills me to do it." He smiles sadly. "I just feel like you're growing up extra fast out there."

It almost wins me over—he is a good dad, and he means well. But like I said. So very needy. So very nosy. "That's what kids do," I say. "We grow up."

"Yes, you do," he agrees. But giving me my space apparently *is* killing him because he adds, "Just be cautious, okay? You have a tendency to throw yourself into relationships so wholeheartedly—your friendships, your crushes, every teacher you ever had in elementary school—and that's such a great quality, but . . ."

It's hard to hear him say all of this, especially when there's nothing to say it about. (Yet!) Fighting back the urge to scream, I say, "Hey, Dad?"

"What, honey?"

"Remember how you *just* said you were going to give me my space?"

"Okay, okay. Oh, but wait—here's an idea: What if you FaceTime me with her, so I can meet her?"

"DAD!"

Finally, he backs off and we switch to topics where I don't have to lie my face off, like my work at the museum (fine), how I'm getting along with Max (fine, mostly), and whether any pizza restaurants around here have managed to pull off a decent Chicago-style deep-dish pizza (no), before we say good-bye and he makes me promise to use my best judgment with Willow. Of course I will. I will be sensible and cautious, and I will carefully assess how things are going at every stage of the relationship.

Just not in the way he thinks.

Once we've signed off, I watch some makeup tutorials, searching for looks I can ask Willow to replicate for me when she comes over, anticipating how it will feel when she touches my face. Halfway through the third video, Max comes in and I quickly pause it and switch tabs.

"Was that a makeup tutorial?" he asks. "Here's a tip: give up and wear a mask."

"Shut up, Max."

"What's with this new obsession with makeup anyway? You never used to wear any."

Huh. I've been wearing makeup since the first day of work;

I *thought* it was strange that he hadn't noticed. But I guess he just didn't care enough to mention it. "Just trying to expand my horizons." I wish he'd go away and leave me alone.

"This is about Willow, isn't it." It's not a question. In fact, I get the unsettling feeling that he was heading this way all along.

"What? No."

"It's definitely about Willow. You're trying to impress her."

"I am not," I say perhaps a touch more defensively than I mean to.

"Copying someone's look and pretending to like their hobbies won't make them like you more," he says. "Just FYI."

"Just FYI." I mimic him in my most pompous voice. "Like you're such an expert. Why are you always trying to undermine my relationship with her?"

"You know how I feel. I'm just trying to protect you." Just like Dad. As if I'm going to be a victim to Willow's every passing whim.

"Well, thanks for the sentiment, but I don't need your protection. Anyway, Willow already likes me plenty, so you can just fuck right off." If he had any idea just who's pulling the strings—how much control I have over the situation . . . well, he'd still be a jerk about it.

"Whatever you say, Makeup," he says with infuriating calm. Before he goes, he tosses a package on my bed. "That came for you this afternoon. It's from Mom. Apparently, she loves you more than she loves me, because I didn't get anything."

"That's because you're a dick," I say, and he laughs and leaves me with the package.

I open it to find two lipsticks, a liquid eyeliner, a palette of twelve shades of eye shadow, and a card. This is so weird. How did she know? I open the card and read it. It says,

> *Dear Zomi,*
> *I heard from Max that you're into makeup these days—looks like your sweetie is, too! I'm so glad you're having a little fling out there in SF—now's the time to experiment with everything: lovers, makeup, jobs, life! Just make sure to use a dental dam if you have oral sex, okay? I know I'm being cringey, but it's important to be safe.*
> *Love,*
> *Mom*

Dear Mom, I imagine replying,

Sweetie *is almost as bad as* bae, *so please never use it again. Or* lover, *for that matter. Please do not talk to me about dental dams and oral sex like you're reminding me to wash behind my ears. Finally, please don't use the word* cringey. *It's literally making me cringe.*
Love,
Nozomi

I do kind of love that she sent me all this makeup. It's nice to have one parent who sees that I need some freedom to live my own life, to experiment—but she's just as annoying and intrusive as Dad in her own way, pumping Max for information about me and giving me unwanted advice and making me feel nervous about lying and worried about whether I can make the lie come true. On top of that, it's like both of my parents are trying to give themselves a do-over through me. Sure, it's sad that their dreams fell apart. But it would be nice if they'd find new dreams for themselves instead of foisting their old ones on me.

18

I AM A MOSSY BOULDER IN A ZEN ROCK GARDEN.

I am calm. I am patient.

I am floating peacefully in time, which means nothing to me, because I am a rock that has existed for—

Forty-six minutes. She'll be here in forty-six minutes.

I drum my fingers on my chin and wait again.

Be a boulder.

A second, a minute, an eternity . . . what is time, after all, to a boulder?

Forty-three minutes and thirty seconds. Gahhhhh.

I can't stand it. I'm going nuts. I'm too jittery to focus on anything online. I can't put on makeup because Willow's going to do it for me. I can't choose an outfit because she's going to help me choose one. Will she expect me to get undressed in front of her? What if—what if she wants to switch tops with me? The thought of us both taking our shirts off and standing in front of each other in just our bras sends an electric thrill through my body. Maybe I should change in the bathroom to show her that we're just friends and I'm not trying to seduce her or anything, because what if she figures out how I feel, and then laughs at me? On the other hand, how am I going to move us toward More Than Friends if I keep pretending that I only see her as a friend?

Forty-three—*what?* Oh, whoops. Forty-two minutes.

Maybe I'll make some scones, out of that Trader Joe's scone mix I saw in the pantry the other day. They'll be ready by the time she gets here. "Come in and have some scones," I'll say as delicious sconey aromas waft from the kitchen. "I just took them out of the oven." And—bonus!—I'll be a baker, just like Arden. Willow doesn't need to know they're from a mix.

Inspired, I bound down to the kitchen. Stephen and Lance are reading their phones and drinking coffee; Max is standing by the sink, guzzling water, having just come in from a run, from the smell of it.

"You smell revolting." I wrinkle my nose and turn away from him.

"Thanks, so do you." He takes one more glug of water and starts heading out of the kitchen. "Are you . . . *baking?*" he says as I pull the mix off the shelf. "Is this because of Willow? You must not like her that much after all."

"Guess what, Max. Fuck you."

"Language," says Stephen absently, and Max smirks at me.

After checking to see that Stephen's not looking, I flip Max two silent middle fingers.

Because the thing is, he's right. My baking portfolio, such as it is, is basically a series of images from *Nailed It!* My confidence wavers, and I read the instructions on the box with a new sense of trepidation. They seem simple enough, but the risk of having to present Willow with a tray full of carbonized hockey pucks is very real. With a dark scowl at Max, I put the mix back on the pantry shelf. "I've changed my mind," I say.

"No! Come on, I'll help you, sweetheart," says Lance, but I refuse because I want Max to feel bad.

Finally, at 9:57 (three minutes early!), the doorbell rings. My heart does a twirl and I fly downstairs to answer the door, shouting, "I'll get it!" On my way down, I'm tempted to beg Stephen and Lance to act normal, but Max is back in the kitchen with them (having showered and changed, thank goodness). If he knows how nervous I am, he'll do everything he can to throw me off my game.

Willow's got a casual weekend look going—leggings, powder-blue Chuck Taylors printed with some logo or other, an oversized sweater, and an artfully messy braid over her shoulder—but she still manages to look glamorous.

She hands me one of the three shopping bags she's carrying: "I didn't know what you had in your closet, so I brought a ton of clothes for us to try."

"Give me those, honey," says Stephen, who was apparently

unable to wait for us to come upstairs on our own and has appeared behind me as if by magic. As Willow takes her shoes off, he exclaims, "Oooh, are those the new Dior Converse?"

"Uh-huh," she says. "Aren't they cute?"

"It's a collaboration between Christian Dior and Converse," Stephen explains on our way up the stairs, anticipating my question. "Haute couture meets streetwear."

"Did someone say Dior Converse?" says Max as we emerge into the kitchen. Feeling the need to show Max how real we are, I take Willow's hand, and thankfully, she plays right along and doesn't look surprised at all.

Willow smiles at him. "Blue ones," she says.

Max whistles appreciatively. "Nice." I watch him warily, waiting for a sneaky comment about . . . I don't know. Something about how he's surprised she'd want to hang out with a fashion fail like me. Or a reference to some NBA player being great at *rebounds*, wink wink, nudge nudge. But nothing comes. Maybe he's decided to be polite.

I'm just extricating Willow from the social niceties, grateful that we've escaped without having to make up any stories or answer any hard questions, when Lance says to Willow, "So, where are you going? We've asked and asked, but this one here has not been very forthcoming." He gestures at me affectionately, and my eyes almost pop out of my head. I've been ambushed! I wonder if Stephen put him up to this. I've been cagey with him about our destination, on the off chance that he mentions it to Cliff, and Cliff tells him that's where Dela's going, too.

Before I can stop her, Willow says, "No, not at all! We're going to the Ice Cream Bar for lunch."

Stephen looks at her as if he isn't quite sure he's heard her right, and I seize up inside. "The Ice Cream Bar?" he repeats. "By Golden Gate Park?"

"That's the one."

"But that's where Dela's going with *her* new girlfriend!" he says. "Cliff just told me yesterday. Did you know that, Zozo?"

My fears are coming to life before my very eyes.

"Uh-huh," I say weakly. "We're actually meeting them there. Double date," I add. Because Willow and I are Officially a Couple and going on a double date is a Thing That Couples Do.

"You're . . ." Stephen looks completely flummoxed now. "But isn't . . . I mean, Dela's girlfriend. Isn't she . . . er, your ex-girlfriend?" he says to Willow.

"Yes, but it's . . . it's fine." Willow stumbles at first but lands it smoothly. "Totally fine. It was tough in the beginning, of course. But things are much better now."

"Still." Max casts a dubious eye at Willow. "No offense, but a double date with the ex? Is that really a good idea? Won't it be kind of awkward?"

"Shut up, Max. Mind your own business," I snap. I knew his manners earlier were too good to be true.

"Hey. Someone had to say it," says Max, raising his hands defensively.

"No, they didn't." I glare at him.

"Seriously, it's fine," Willow says easily. "I wouldn't be doing this if I weren't totally okay with it." Max doesn't argue, but I can tell from the way he's searching her face that he doesn't believe her. And now I'm afraid that Stephen and Lance don't, either.

"Well! You've clearly got a lot of clothes to try on, so don't let us keep you!" says Lance in a voice so bright it makes me want to squint. "Up the stairs you go!"

"I'm so sorry about that," I say as I help Willow lay all her clothes out on the bed.

"Don't worry about it. I'm sure Max is afraid you'll get hurt because I'm still obsessed with Arden. And he'd be right, if you and me were for real. Because it *will* be awkward. Ugh, it *better* be awkward, anyway."

"Right. Of course." Ouch. If Max was trying to protect me, it's already too late.

It takes a minute for me to recover—and despite Willow turning on some music, another couple of minutes to relax, because bras and bodies. But Willow says she's good with what she has on, so it's just me. Whew! That sure simplifies things! I'm definitely not disappointed that we won't both be shirtless in front of each other. Not at all.

"Here, try this top with the jeans you have on," she says, and holds out a cream-colored boatneck T-shirt.

I take the shirt, turn my back, inhale, and undress. I pick up her shirt and sneak a peek at her; she's absorbed in her phone. Oh well. I didn't really think I'd catch her casting discreet but longing looks in my direction, did I? But then I slip the soft cotton shirt over my head and realize that I am now putting something next to *my* skin, that has been next to *her* skin—next to her stomach, her back, her boobs . . . well, her bra, anyway—and suddenly I feel a lot better.

"Mmm, that's not quite right," says Willow when she sees the top on me. "How about this"—she hands me a pair of black skinny jeans—"and . . . this."

An oversized plaid shirt?

"I know, I know." She grins when she sees the look on my face. "But plaid is super in right now."

But that outfit doesn't quite work, either, and we try another outfit, and another, and we're on Outfit #5 when Willow gestures frantically at me to turn down the music.

"Are you sure that Dela said lunch at one o'clock at the Ice Cream Bar?" she asks, frowning at her phone.

"Yeah . . . ?"

"You're *sure*?"

"Well, yeah." Of course I'm sure.

"She didn't say, for example, bike riding at eleven o'clock in Golden Gate Park?"

"No, definitely not." That's an oddly specific hypothetical. "Why?" I ask, nervous.

Willow drops all pretense of being calm and thrusts her phone at me. "Because, Nozomi, they're on their way to Golden Gate Park right now. Like right this very instant! They *lied* to us!"

I look at Arden's story—a photo of herself smiling next to a bicycle, her hair wrapped in a silky lemon-yellow scarf, with the caption: **Headed to Golden Gate Park to meet my girl!** I can almost hear the music in the background: Dun-dun-*dunnnn!* [Extreme closeup of Nozomi's and Willow's stunned faces!]

I feel a spike of resentment at Arden. Leave it to her to ruin my morning alone with Willow. Just when things were really starting to click!

Scrambling to de-escalate the situation, I say, "It was probably a last-minute decision."

"Well, they should have told us, then, shouldn't they!"

"But . . . but that's okay, though, right? They haven't canceled lunch. Let's just concentrate on that. Speaking of which, what do you think of this shirt with these—"

"And bicycling in Golden Gate Park! I cannot *believe* her." Her nostrils flare and her eyebrows lower menacingly.

"Um. What's wrong with bicycling in Golden Gate Park?" I quaver. Too late, I realize my mistake; Willow goes *off,* and so does my opportunity to keep things under control.

"It's what *I* did with *her* for *our* first date," she fumes. "How dare she do this to me! Don't I mean *anything* to her? Is nothing from our relationship special to her?" Suddenly, her lip trembles and her eyes well up as her fury threatens to give way to anguish. "I don't understand why she's doing this," she says, her voice thick with impending tears. Then after a pause, "No. No. I will *not* cry. I won't. I *won't,*" between clenched teeth. She blinks ferociously and grabs a tissue and dabs carefully at her eyes, taking long, measured breaths until finally, she lets out one big whoosh and sort of shimmies her shoulders, as if to dislodge any remaining heartache.

"Okay. All better." She glances at my face, bites her lip, and says, "We don't have time for foundation or concealer—wait, no, maybe this stuff, really quick. It's practically transparent, so we don't have to worry if the shade isn't a perfect match." She hands me a tube and instructs me to put a tiny bit on. I take it with a slight sense of foreboding. There's an urgency in her voice that I don't like.

As I spread the goop on my face, she surveys the outfit I have on currently—denim capris (mine) and an embroidered top (hers)—and pronounces, "That's actually perfect. Okay, let's call a Lyft. We have to move fast if we want to catch them."

"Catch them?" I was afraid of this.

"Nozomi, we have to do everything in our power to prevent them from getting closer."

"But . . . but won't it look like we're stalking them?"

This appears to give her some pause, but she waves it off. "They deserve it. You *know* she posted that story for me to see. Does she think I'm going to just sit back and let it happen?"

"But what if she's just trolling you? You don't have to—"

"Please?" Willow takes my hands in hers. "Come on, it'll be fun. It'll be an adventure. A fun, spontaneous adventure. It'll be a bonding experience!"

Well, when she puts it that way . . . I imagine us on a madcap ride through the park, searching for Arden and Willow.

Maybe we'll spot them in the Botanical Garden and hide behind bushes as we follow them around, giggling as we place ourselves in an impossible-to-miss spot so they can see us kissing each other. And then just like in the movies, the fake kiss will become infused with real desire, and we'll find ourselves suddenly bashful and shy . . .

My hands are still in Willow's, and she's looking at me with bright-eyed anticipation. "All right," I say.

"Oh, yay!" She gives me a quick hug, then pulls back and beams at me. "Thank you. You're such a good friend."

"It's no big deal," I say. "You're right. It'll be fun."

"No, really, I mean it." Willow takes my hands in hers again. "Thank you."

All this holding of hands . . . I can feel myself starting to blush. So I let go and cover my face in mock exasperation to hide it.

"Hey. Look at me." I feel Willows hands again, and as she gently pulls my hands away from my face, I open my eyes to see her looking right into them, her gaze steady and searching. Whoa. I smile shyly, heart pounding, a little confused but ready for anything.

"I wish we had time to do your brows and lashes," she says finally. "But we should really call that Lyft."

19

ARDEN POSTED A LIVE VIDEO OF HERSELF AND
Dela at the Golden Gate Park carousel a few minutes ago, so it
seems like as good a place as any to start. But when we arrive,
panting on our rented bikes, they are not among the riders
who empty into the plaza when the carousel comes to a stop.

"Dammit," Willow mutters. She checks Arden's stories for
another clue, but there's nothing new. "Okay. Okay. Where
else?" She gazes into the distance, tapping her fingers on
her lips as she thinks, then turns to me with her eyes ablaze.
"The Japanese Tea Garden." We leap onto our bikes and barrel through the plaza, scattering pigeons and small children.
We glide downhill and huff and puff uphill, past playing fields,
meadows, and thick groves of oak trees and eucalyptus. Willow clears the path ahead of us, bellowing "On your left!" and

"On your right!" at joggers, roller-bladers, and parents with strollers who leap aside and shout at her. I trail in her wake, calling "Sorry! Sorry!" and absorbing a barrage of dirty looks and muttered comments about disrespectful teenagers.

But there are no bicycles parked in front of the Japanese Tea Garden. "The de Young Museum!" Willow cries, and we ride over. But there's no sign of Dela and Arden there, either. The next twenty minutes is basically a grim, high-speed bicycle tour of Golden Gate Park where we stop at each attraction just long enough to ascertain that Arden and Dela aren't there, after which Willow makes a prediction about where Arden and Dela will *really* be, and we leave. We stop by "The polo field!" "The bison paddock!" and "The beach chalet!" until finally she makes a prediction that sticks: "The boathouse!"

Willow spots Arden's bike locked to a rack in front of the boathouse almost immediately. As we lock up, she seethes. "I *cannot* believe they came *here*, of all places. This is where we had our first kiss!" The seething continues for a minute, but then something dreadful seems to occur to her and she turns to me, her eyes desolate. "What if I'm wrong? What if they really are meant for each other?" The furious energy that propelled her through the park seems to drain out of her, and she droops against me, resting her head against mine. "I don't know if I can do this."

This is it. This is my moment. Tentatively, so as not to disturb the scales that are starting to tip in my favor, I put an arm around her and give her a gentle half hug. "Maybe it would be healthier to go somewhere else," I say. "We can focus on having a good time, like you said. I used to love the observation tower at the de Young. Or maybe we could just chill on the grass somewhere."

"Maybe," Willow says quietly. "This is really nice right now, actually. Just sitting here with you. It's helping me calm down."

AAAAAHHHHHHH!

"Oh, good," I say, and lean back against her just the tiniest bit and try hard to exude a calming aura. I concentrate on soaking up every drop of this delicious moment so I can take it out and savor it later—the sun on my face, her back against my arm, just like a real couple. Just like I dreamed of at the beginning of the summer. Soon I'm adrift on a fantasy in which Willow and I have our first kiss—we'll be laughing about trying to outsmart Arden and Dela, and she'll admit that she doesn't feel the same way about Arden as she used to. And I'll say, "Oh?" And she'll say, "It's because of you," and I'll say, "Well, I'm glad I could help," and she'll say, "No. I mean I'm in love with you," and then we'll lock eyes and lean toward each other, and—

"Okay, I've made up my mind. I know I'm being an obsessive asshole, but I have to see this through. I have to show her that she's making a mistake."

No! No-no-no-no-no-no-no! "Are you sure?" I ask. "It won't upset you too much?"

But Willow's face has taken on a steely-eyed determination. "No, I'm ready for this. She wants to bring her new girlfriend here? Fine. I've brought mine. Let's see how she feels about that." She slips her arm around my back and gives me a quick squeeze and a peck on the cheek, and I know I'm pathetic, but I have to restrain myself from putting my hand to the spot where her lips touched my skin.

I figured our rowing expedition would be fun and romantic, at least—I had visions of a lazy little float around an idyllic little pond, the kind of leisurely, refined activity you might expect to see in a movie featuring girls in gauzy white dresses and straw bonnets, shot through a soft-focus lens.

I was wrong.

We're led to our boat by an outdoorsy-looking white guy in a forest-green T-shirt and khaki shorts named Chip or Tyler or Huck or something, who gallantly holds our hands as we teeter aboard. The boat is docked pointy-side in, so all I have to do, Chip-Tyler-Huck tells me as I sit down with my back to the dock, is turn it around and we'll be on our way. Easy-peasy. I smile at Willow and take an oar in each hand. She smiles back expectantly, and my heart flutters. This isn't so bad after all.

A few minutes later, I'm sweating and cursing and struggling to maneuver the boat backward away from the dock without whapping anyone else with an oar. (To be fair, the other boater should have known better than to get within oar-whapping distance. I'm sure that's a violation of safety rules.)

"Get those oars in a little deeper and apply even pressure throughout the stroke!" Chip-Tyler-Huck calls cheerfully as I flail about.

What does he think I've been *trying* to do?

Willow, in the meantime, is helpless with laughter, which does nothing to quell my mounting frustration and humiliation. At least she's having a good time. She'll associate me with mirth and merriment, in addition to utter incompetence.

Finally, we get far enough out on the pond for me to work the oars and not have to worry about causing a waterfront catastrophe. I pause to wipe my brow and catch my breath—rowing is shockingly hard work—and look around. According to Chip-Tyler-Huck's orientation and safety speech, this wooded island behind me takes up most of the lake, and the thing to do is to row around it. It's something I think I might enjoy quite a lot, actually, if it didn't involve so much rowing.

Willow begs me to hurry. "They can't be far ahead," she says, craning around me to scan the stretch of water in front of her. I'm about to raise a protest when she muses, "I think what we should do is get within sight of them and when they look over, you could lean forward and kiss me. I mean, if that's okay with you."

You could lean forward and kiss me . . . Without warning, I feel the phantom sensation of her waist against my forearm, her hip under my hand, her head on my shoulder. It makes me woozy with desire.

It is more than okay with me.

Don't get me wrong. Rowing is still a nightmare. I'm still hot and sweaty and worried about ruining Willow's nice top and I think I might be developing a blister on my right hand. But I discover that it's not quite as stressful when we're alone and Chip-Tyler-Huck isn't shouting helpful tips at me every few seconds. We glide past little beachy landings and under a stone bridge, and we're just coming up on a Chinese pavilion when Willow says, "I see them!"

Thank god.

"Okay, just a little farther—I think they've stopped to look at the waterfall."

"If we get between them and the waterfall, they can't miss us," I say. Plus, it looks so nice and shady by the shore, and I won't have to turn the boat ninety degrees or execute some other ridiculous maneuver to make sure they get a good angle on our kiss. I forget my aching arms and burgeoning blisters, and redouble my efforts. Every stroke is bringing me closer to feeling her lean into me again, feeling her lips on mine.

It's a romantic little spot with the (clearly fake, but still very pretty) waterfall on one side and the lake stretching out on the other. An older white couple are tossing crumbs to a pair of mallard ducks right in front of us, and the ducks are bobbing and quacking and wagging their little ducky tails with charming enthusiasm. A flock of Canada geese floats serenely on the other side of a jetty behind us, and a few of them have drifted over and are watching the ducks and their antics with detached amusement.

"Has Arden seen us?" I ask.

"Definitely," says Willow. "Are you ready?"

"As I'll ever be." My heart starts racing. Our first (fake) kiss. This is always the moment in the movies where the pretend couple comes face-to-face with their undeniable attraction to each other—the before-and-after moment—the turning point. I have to make it good. No, not just good. I have to make it real.

I grip the sides of the boat for balance and it rocks gently as I shift my weight forward, slowly, slowly. Willow leans toward me, smiling, meeting my gaze; we're so close now, I can see myself reflected in her eyes, and I pause for one tantalizing, terrifying, exhilarating moment—

And then the geese attack.

It turns out that the mildly amused geese we saw earlier were actually the advance guard for a vicious band of goose marauders who have decided as one to crash the duck party, and what's worse, seem to have used some sort of secret goose communication system to alert every goose in the surrounding area to the plan. They close in on us with astonishing speed, in obscenely large numbers, and our tranquil, romantic little cove becomes a hurricane of flapping, honking, hissing monsters, churning up the air and water all around us and ruining everything.

"Get us out of here!" Willow keeps shrieking.

"I'm trying!" I shriek back, but the boat has turned itself pointy-side-toward-shore because why not, and there are geese literally everywhere, which makes putting the oars in the water an exercise both in animal cruelty and self-endangerment. There's nothing to do but keep screaming, really, and pray we don't get pooped on.

I don't even know how we manage to escape, but I do know that once we're clear of the goose juggernaut, I hate geese, I hate rowing, and I hate the smudge of goose poop on my butt from where I sat on it on my bench. I also hate Dela, who I bet thinks the goose attack was the funniest thing she's ever seen, and Arden, who will probably pretend she was worried about us.

"I'm so sorry," Willow says. "This was a bad idea. I never should have suggested it." She hands me a wipe from her bag, and I do my best to wipe my pants off while she cleans the bench for me.

"It's okay," I lie, and she gives me such a penetrating stare that I amend, "It was okay until the goose blitzkrieg."

"The goosekrieg," says Willow.

We look at each other and smile. The smile turns into a chuckle, which blossoms into wild, hysterical laughter, and soon we're collapsed against each other and giggling uncontrollably.

When the laughter fades, the sensation of Willow's arms on my knees, and our heads on each other's shoulders, sharpens. I feel her back rise and fall as she sighs contentedly.

I should kiss her. Now would be the perfect moment. *Dela and Arden are still watching,* I'll say. *Should we . . . ?*

Willow must have the same thought, because she lifts her head slightly and says, "Dammit. They're gone. That would have been the perfect moment for a kiss."

Dammit.

Willow insists on rowing the rest of the way around the lake, to make up for the goosekrieg incident, but I really don't want to start the hunt again.

"They've already seen us together having fun. Wasn't that the point of coming here?"

"They saw us getting attacked by geese and screaming our heads off."

"They also saw us laughing about it. I'm sure they did. We can spin the whole thing as a hilarious romantic adventure," I argue. "We don't even have to go to lunch. I'm sure we'll have plenty of other chances to be girlfriends in front of them." And more time to be together without them now.

Willow remains unswayed. "Maybe, but I think the more time we spend in front of them, the better. It's kind of the point of the plan, isn't it?" Well. *Her* plan, anyway. Reluctantly, I agree.

But it only takes a minute of hard rowing for her to decide maybe we *can* wait till lunch to catch up with them. "Now I'm *really* sorry I made you row," she says, examining her palm for blisters. "Why didn't you say something? You have to let me make it up to you somehow."

What I want to say is, *You could make it up to me by kissing me.* What I actually say is, "Don't worry about it. It was fun," even though that's a lie. The truth is, I'm not really sure why I didn't say anything. *Because your enormous crush has made you into a doormat,* I can hear Max saying. *Because sometimes you have to make sacrifices in the service of your dreams,* I argue back in my head. Besides, it wasn't a total loss. We're having this moment right now, aren't we? And we got to laugh together, which everyone knows is important. And we had an almost-kiss moment—and Willow knew it. Okay, so maybe she didn't *feel* the same way about it that I did, but she obviously sensed the *potential* for romance. That has to mean something.

20

WILLOW AND I TURN THE CORNER ONTO COLE
Street just in time to see Arden and Dela go into the Ice Cream
Bar, and Willow practically rubs her hands together with glee.

"I am so ready for this, Nozomi. *So* ready."

I, on the other hand, am not. I feel exceedingly *un*ready, if
truth be told. In the time between the goose attack and now,
we've gone over an exhaustive list of conversation topics and
hypothetical situations, plus when and how much we should
kiss, hug, and hold hands. But the fact is, a lot of it is going
to have to be improvised. And I am not to be trusted when it
comes to improvising.

As we near the shop, Willow slows down. "Riiiiight here."
She smiles softly at me, turning me slightly away from the
plate-glass window, and says, "Okay, kiss me."

"Right now?" I croak.

"Well, yeah," says Willow, her gaze still fixed lovingly on me. She strokes my cheek and murmurs, "This is part of the plan, remember? We want Arden to think we're kissing even though we don't know they're watching."

We did talk about this, and her touch should be making me wild with desire, but . . . it doesn't feel right. It's probably goosekrieg PTSD. Or maybe . . . maybe it's because I was so close to kissing her for real before, I want our first kiss to feel more like that. I don't want to perform it. I want to *want* it.

"Are you sure they're watching? How do you know?"

"Trust me. I know Arden. She'll have been waiting for us to show up, and she'll be watching," Willow says with authority.

"Okay," I say uncertainly.

"Okay. Here we go. Kiss me, baby." She gives me a playful smile, and I take a deep breath and go for it.

Our lips meet. It's a bit tentative. Of course it is. It doesn't feel natural, the way it did back at the lake. I wish we'd gotten to kiss at the lake.

"I'm not sure that was enough," she says against my mouth. "Should we do another one?" How can I say no? Maybe I can make this one better. I kiss her again, a little more force-fully this time, and she responds by sliding one hand over my shoulder and one hand around my back and pulling our hips together, and my arms tighten around her, and I take it back about this being a weird situation, it's pretty good, amazing, even, and as her fingers move up to the nape of my neck, I have just enough time to hope that she's starting to lose herself in this kiss the way I am before she pulls away from me, laughing. "Wow," she says. "That was unexpectedly hot."

I would prefer it if she weren't so surprised, but let's focus on the positive: she thought it was so hot, she had to shut it down! Maybe she'll go home and remember that kiss, the warmth and pressure of her lips on mine—no, wait, I mean *my* lips on *hers*—and wonder what it would be like to kiss me again. Maybe she'll smile fondly and think to herself, "I think I might be chasing the wrong girl."

Maybe she'd even be open to another kiss right now.

I clear my throat and ask her, "Another one?" very casually, as if I'm trying to decide how many cupcakes we should put on our shared dessert plate. Please let her want another cupcake.

"Nah, I think that's enough. We don't want to overdo it."

Right. Of course. There's an audience to play to.

"Okay. Let's make Arden regret the biggest mistake she ever made." Willow takes my hand and we push through the door.

Arden and Dela are waiting just inside, and one look at Arden's face is enough to let me know that she did witness that kiss, and that she thought Willow was into it. Which is encouraging.

"Heyyy!" Willow gets her greeting out first, and her voice is at its light and melodic best.

Not to be outdone, Arden answers with an equally enthusiastic, "Heyyyy!"

Dela doesn't say anything, but she meets my eye and grimaces, which is oddly comforting. At least someone besides me is feeling out of their depth here.

We head toward the counter, and Arden says innocently, "Were you at Stow Lake earlier? I could have sworn we saw you. Near Huntington Falls, I think."

But Willow wasn't kidding outside when she said she was ready. "Oh my god, really? We did go to Stow Lake! We had this *wild* experience right by Huntington Falls. Did you see two girls being attacked by a flock of killer geese? Because that would have been us."

"We *did* see you, then! Are you okay? You looked like you were really freaking out. We almost tried to rescue you, but—"

"We *were* totally freaking out! Screaming our brains out—I'm surprised you didn't hear us, in fact. It was hilarious! Right, Nozomi?"

"Right!" I say. "So, so funny! We laughed so hard!" I laugh a little, for good measure. Arden raises her eyebrows and Dela narrows her eyes. Oof.

"Right? Don't recommend . . . but highly recommend," finishes Willow with a smile. "Anyway, I'm starving! Let's order."

We walk to the register and look at the menu. I go first and ask for a grilled cheese, and I'm about to order a scoop of butterscotch swirl in a waffle cone when Arden jumps in and orders a banana split for dessert for the four of us, saying to Willow, "We used to get this all the time, remember?"

Willow is unfazed. She says, "I think Nozomi and I will get something to share. What looks good to you, Nozomi?"

"Um." I was really looking forward to that butterscotch swirl, but I feel like I should support Willow in front of Arden. I take another look at the menu, which lists everything from brownie sundaes and homemade ice cream sandwiches to candy-cap-mushroom-flavored soda and tobacco-infused syrup. I end up suggesting a butterscotch milk shake, which at least has butterscotch in it.

"Good choice," says Willow. "I've never had that one. Arden doesn't like butterscotch, so we never got it."

"And *we* can get a root beer float," Arden chimes in almost instantly, looking at Willow even though she's ostensibly talking to Dela, "since Willow hates root beer so much and I've never had a chance to try it."

This is getting very stressful. I hazard a glance at Dela, who meets it with raised eyebrows, just for a moment, before staring intently at the other flavors in the freezer case in front of us. I wonder if she wanted something besides a root beer float.

We finish our order without further incident, thank goodness—another grilled cheese for Dela, a black bean burger for Willow, and a BLT for Arden—and grab four spots at the counter at the back of the shop.

Almost immediately, Arden starts again. "So. I'm just gonna

be honest and say out loud what's going on."

My heart leaps into my throat. She knows. She's figured out the plan and she's going to call us on it.

"I have to admit I was kind of surprised that you found someone so soon after we broke up," she says, addressing Willow as if I'm not even here.

I hold my breath, waiting for her to finish: *In fact, I'm so surprised, I don't believe you two are for real. There's no way you would ever slum it with a girl like Nozomi. I know I wouldn't. And neither would Dela.*

Okay, that might be my insecurities talking.

But Arden doesn't say any of that. She doesn't say anything at all. *That* was her big announcement? That she didn't expect Willow to find someone new so quickly?

"Well, you know how it is, I'm sure," says Willow airily and with more than a little venom. "You meet someone new and you just get swept away, don't you? You just forget everything that's ever happened in the past."

Arden's smile turns wooden.

"It escalated very quickly," I add hastily. "Unexpectedly. Right, Willow?"

"*Very* quickly," Willow agrees with a sly smile in my direction, and her voice is so loaded with meaning that I shiver involuntarily, as if what she's suggesting has actually happened.

"It was pretty much the same with us, too," Arden says almost belligerently. "Totally swept away."

Dela looks at her in—surprise, maybe?—and opens her mouth, but Arden starts again before she has a chance to say anything.

"I mean, we worked together for a whole semester before anything happened, so I guess I can't say it was *sudden*. But I feel more and more . . . smitten these days," she says. The hard smile is gone, and she's lavishing an adoring gaze on Dela. Dela smiles back warily.

I can't stand the mounting tension. I have to change the subject. "Boy, I can't wait for that grilled cheese sandwich," I say brightly. "I love grilled cheese. Yum. Yummy-yum-yum." Oh my god. What am I saying.

Arden gives me a long, thoughtful stare, and I begin to worry again that she's wondering how in the world Willow could ever fall for me, for the kind of girl who says *yummy-yum-yum*. I'm beginning to wonder myself.

"Hm. Well. Anyway, I'm glad we can all be friends. It makes everything so much easier, doesn't it?" she says. "No hard feelings, or whatever."

"Mm-hmm," says Willow with a tight smile. "No hard feelings at all."

Silence has fallen again, thick and heavy and swarming with the hard feelings whose existence Willow and Arden have just denied. I don't know how much longer I can take this fake-friendly lunch we're having—it's not at all like the hilarious larks that you see in movies. I start squinching and unsquinching my toes inside my shoes, just to have something to focus on besides the overpowering sense of doom that's threatening to crush the air out of my lungs.

Squinch, unsquinch.

Squinch, unsquinch.

Squinch—

"You know what?" Arden says. "I'm so sorry, but I think Willow and I have some issues we need to sort out. Do you mind if we take a moment?"

Dela and I look at Arden, stunned.

But Willow is right with her. She says frostily, "What if I don't want to talk to you?"

Arden stares her down. "Do you not?"

"Well, I—no. No, I do not."

"Maybe you should, though," says Dela. Now we all gape at her.

"What?" says Willow.

"I said maybe you should talk to Arden. It makes more sense than sitting here and pretending everything's fine when it's clearly not."

What is WRONG with you? I want to shout at Dela. *It does NOT make sense. I think maybe Willow should NOT talk to Arden.* Doesn't Dela understand that she's opening the door to the demise of both our relationships? (Well, okay, her actual relationship with Arden and my possible future relationship with Willow?)

Willow opens her mouth, then shuts it, then opens it again, hesitates, and says, "Well. Fine. I have nothing to say, but if that's really what you want, Arden, I guess I can cooperate." She turns to me. "Nozomi, is that okay with you?"

I don't feel like I can say, "No, it's not okay with me at all! This was *not* part of the plan!" without looking like I've completely lost the plot, so I nod and say, "Sure! Whatever you need to do."

"Okay, then." Willow stands up and raises her eyebrows at Arden, who does the same. Then she leans over and kisses me, which takes me so much by surprise that I don't even have the presence of mind to enjoy it, let alone kiss her back properly. Arden does the same to Dela—only their kiss is longer and hotter, and as it goes on, I can tell Willow is considering kissing me again, which—I can't believe I'm saying this, but I hope she doesn't. Thankfully, Dela pushes Arden away and says, "Go," and Willow and Arden leave the restaurant and stalk off together with their arms crossed and their mouths drawn into angry frowns.

Then it's just me and Dela alone at the counter, drumming our fingers, squinching our toes, and looking anywhere but at each other.

21

THE FOOD FINALLY ARRIVES, AND FOR A SECOND I wonder if we should wait for Arden and Willow, but Dela tucks right into her grilled cheese, and it looks so good—crispy and brown and buttery on the outside, golden and melty and gooey on the inside—that I give in and start on my own.

"Mmmm, this is heaven," I murmur, but I'm drowned out by Dela, who says, "What an unmitigated disaster."

"No, that's not true," I say, only half joking. "This grilled cheese is delicious."

Dela grins. "Point taken. With the exception of this delicious grilled cheese, lunch has been an unmitigated disaster."

I can't help smiling back. I never thought I'd feel solidarity with Dela, but here we are.

She goes on. "Seriously, what were you thinking, asking to

do a double date with me and Arden? I don't know why Arden went with it, to be honest. It's obvious that Willow's not over her. And I know she's not over Willow. I know she's jealous of you."

Arden's jealous of me?

Arden . . . is jealous . . . of me?

That must mean she thinks I have a chance with Willow.

I have a chance with Willow!

Oh, whoops. Dela is still talking. ". . . and I'm not gonna judge her just because she has feelings. But I am *not* okay with the two of them jerking us around and using us as trophies or weapons or whatever. I don't know about you and Willow, but I *know* Arden kissed me goodbye like that for show."

"Hm." The disappointment I felt when Willow decided that Arden had seen enough kissing comes rushing back. Dela's been feeling this, too, I realize.

Though if things work out the way I want, neither of us will have to feel this way.

The root beer float and the butterscotch shake come up at the counter, and we fetch them. Dela eyes the float distrustfully before taking a tiny sip and making a face.

"I thought you liked root beer," I say. My butterscotch shake is uhhh-mazing, by the way.

"I never said that," she says. "Arden ordered it without asking me, remember? As a passive-aggressive fuck-you to Willow."

"Oh. Right." I regard my shake, which now looks like

Willow's passive-aggressive fuck-you to Arden, though that's not going to stop me from slurping it right up. "You want some?" I offer it to Dela, who wrinkles her nose.

"I don't like butterscotch, either."

"Do you like *anything*?"

"I like grilled cheese."

"Dessert, I mean," I say, rolling my eyes.

"I like lemon meringue pie."

"*Lemon meringue pie?*" I can't help laughing.

"What?" she says, looking offended. "What's wrong with lemon meringue pie?"

"Nothing," I say. "It's just—well, it's such a bright and sunny dessert. And fluffy. And sweet. And only a tiny bit tart. It doesn't match your personality."

"And you can say this because you know me so well."

"I know you well enough."

"Oh, really." She leans back and crosses her arms. "What's my personality, then?"

"Dark. Sour." I leave out "pretentious." I don't need to be mean. "You should like . . . dark chocolate cake with sour cherry filling. Except you don't like chocolate, so maybe something like sour cherry–infused espresso."

She rolls her eyes and grins. "So, bitter, too."

I take a big sip of my milk shake. "I don't hear you denying it."

"Ha-ha." She takes her phone out and types. "Sour cherry-infused espresso isn't even a thing!"

"I didn't say it was."

Another minute goes by, and without warning, Dela says, "You know what, I never should have agreed to this mess. I *knew* it would end badly, but I let Arden convince me it would be okay. Who knows why. Anyway, I think I'm gonna bail."

She gets a to-go box and paper cup for Arden's food and root beer float and asks the server to hold them for Arden. Then she nods at me. "See ya," she says, and leaves without waiting for me to reply.

I don't want to go. What if Willow and Arden come back, realize that Dela and I have left, and decide in our absence that the two of them should get back together? I wish Willow had agreed to cancel lunch and we'd stayed on the lake. It would have been so nice, just the two of us.

Eventually, though, I give up and ask for a to-go bag and a paper cup. I draw a big heart on the bag for Willow, but I take the milk shake with me. Dela might not like root beer, but I love butterscotch. And anyway, Willow owes me for all that rowing.

22

OAK VISTA CONTINUING CARE COMMUNITY IS
nestled in the foothills of the Santa Cruz Mountains. Hundreds
of years ago, the Spanish Mexican ranchers used to graze their
cattle here, and I can still see a few cows scattered on the
slopes as we pass through what Stephen never fails to tell us is
land owned by Stanford University. In the winter, it looks like
Ireland (or what I imagine Ireland looks like, anyway): bright
green hills as far as the eye can see. But now, in the summer,
the sun has burned everything to a dusty, dull, dead-grass-
brown; I try to see it as golden, or blond, or even just plain old
yellow, but it resists all my efforts to cast it in a better light.

The pretense is that we're going on an exploratory tour,
but in reality, Stephen has already made up his mind. Max and
I have been instructed to rave about how amazing Oak Vista

is, how beautiful the residences are, how delicious the food, how interesting all the activities. The plan is to continue singing Oak Vista's praises in front of Baba every now and then for the next few weeks until Dad arrives, at which point he and Stephen will take Baba out for a nice meal and tell her they'd like her to move there in the not-too-distant future. They keep insisting that Baba will take it better this way, but I'm still not convinced.

Despite the brilliant sunshine outside, the atmosphere in the car is decidedly grim. Baba is staring sulkily out the window; apart from her unmistakable opposition to the whole idea of this field trip, she's furious with Stephen, who snapped at her when she criticized his driving, and then snapped at her again when she made a comment about him and Lance eating out too much. Stephen probably would have had more patience, but he's annoyed because Lance had to leave town unexpectedly for an emergency on-site consultation on one of his buildings. Max is hungover from going out with some college buddies last night and is in a foul mood.

Me, I'm cranky because Mom called this morning to tell me that she was going to send me links to some options for bedroom furniture from Ikea. It seemed like good news, but two sentences later, she bait-and-switched me. The bedroom conversation was happening because—surprise!—she's planning to move into Mr. Jensen's house, and his spare bedroom is going to become my bedroom.

"Isn't that great, Zozo? I can't wait to decorate it with you," she gushed.

"You're moving *in* with him?" I stared at my phone in disbelief.

"It's bigger than the one you have at ho— I mean, at Dad's house."

"You only started dating him in May! You're not even legally divorced yet."

"I am an adult," she replied, as if being an adult excused everything, "and I've told you many times that I only left because I finally realized I had no other choice."

Ah yes. The April Epiphany, when she read a self-help book and decided that the marriage was unsalvageable and she needed to "save herself," followed quickly by the May Departure and Dating Spree, when she began "finding herself."

"I'm not staying at your boyfriend's house," I said, and hung up.

In sum: it's been a shitty morning for everyone.

Thank goodness I can distract myself with something fun. Not long after I got back from the Ice Cream Bar, Willow called. I'd been afraid that she was going to make a joyful announcement that our plan had worked, and that she and Arden had settled their differences and gotten back together. But in fact, she informed me that she and Arden hadn't been able to stop fighting. What's more, she felt terrible for abandoning me in the shop with Dela and wanted to take me sightseeing to make up for it. Was sometime this week okay?

Just the two of us on a real, honest-to-goodness, not-just-for-show, not-just-for-Instagram-likes date? Hmm, let me think . . . (which is to say, YES!!!) Okay, so it's not precisely one hundred percent a date in the sense that she wants to take me in her arms and kiss me senseless. But you never know, do you? Anyway, given her fight with Arden yesterday, it's the perfect opportunity for me to shine.

I look out the window and let the glow of anticipation transport me to a sunset picnic at Lands End, a catamaran ride on the bay, a redo of Golden Gate Park where we actually slow down and enjoy it. By the time we pull into the parking lot at Oak Vista, I'm so completely wrapped in a cocoon of possibilities that when Stephen asks me what I'm looking so dreamy about, I say, "My date with Willow this week," and I don't remember until after I've said it that it's not *exactly* a date.

We're greeted in the lobby of the sprawling main building by a lady in a smart suit, understated makeup, and a flawless French twist, and I have to put the dream on hold.

"I'm Celia," she says, and when Max and I introduce ourselves, she exclaims, "Well, aren't you lucky, Grandma! Remind me to tell you about all the family activities we have here for when your grandchildren visit."

Baba laughs and says, "I'm not going to live here. I'm just here because my son wants to tour."

Her laughter feels a little false, though, and when Stephen clears his throat and says, "Keep an open mind, Mom. I think you'd really love it here," her eyebrows settle into an angry V.

"Of course, it's a decision you'll want to make as a family," says Celia with practiced calm. "But I think you'll find that we have a wonderful, welcoming community here."

"Doesn't that sound nice, Mom?" says Stephen, and he smiles hopefully at Baba, but her eyebrows remain stubbornly V-shaped.

Celia shows us the fitness center, the library, and a condo unit before calling a golf cart to take us around the grounds. She points out swimming pools, tennis courts, hiking paths, and a "sustainable, organic, artisan" community vegetable garden. She encourages us to admire the sweeping views of the wooded foothills. I don't even have to pretend to be impressed. I generate so many oohs and aahs that Max elbows me and tells me to tone it down.

Baba, however, glowers at everything as if she finds it all deeply, personally offensive. She keeps up a constant grumbly commentary as the tour goes on: too many white people, too many rich people, ugly paint colors, no space for her to garden.

"But there was a garden just back there," Max says.

"It was not so good. So many tomatoes," she says darkly, as if tomatoes were the fruit of the devil, as if they weren't one of the only two vegetables in her own garden (the other being cucumbers).

Once the tour is over, Stephen suggests a walk on one of the paths that meanders through the hills on the property—Baba loves a scenic nature walk—but it's hot and uncomfortable and

Baba grouses about sunburn and dehydration.

"I bet it's so pretty in the winter, though," I say. "All green and everything."

"The path will be muddy," she says.

"The path is paved," Stephen points out, his voice strained.

"It will be slippery and dangerous."

Back in the lobby of the main building, an attendant offers us a choice of water, sweet tea, and cold oolong tea. Stephen tries to spin it as Asian-friendly, but Baba sniffs, "Oolong-cha. It's Chinese, not Japanese."

"I saw a flyer for a chess club," Stephen ventures. "You like chess, right?" I have to hand it to him. He really doesn't quit.

She sniffs. "I doubt anyone can beat me."

"It's mostly men who play chess, anyway," Stephen muses, and a spark flares in Baba's eye.

"I can beat any man," she snaps.

"Probably," he replies mildly, and as Baba boasts about how she was the chess champion of her school, and rants about how men who play chess think they're so smart, Stephen smiles at me and Max.

Baba may be difficult and infuriating, but I can't deny how awesome she is, too.

We go around a bend in the freeway headed north, and the weather changes abruptly as we enter another microclimate. The sky shifts from pale blue to pale gray, and the tops of the Santa Cruz Mountains disappear under billows of fog that tumble over the peaks and spill down the sides like the foamy crest of a giant wave. Stephen glances over at Baba, who has fallen asleep in the front passenger seat.

"How do you think that went?"

"Could've been worse," answers Max. "I guess she can go and win all the chess tournaments."

"It would give her a positive reason to move. Nothing gets her going like the possibility of kicking someone's ass," Stephen says, and then adds with a wry grin, "If you can call wanting to beat people at chess a positive reason."

Baba stirs a little, which shuts down that avenue of conversation.

Do they have actual tournaments, though? Or will it be more like the soccer league I played in as a kid, where no one keeps score and everybody gets a trophy? Poor Baba. We're already treating her like a child; she'll hate it if they treat her that way at Oak Vista, too.

I lean forward and look at her face. She has a brown spot near her right eye, and tiny wrinkles crisscross her chin, the corners of her eyes, and the area around her mouth. Her jaw is slack and her mouth is open a little, and her brow has relaxed out of the furrow she's held it in for most of the afternoon. I've always thought of her as fierce and full of fighting energy, but she looks so vulnerable now, when she's asleep. It's going to be hard for her to leave her home, her garden, and her neighborhood where she never felt out of place for being Asian. Of course she's trying to convince us—or herself, maybe—that she doesn't need to move. Why is she so stubborn about it? I don't know if she really believes that strongly that she's okay, or if she knows on some level that she's not but hopes she can bend life her way through sheer force of will. Honestly? I admire her determination. I just wish she could see how it's messing up her life—and ours, too.

23

ONCE WE'VE DROPPED BABA OFF AT HER HOUSE and returned home, Stephen goes straight to his office to call Dad and give him a full report. I follow Max to his room.

"What?" he says. "Why are you following me?"

"Can I talk to you for a sec about Mom?"

He groans and rubs his forehead. "I've had a splitting headache ever since I woke up this morning, and that walk in the sun with Baba didn't help. Can't it wait?"

"I've *been* waiting. I didn't talk to you in the car, did I?" Max looks longingly at his bed, and I add, "I promise it'll be quick. Please?"

"Fine," he says heavily. He trudges to his bed and lies down carefully, draping his arm over his eyes. "What is it?"

"Did you know she's moving in with Mr. Jensen?"

"What?" This shocks him into dropping his arm and lifting his head to face me. "Seriously?"

"Yep."

"Ughhh," he says, and back down he goes.

What, that's it? One semi-animated expression of disbelief and a defeated groan? Then I remember that he's hungover, so I wait another beat. But there's nothing more. No outrage, no agitation, not so much as a mumbled "what the fuck."

"Well?" I prompt him.

"Well, what?"

"Well, what do you have to say about it? It's barely even been like two months since they started dating! Even if you pretend the whole idea of her and Mr. Jensen isn't gross and weird in the first place, don't you think it's too soon? Don't you think she should live on her own for . . . I don't know, longer?"

"Can you please stop with the screeching, Zomi? Just take it down like fifteen notches?"

"I'm not screeching," I protest.

"Every syllable that comes out of your mouth feels like you're taking an ice pick to my skull."

I open my mouth to argue but think better of it. Stay on topic. In my lowest, quietest, calmest voice, I say, "Don't you think it's weird? What should we do?"

"Yes. Nothing."

My head practically explodes. "What? Why? Aren't you even a *little* bit upset? It's been two months, Max. Two! Months!"

Max winces. "Quiet? Please?"

"Oh. Sorry." Oops. "But aren't you? Upset, I mean?" I ask. Then I say the thing I've been wondering about for weeks now. "Do you think . . . do you think maybe she had an affair? Like started seeing him *before* she moved out?" I hate to think that Mom would actually cheat on Dad. I hate it so much I actively try *not* to think about it. But it's not impossible, is it?

Max doesn't say anything for a while. Then he breathes in slowly, as if he's getting ready to say something important—and holds it for a second, then seems to change his mind and breathes out. I try very hard not to want to smother him with a pillow as he takes two more long, slow breaths, until I lose my patience and say, "Can you say *something*?"

Finally, he says, "Of course I'm upset. I think it's fucking disgraceful. But what am I supposed to do about it, Zomi? Sue her? Have a temper tantrum? She's forty-eight and she's gonna do whatever bonkers, random shit she wants, and we can't stop her. The sooner you accept that, the better."

"But it's . . ." I cast about for the words to explain my outrage. "It's wrong. It's disrespectful. To Dad. Don't you think? He didn't choose to get divorced."

Max raises his arm enough to reveal one open eye, with which he gives me a long, hard look. "You *do* know their marriage was a literal garbage fire, don't you?"

"But Dad tried to make it work. He asked her to go to marriage counseling. She could at least respect that."

Max stares at me for another moment before he crosses his arm back over his face and heaves a massive sigh. "Trust me, Zomi," he says. "If Dad is delusional enough at this point to feel disrespected by Mom moving in with Mr. Jensen, he deserves the disrespect."

Which I think is unfair and mean, but I get the sense that we're scraping the bottom of Max's very limited barrel of patience, so I don't argue.

"She expects me to stay there on her nights," I tell him instead.

"Ha." He snorts. "Big L."

"Yeah, I knew you'd think it was funny, you jerk."

"I think it's hilarious. Thank you for that."

"Fuck you."

"Fuck *you*."

With a sigh, I turn to go.

"Oh, hey. One thing," he says.

"Yeah?"

"I've been meaning to tell you. Willow's definitely not over her ex. In fact, I'd go so far as to say she's obsessed, and you should get out before it gets ugly."

What—how dare he? "What are you talking about?" I splutter. "Based on what evidence?"

"Um, for starters, you went on a *double date with her ex* yesterday."

"So? She's totally over Arden. You heard her say it yourself."

Max lifts his arm just enough to skewer me again with one eye. "And you believed her? Jeezus, you're more gullible than I thought."

"I am not gullible."

"Mm-hmm. Right."

"I know what I'm doing," I insist.

"You have no fucking *idea* what you're doing. If you did, you wouldn't be dating this girl. I know you're not the sharpest crayon in the box, but it's like you're closing your eyes on *purpose*, and—"

"I'm not really dating her, okay?" I shout, unable to take it anymore. He flinches, and maybe it's mean of me, but *yeah*. He deserves it for insulting me like that.

"Okay, what?" he says. "And can you not yell?"

In addition to petty (but sweet) satisfaction, I'm flooded with a strange exhilaration—or maybe I'm just relieved to be able to tell the truth—and the whole story, the whole plan comes pouring out. "See?" I finish. "I have a plan, and I'm totally in control. It's like in those movies where—"

"Are you telling me you're trying to have a relationship based on a romantic-comedy trope? Here's a clue for you, Zo: those aren't documentaries."

Well, when he puts it that way, in that tone of voice.

"Listen, though. It's *going* to be real. We're going on a real date this week! She's taking me wherever I want to go in the city."

"Does *she* think this is a date?"

"I mean. Not exactly. But it's not a *fake* date."

"I hate to break it to you, dear sister, but if she doesn't think it's a date—especially if she's thinking about someone else the whole time—it's not a real date."

Leave it to Max to poke holes in the only thing that's making me happy right now.

"All you ever do is try to bring me down," I say irritably.

"You only see what you want to see, so I'm trying to show you what I see. It's for your own good. Look at the facts, Zomi. Live in the real world, for fuck's sake."

"I do live in the real world."

"You're literally trying to turn your life into a movie. Like you think everyone's going to get a happy ending. And I'm telling you that in the real world, that's not possible."

I've had enough of this. "I thought you had a headache and wanted to be left alone," I say.

"Trust me, I would like nothing better. And I've said all I have to say, so you can go now. Goodbye."

I don't care what Max thinks. He's the kind of guy who's so jaded and cynical, he sees Mom moving in with her not-even-two-months-new boyfriend—before she's even moved all her stuff out of our house—and goes, *oh well, just accept it,* instead of freaking out like a normal person who understands that that's not how people are supposed to act. It's not like I'm *unaware* of Willow's feelings about Arden. It's not like I don't understand that this might not work. It's just that I expect the best out of life, and he expects the worst.

Only . . . it's hard to be optimistic and hopeful about my plan when Max the killjoy keeps reminding me of all the ways it could fail. Ugh. I hate him.

24

ONE OF THE MORE UNUSUAL PIECES IN THE museum's collection is a big, empty glass cube with a metallic sheen, mounted on a Plexiglas stand and entitled . . . wait for it . . . *Glass Cube*.

Why? I want to ask the artist. How am I supposed to explain this to kids? How is this art?

I'm sitting in front of it and slogging through articles comparing the artist's work to Stonehenge (*What???*) and crammed with gobbledygook phrases like "an agent for the dematerialization of the object" when Willow texts.

Help me stop thinking about Arden? I hate it SO MUCH

I look at *Glass Cube*. I should really stay here and figure it out. I text her a photo of it and type:

Tell me what this means

Willow: wtf 😫

Come down here and talk to me

Pleeeease

With a sigh, I go; I've discovered I'm pretty good at cheering Willow up. I love that she relies on me this way, and I love being the one she trusts with her secrets, but I do sometimes wish she didn't have *quite* so much to share. Especially since the bulk of what she shares are sad thoughts about Arden. I mostly nod and say nothing, which has led her to believe that I am wise and thoughtful.

I've been thinking about what Max said, though, about facts and the real world, and with our practically real date on the horizon, I've resolved to try something new.

When Willow sighs and tells me "I've been better lately, but I also keep thinking about her birthday party. We definitely have to go, but it's going to be so hard to go and see her with Dela," I'm ready.

"You know how we said that Arden would want you back after she saw you looking happy with me?" I begin, and she nods. "I think maybe *looking* happy isn't enough. What if you focused on being happy without Arden for real, instead of acting? Like, if you forgot about getting back together with Arden? Hear me out." I put my hand up when she starts to protest. "You can still get back together in the end. But there's all these movies where couples break up and they only get back together after *both* of them, like, grow or whatever. And then they each see the other person at their best, and *that's* what

185

brings them back together."

Willow nods slowly. "You know what? You're right. Faking being happy in front of her *is* making me miserable. I've been obsessed with her, and it's not good for me."

"Yes, exactly! You need to stop worrying about her all the time and try to find happiness where you are. So like, when you're with me—for example—try to be happy with *me*, instead of being sad that you're not with Arden."

"Yeah, I get what you're saying . . . hey!" Her face lights up. "Our sightseeing trip tomorrow will be the perfect place to start!"

"Yes!" I say, elated. This is just what I was hoping for.

"Okay. I'm going to do it. I won't talk about Arden, I won't think about her—nothing. I will be totally, one hundred percent in the moment."

"Exactly!"

Willow sighs. "It'll be good to feel that way again—really, truly happy." Then she looks worried. "Do you think I'll be able to?"

"I know you will," I say stoutly. "I'll be with you, won't I?"

"Yeah, you will." She smiles. "I'm so glad I met you. I don't know how I would have made it through these weeks without you."

My mind goes blank, like it always does whenever she says something like this, so I just smile modestly.

"Life is so ironic, isn't it?" Willow muses. "Being happy *without* Arden is the only path to being happy *with* her."

"Mm-hmm!"

Sigh.

When will she open her eyes and see the path to being happy with *me*?

Stanford Cal Pomona Northwestern
   Please let me give birth to a healthy baby
   a long-term relationship
   I wish I was an Oscar Mayer wiener

I look at the growing pile of folded wishes, a rainbow of delicate winged creatures on the table. Stephen finally showed me Dela's drawing of how the installation will look: it's a grove of bamboo trees in ceramic pots, glowing in fairy lights with origami wishes suspended from every branch; at the center is the pavilion, a vaguely Asian-looking gazebo made of blond wood with a spiral staircase leading to an upper deck, where a flame burns in a glass bowl. It's a space for wishes to be honored, showcased, and tenderly cared for before being released to the heavens. It's magical. Hopeful. And still baffling to me that it was all born in the mind of Dela the Harbinger of Doom.

"Have *you* made a wish?" I ask Dela.

She shrugs. "I don't really believe in that kind of stuff."

Again with the prickly cynic act. "You must have made one." This is the mind that dreamed up the Tanabata Pavilion in the first place, the heart that insists that each and every one of those wishes I lost is given back its chance. I refuse to believe that a person with that mind and that heart is as staunchly anti-wish as Dela makes herself out to be.

But she just shakes her head. Infuriating.

"Well, then why are you doing this?" I challenge her. "Why are you sitting here folding all these things?"

"Because you ruined all the original ones," says Dela.

"You know what I mean. Why are you doing *this*?" I gesture around at the wishes.

She shrugs.

I hate having conversations like this, where it's all me trying to keep it going. Why does she have to make this so hard? I know we're not the Best of Friends, but I would think that after the whole Ice Cream Bar incident, things might be a little less hard. I press her, mostly because there *has* to be more to her than what she's showing me. And, I'm sorry-not-sorry to say, a little bit out of spite.

"Did you fold all of the old ones yourself?"

"Some of them."

"Who did the other ones? Your dad?"

"My mom."

"Oh. Well, can you get her to help us fold these ones, then?"

"Nope."

"Why not?"

"She's dead."

Oh. Of course. This, I realize, is why it got so awkward way back when I asked if Dela's mom was Japanese. I feel like such an oaf. How do I keep missing these things? Why don't I ever think before I open my big mouth?

Is this why Dela is so angry all the time? I can't help thinking about Mom and how angry I am at her for all the things—but it's better than being angry that she's dead. Dela and I keep folding wishes, with the fact of her mom's death spilling silently into the room and surrounding us until I think I might suffocate in all the unspoken emotions.

Finally, I say, "I'm sorry."

I look down at the crane in my hands. I've just finished folding it and pinching the narrow corner of the neck to make a beaked head. I tug on the tail and the head a little, to make the wings flap, and I imagine it taking flight, rising up into the sky, to the River of Heaven and Princess Orihime's father, Tentei, whispering into his ear. Before I can stop it, a question comes out. "Was one of these wishes hers?"

There's a long pause before she says, "A thousand of them were," and then I know what happened. But Dela tells me anyway. "She died last year. Cancer."

"The ones that were in that box. When I knocked into you. The ones that blew away . . ." I'm afraid to finish the question because I know what the answer is. There's an old Japanese belief that if you fold a thousand origami cranes, the gods will grant you one wish. And there's a story about a girl who folded a thousand paper cranes while she had cancer. But she died anyway.

Dela nods, and my whole body suddenly feels as tired as hers looks. No wonder she was so upset when they all blew away.

"Only some of them were ours, though. I kept a few for myself and burned the rest. Most of the ones in the box were from this list." She gives the spreadsheets a shake.

That makes me feel a little lighter, but not much.

"I entered the concept art and an essay in the grant contest while she was sick. Then she died, and the next week, I found out I won. Victory. Woo-hoo." She pumps her fist and smiles grimly at the pale purple butterfly in her fingers. She presses her lips into a line and blinks hard a few times.

"Oh." I feel my own tears welling up, and my voice goes hoarse around the lump that's risen in my throat. "That's awful."

"Yeah, well." She glances at me, then quickly looks away. "Stop crying. She's not *your* mom. I'm fine." She sniffs and grinds at her eyes with the heels of her hands.

"You're not fine. And I'm not—I don't—I didn't *mean* to cry," I say a little defensively. "You can't get mad at me for that."

"Can't I?" Her voice sounds strangled, and she takes a few shaky breaths. "Shit."

"I'm sorry. I didn't mean you *can't*. Of course you can. I just meant—"

"Can you just shut up for a sec?" Dela growls, and I can tell she's losing her battle for control, but I don't know what I can do to make her feel better. I want to tell her it's going to be okay, or to encourage her to look at the bright side. I also kind of want to run away, because it's really uncomfortable to watch someone cry. Because it's not going to be okay, not the way she wanted it. It's excruciating, not being able to do anything about all that pain. But miraculously, I squash all the things I want to say and sit there and let her cry.

Finally, she starts taking slow, deep breaths again, and sniffles. "Can you get me some tissues or something?" she asks, her voice muffled by her arms. I run to the bathroom, relieved to have something to do and a little annoyed with myself for not having thought of this on my own.

When I return and offer her a giant wad of toilet paper, she takes it silently, tears off a bunch, and honks her nose a few times, so loudly that under different circumstances I might be tempted to laugh. She dabs at her runny eye makeup with the rest. "I must look like shit," she says.

I shrug. "I mean. You just cried your eyes out, so I'd say you're entitled to look like shit."

"Ha." She blows her nose again. "My mom would have said the same thing, probably. She was unflinchingly honest." She makes a noise in her throat that sounds a little like a laugh, and a little like a sob. "Except for when she didn't tell me she was dying."

"She knew? And she never told you?"

"She did. Toward the end, the last couple of months. Right after I submitted my entry for the contest. It wrecked me, and not just because I was sad she was dying. I felt like all that optimism, all the hope, all the work that went into the origami had been for nothing. And then after she died, I found out that she'd known the whole time—the whole time I was designing the pavilion, the whole time we were folding all those cranes, for months, she knew—and my dad knew—that she was going to die. They let me hope and wish and dream, and they knew it wasn't going to come true."

Wow. "Are you mad at her for not telling you earlier?"

"Some days I think I understand what she was doing. Some days I'm still furious that she lied to me and let me keep hoping for so long. My dad, too. And then I feel guilty about being mad because she was only doing what she thought was best."

"Stephen and my parents say that's a Japanese thing," I tell her. "You hide bad news from people to save their feelings."

Dela nods. "That sounds just like my mom." Then she adds, "Though, you know, looking back, I should have figured it out myself. She kept getting thinner and weaker, and she stopped doing chemo and radiation . . . but I didn't want to see what I didn't want to see."

"Ha," I say, without really thinking. "That sounds exactly like what Max said about . . ." Just in time, I stop myself from saying "me and Willow."

"About what?"

"Nothing," I say hastily. "I shouldn't have said anything." What is *wrong* with me? First I blunder into making her tell me her mom is dead, then I almost tell her about Willow, which is a) wrong and insensitive, and b) obviously not an option.

"Tell me," she says.

"No, really. It's so different from your situation, it's like, offensive."

But she seems to take this as a challenge. "Try me."

"No."

"Come on," she insists. "I could use a change of topic."

Ugh. I can't tell her the real story. What else might Max have been talking about? Who else only sees what they want to see? Then it comes to me. "My grandmother. He said the same thing about my grandmother."

"Oh, right." She nods. "The whole retirement home thing?"

Of course. Because Cliff's been working at Baba's house. He's probably told Dela about the job and why Stephen's hired him to do it.

"Yeah, that," I say, relieved that I won't have to go into it. "She thinks she's going to live at home forever."

"That's not *that* offensive."

"No, I guess not," I say. "I didn't want to upset you. Especially after I kind of pushed you into talking about your mom in the first place."

She honks her nose again and says, "It's fine. I'm tired of people trying not to upset me all the time. Honestly, *I* don't even know for sure what's going to upset me from day to day. I might have been able to handle you asking about my mom on a different day. As long as you don't tell me everything's going to be fine, or that my mom is in a better place now, or everything happens for a reason, you can say whatever you want, and if you upset me, I'll tell you."

"Okay. Cool." That's . . . mostly reassuring, I guess. I do feel kind of proud of myself for having earned her trust.

We go back to folding. Eighty wishes later, we tidy up the work space, I snap off the lights as we exit, and Dela locks the door and says, "Thanks."

"Huh?" The movement sensors turn the hall lights on as we pass through them into the atrium.

"For listening. For getting it about my mom. And for not pretending everything's fine."

"Oh. Uh. You're welcome." We're walking through the atrium now, and it lights up, the white walls glowing softly.

"There's just not that many people I've been able to talk to about this," she continues.

"What about Arden?"

Dela shrugs. "I know Arden implied that we're super serious or whatever, but things are actually pretty low-key with us. I'm trying to keep it light and fun."

"Yeah, I'll bet, Lemon Meringue. You're so soft and sweet and sunny."

A burst of laughter escapes Dela's lips, which I suddenly notice *do* look soft and sweet. They don't match the rest of her prickly personality. I look at her, all gloomy and brooding in her black moto jacket, black jeans, and Doc Martens, her short hair simultaneously spiky and silky and blowing in the wind over her wide, dark eyes as we step onto the sidewalk. I'm starting to see why Arden might be attracted to her.

I lock the door and turn back to see those eyes fixed on me. "Seriously, though. Thanks," she says.

"You're welcome."

Dela's hug is quick, and I barely have time to respond and hug her back before she releases me and turns away. "See you tomorrow," she says, and walks off without a backward glance. I'm left with the lingering sensation of surprise, the scent of her leather jacket, and the feel of her cropped hair against my cheek.

25

AFTER BINGEING A SLEW OF ROMANTIC COMEDIES last night for moral support and reminding myself over and over of Willow's decision to focus on being in the moment with me, I wake up feeling better than ever about tonight's date. I spend extra time on my hair and makeup, and with my black skinny jeans, a new pair of boots, and a new oversized sweater that looks a little like the one Willow wore when we went to Golden Gate Park, I feel like I'm at the top of my game when I leave the museum. I low-key wish I weren't skipping out on Dela, especially after what happened yesterday—she was definitely Not Pleased when I said I was going out with Willow instead of folding today, and I don't blame her—but a date is a date.

When I announced my plan the other day for Willow and

me to ride the cable car from the turntable at Market Street all the way over the hill and down to the Hyde Street turntable, Stephen advised against it, citing long lines of tourists. Max laughed and asked if I was trying to win Worst Date Idea of the Year. So naturally I begged Willow to do it, just to spite him.

I concede now that this may have been a mistake. We've been here thirty minutes and we've only made it halfway through the line. Instead of flirting, we've been staring at our phones, and I keep wondering if she's checking Arden's accounts despite her vow not to. Oh, and there's a street preacher shouting at us from a few yards away about how the end times are nigh, and how homosexuals, baby-killing abortionists, Jews, Muslims, and other heathens need to REPENT NOW or we're all doomed to the fiery fires of hell. Not quite the romantic experience I'd hoped for.

But as we near the front of the line, the preacher starts going off on the evils of alcohol and marijuana, and Willow finally looks up from her phone and grins at me. She says, "The first time I got drunk, I cut my own hair."

"No."

"Yeah." She laughs. "It was at my friend's house. Her fifteenth birthday party. I woke up the next morning and cried so hard."

Then it's my turn. "I got drunk with my friend and we made avocado masks and fell asleep before we washed them off. It was so gross—guacamole all over the sheets and the pillows." Willow gasps in horrified delight. "Right?" I say, pleased. "Her mom was *furious.*"

"I drunk-hooked-up with Arden at the *Midsummer Night's Dream* cast party . . . We were already so into each other, though, it hardly counts as a drunk hookup."

I want to remind Willow that she's not supposed to be talking about Arden, but it feels petty and jealous, so I keep my mouth shut as she tells The Story of Arden and Willow from the moment they met at the first read-through of that *Midsummer Night's Dream* production. She tells me how Arden *became* Oberon, the Fairy King. How Willow offered to rehearse lines together, with her standing in for Oberon's queen, Titania, which was when she learned that Arden's boyfriend had recently broken up with her because he couldn't handle how smart she was. How, after weeks of flirting, while Willow was doing Arden's makeup on closing night, their eyes had locked— and how incredibly sexually charged that moment had been. How Arden, high from a magnificent closing performance, and Willow, tipsy on peach schnapps, had practically thrown themselves at each other at the party. And how—again—she couldn't understand how Arden could just toss that kind of magic away.

"Okay, I'm sorry. No more Arden talk," she says. Finally. Though at least she's not so clueless that she doesn't even notice when she's breaking her promise. "Have you ever had a drunk hookup?"

"This girl Helena," I hear myself saying, maybe because I'm so glad to have the spotlight back on me instead of Arden.

"I thought she was so hot, and I was afraid to talk to her until I got wasted at this party and—" Wait. Maybe I shouldn't tell this story. First of all, it's about Past Me, Beige Wallpaper Me— the opposite of the self-confident, sophisticated me I've been working so hard to become. Second, I don't want to dig into all that humiliation in front of Willow and reveal Past Me in all her misery.

"And what?" says Willow. "What happened?"

"Oh, we hooked up, obviously. And . . ." I try for the truth. "And it was kind of a disappointment." I try to say what happened next and find I can't do it. "She was the worst kisser," I lie. "Way too much tongue."

Willow shudders and makes a face. "Blech."

The best lies contain an element of the truth, though, so I layer it in and spin it with my new, confident attitude. "Then I overheard her talking later and she had the nerve to say that I wasn't pretty enough for her. Can you believe it?" Ouch. Even with the spin, it still stings.

"What a bitch!" says Willow with genuine outrage, and I'm surprised by the relief that floods my body. I realize just how desperately I wanted her to react this way, and how nervous I was that she might say something horrible, like, *I can see her point.* "How could she say that about you? You're *so* pretty! Plus you're sweet, and smart . . ." She trails off and looks closely at me, glances at her phone, and then at the line for the streetcar, and says, "I'll be right back." Then she dashes down the street.

Five minutes later, she's back, brandishing mascara, and—I

squint at the package—something called mascara primer. "Makeover time!" she sings. "This is just cheap crap from Walgreens, but it'll do for now. I'm going to make you look so good—not that you don't already look great, obviously. But when I'm done with you, Helena's going to be so sad she let you go, she'll cry herself to sleep for a week."

I don't have the heart to tell her that Helena doesn't follow me, so she won't see any photos I might post, but I'm certainly not going to turn down a makeover, especially since the first one got cancelled by the Golden Gate Park caper. So I do a little squee and allow Willow to transform me into a vision of beauty.

Willow works quickly and efficiently. I can't help wishing Max could see us. This is turning out well after all. She has me reapply my lipstick, and asks me for my eye shadow—luckily, I've taken to carrying it around with me just in case, for moments exactly like this. She considers it for a moment and instructs me to close my eyes.

"I've been thinking of applying to cosmetology school for next year," she says as I feel the silky little brush gliding across my eyelid.

"That's awesome!" I say.

"Yeah. But my parents will flip. They want me to be a doctor."

I can't help laughing. "Your parents really *are* an Asian stereotype."

"I know, right? My mom's mad that I'm not taking

multivariable calc this summer. Or doing the UCSF junior pre-med program. She keeps saying I'm wasting my true talents. And during the school year, my dad is always emailing my teachers to check on my grades and ask what I can do to ensure that I stay at the top."

I remember how she "forgot" to apply for that research internship; it all makes sense now. I'd push back, too. "Oh my god."

"Yeah." She sighs and starts doing quick little brushstrokes, blending shades.

"I bet you wish you had white parents," I say.

Willow giggles. "Ha! Not to stereotype, or anything."

"It's our lives," I say into the dark. "We should get to choose what we do with them."

I hear her sigh again, and she says, "Yeah, but here's the thing. My mom grew up really poor. Like, her parents almost gave her away to another family. That kind of poor. And now I have all this opportunity, so of course she wants me to use it to become like, financially secure. Okay, open your eyes a sec."

"Wow." I open my eyes.

"Right? How do you go against that without feeling guilty?"

She snaps the palette shut, takes the wrapping off the primer, and begins applying it to my lashes.

"Do you think I'm being a spoiled little rich girl? Like, First World Problems, and all that?"

I think about kids who've lost entire families to war and

famine. Kids who don't know where their next meal is coming from. Willow's own mom. Even Dela, whose mom is dead.

"Um. I guess?" I say. On the other hand, that doesn't make her problems any less real, and that's what I tell her as she brushes on my mascara.

She smiles at me so tenderly that I feel a little internal quiver. "Thanks, Nozomi. You always know just what to say to make me feel better. Hey, here comes the trolley! Perfect timing!"

Willow hastily shoves the makeup into her bag as the cable car disgorges its passengers. We watch the Muni workers guide it onto the turntable, grasp the railings on each end, and rotate it 180 degrees. We sit on the benches lining the outside of the trolley, just like I hoped we would, and smile at each other as the city goes by. *You always know just what to say to make me feel better.* No one's ever said that to me before. I've been here for her just like I said I would. And she's noticed.

What has she done for you, though? I can hear Max saying. *All she really cares about is Arden.*

She's not my actual girlfriend yet, so she's not obligated to do anything, I reply in my head. *And she only mentioned Arden once.* I think she's allowed one story. She's only human, after all.

Anyway, she *has* done something. She did my makeup to make me gorgeous so Helena would be jealous, didn't she?

And I do look gorgeous. My eyes look bigger and brighter, and my lashes look long and thick and lush, just like the mascara ads say they're supposed to. I tell her this and she laughs:

202

"The magic of makeup!" At the crest of the hill, just before we begin the stomach-dropping descent toward the bay, Willow puts her arm around me and we smile, cheek to cheek, at our faces on the screen, and I drink in the feeling of our bodies touching. Then she says, "I'm going to kiss you now, okay?" and I nod, and when I feel her lips on my cheek, my eyes flutter shut on their own, and it feels so natural when my lips meet hers for a second kiss that when she pulls away and turns immediately to her phone, I feel like I've been slapped.

"We look so good in this kissing one," she says as she posts it with the caption, My 🖤 "I know I promised I wouldn't bring Arden up again, but she's going to freak when she sees this."

"Mm-hmm," seems like the easiest way to keep my voice from betraying me. That second kiss felt so real, even if the first one wasn't. I wish she'd come to her senses and kiss me for reasons other than "Arden will be so jealous."

"Okay, okay," Willow says, apparently reading my mind. "Ugh, I can already feel myself getting all stressy again. Whooo!" She shakes herself out, getting rid of those pesky Arden vibes. "Okay. No more, I swear."

It's okay. It's okay. I just have to be patient with her a little bit longer, since she clearly needs to process all of this before she can move forward. The best thing I can do right now is be a good listener. We're at the point in the movie where the real connections are happening. The trust is there. The heat is there. The real kiss is just around the corner.

I can feel it.

Just around the corner.

We snap a few more photos at the Hyde Street turntable and grab a Lyft to Hawk Hill, just north of the city in the Marin Headlands—the best spot for a Golden Gate Bridge photo op, according to Willow. The bridge glows in the setting sun, which casts a soft pink light on our faces as our hair blows in the wind. It's gloriously romantic, and as we stand with our arms around each other, posing for a photo taken by a nice tourist couple, residual heat from the cable car kiss surges through me and I feel like I *have* to try again. I can almost feel her lips against mine . . . Oh, what the hell. I'm going for it.

"Hey, can I kiss you?" I don't bother trying to keep my voice light and friendly.

"Huh? Oh, sure, go ahead!" she responds as if I had, and offers her cheek.

Oh. Okay. Cool, cool, cool. It's still a kiss. I'll make it quick. Just . . . a quick . . . kiss on the . . . but once I'm there, once my lips brush her skin, I can't help lingering a little longer than necessary—maybe even a lot longer than necessary—breathing her in and allowing myself the tiniest of fantasies: when I pull away, she'll turn, pull me to her, and kiss me back.

"Aww," she says with a smile. "Now me!" and gives me a peck on the cheek in return. Sigh.

But! Wait!

In the split second before she got all jolly and friendly, I looked into her eyes, and I'm pretty sure—I'm almost certain—I saw something there: desire. Real emotion.

That friendly little peck? Maybe she's pretending, too. Maybe she's as nervous as I am.

But the moment—if that's what this is—doesn't have a chance to bloom, because the tourist lady comes rushing over with my phone saying, "It's ringing! Do you want to answer it?"

I take it with a sigh. Our moment will have to wait, I guess. "Hello?"

"Zozo, it's Stephen. I'm so sorry to interrupt your date, but Baba's missing."

Stay calm, I tell myself. *Stay calm.*

I turn to Willow, who's frowning down at her phone and texting madly, her thumbs flying.

"Hey, um," I say hesitantly. "There's this, um, family emergency and I have to get back home."

"Hmm?" Willow looks up from her phone. "Sorry, I didn't catch that. Did you say you had to get home?"

"Family emergency," I say again, and realize that this sounds like a made-up reason—the kind of thing you say when you want to bail out of a bad date, which is definitely not the case. So I add, "My grandmother has wandered off and gotten lost. Possibly. I need to go and be at the house while my uncles and my brother search the neighborhood."

"Oh my god, that's awful!" she cries. "Come on, let's get a ride."

As we wait, I look across the bay. Two hours. According to

Stephen, that's how long ago he called Baba to remind her he was taking her grocery shopping after work, and that's the last time anyone knew where she was.

Fog swirls in from the ocean like something alive, streaming down the hills and curling around the spires of the bridge. The rosy hues of twilight have faded to gray. Lit windows and streetlights are beginning to sharpen themselves against the dark settling over the city. And Baba is out there somewhere, lost.

Stay calm.

Once we get into the city, Willow says, "Hey, do you want me to come with you? Like to sit with you or whatever, for moral support?"

"No, it's okay," I tell her. "You don't have to."

The prospect of sitting alone in a quiet house with Willow by my side and offering me emotional support is tempting, but I'm not ready to drag her into the family drama. What if it turns her off? What if she thinks, *Whoa, don't want to get involved with all of* that.

"Okay, if you're sure," she says slowly. "Just let me know if you change your mind, okay? I'm serious."

"I will," I assure her. I hope she doesn't feel rejected or anything. She does seem really sincere about wanting to help, but I just . . . I can't picture her in the middle of the chaos that's unfolding right now.

The car pulls up in front of Baba's house, and Willow gives

me a warm hug. "Don't worry. I'm sure they'll find her. She'll probably show up a minute after you walk in the door."

"Yeah, probably." I give her a weak smile, and she waves and disappears as the car goes around the corner.

I let myself into the house. It's nearly dark now and the temperature is dropping fast, and there's been no word from anyone for a good half hour. I imagine Baba wandering around out there, lost and scared. She'll remember her address if someone finds her, right? Then I remember that Stephen once said she's been going to the bank and taking out tons of cash lately, thinking she needs it to pay her bills. No one would mug a little old lady like her, would they? *Please, Baba, be okay*, I say to the window. *Find your way back home.*

I can't concentrate on any of my social media, and I don't have Baba's wifi password, so I can't watch videos. I know it's important for someone to be here in case she comes home, but I feel like I'm not doing enough. I try texting Willow, but she doesn't answer, and I'm surprised by how lonely that makes me feel. Maybe I should have had her come and sit with me after all. I wonder what would have happened between us if Baba hadn't gone and gotten herself lost.

And then I feel guilty. None of this is Baba's fault. Where *is* she? When is someone going to call?

Out of desperation, I pull out a cookbook. Maybe I'll bake some cookies to distract myself. That's a good idea. People will appreciate having something warm and comforting to eat when they get back. With Baba. When they get back with Baba. I rummage around on the cabinet shelf labeled BAKING INGREDIENTS.

Lucky for me, Baba has a chocolate chip addiction. I find four half-empty bags of chocolate chips, which should be enough for a double batch.

I read the directions and get out all the ingredients. I mix up the dry ingredients like the recipe says to. Then it says to beat room-temperature butter with the sugar in a separate bowl until fluffy, three minutes. Then add the eggs, and *then* put it all together. That's ridiculous. I don't have time for all that nonsense. I dump everything in and turn on the mixer.

The dry ingredients explode out of the bowl, which starts rattling violently and going *ga-gunk, ga-gunk, ga-gunk* like it's alive inside and trying to work itself free so it can attack me. I shriek and turn it off, and as the silence and the flour settle, the doorbell rings.

Maybe it's the police, and they've brought Baba home. I rush to the door and throw it open to see Baba, thank goodness, and . . . Dela?

I blink in surprise, and Dela blinks back. "Um. I found your grandma," she says, and steps inside.

26

BABA PEERS AT ME AND SAYS, "NOZOMI, WHAT happened to you?"

"What happened to me?" I echo in confusion. For a moment, I wonder if the worry has aged me or if the mixer somehow gave me a bloody nose, but then Dela, with a glint in her eye, gestures toward her face. I raise my hands to my own face, and my fingers come away white and powdery.

"Oh. Uh. Baking," I mumble, and close the door behind them.

At that very moment, I get texts from Stephen, Lance, and Max, all with the same content: Late-breaking news! Dela has found Baba and should be arriving on the doorstep any second now!

Lovely. Thanks for the update.

"Are you okay, Baba? What happened?" I ask as Dela ushers Baba into the kitchen and pulls out a seat for her. Baba looks around, bewildered.

"I didn't leave it in this mess," she says.

"No, sorry, Baba, that was me," I explain quickly. I don't want her worrying that maybe she *did* leave it like this and doesn't remember. "I was trying to bake cookies."

"*Trying* being the operative word, apparently," says Dela as she busies herself pouring water into the kettle and pulling a container of green tea off the shelf labeled TEA.

I ignore her. "Baba?" I ask again. "What happened? Where did you go?"

"I went to the post office and the bank," says Baba, immediately on the defensive. "But they've moved! They should tell people before they move," she says with a frown, her eyebrows drawn as far down as I've ever seen them. "And they've changed the street signs. It's hard to see in the dark which way to go."

"Luckily, I happened to be in the neighborhood, so we walked back together," adds Dela. "My dad left something here and I was coming to pick it up." She holds my gaze for long enough to confirm that their encounter wasn't just a wild coincidence, and I feel such a rush of gratitude that I almost hug her. Except how did she get roped into this?

"He is a very forgetful man," Baba says, shaking her head. She turns to me and says, "Every couple of days, he comes to get something he left behind. He's lucky you are looking after him." She chuckles.

Dela smiles at Baba, and there's a familiarity there that surprises me. "He's incorrigible."

"It's too bad you don't like boys. You would make the good wife," Baba replies, which *doesn't* surprise me, and I can't help bristling. Stop. Calm down. I'm supposed to be feeling sorry for her right now. But I still feel resentful and hurt, and when I see Dela, I'm embarrassed as well.

"She'll make a good wife no matter who she marries, man or woman," I blurt out. "Because she's smart and talented and she cares about people. Not because she can keep track of her dad's stuff and make tea." Dela's cheeks turn pink. Mine are probably turning pinker.

"You young people have your opinions. I have mine," says Baba mildly. I have to stifle the urge to strangle her, despite her being a frail, lost old woman who is also my grandmother.

I'm sorry, I mouth at Dela, who nods, her face a mask.

I find the vacuum cleaner, and as I clean the flour and sugar off the kitchen floor, I wonder if it's worth arguing with Baba, if she would even listen right now. It's the same old calculation: what will it cost me to be my truest self around my grandmother? It's so hard, and I'm so tired of making it. But tonight, I'm beginning to see another side: What will it cost her? Is it worth challenging her that way when she's already struggling?

The kettle starts whistling. I get down the teapot and cups and Dela pours the boiling water into the teapot, swirls it around, and pours that water into each of the teacups before measuring the tea into the teapot and pouring all the water back into it. Watching her calms me.

Okay, maybe now isn't the time to make a stand about LGBTQIA rights, or feminism, or anything. Now is the time to take care of Baba. If Dela can keep her mouth shut, so can I. I will be as calm and collected as she is.

"Hey, Nozomi?" she says quietly.

"Yes?" I try to be zen and serene and open to whatever the universe may send me, to whatever Dela may have to say about Baba, about this situation.

"You look like a ghost. You should probably wash your face."

After I return from scrubbing off the flour and, in the process, all my makeup, and combing out my hair, Dela pours the tea into the teacups. I collect a couple of stray chunks of butter that have escaped the bowl and made it onto the countertop, and after weighing my options, I rinse them and put them back in the bowl.

"Not a baker, huh?" Dela deadpans.

"I was *trying* to do something *nice*," I retort.

She gets up and peeks into the bowl. "You're not supposed to throw everything in all at once. You have to use room-temperature butter and beat it with the sugar. Then you add the eggs, and *then* you add the flour."

"Thanks. Very helpful," I say. "I'll remember that twenty minutes ago."

"You can pour out everything but the butter and start over," she says. She pokes the chocolate chips and wrinkles her nose. Right. She doesn't like chocolate.

"I didn't know you were going to be here, or I would have made something else," I protest.

I can see Baba eyeing the chocolate chips, so I pour some leftovers into a little bowl and offer them to her. "Here," I say. "You deserve a treat. You've had a rough evening."

"Ah! Thank you, Nozomi. You're a good girl," she says.

Dela and I find a recipe for snickerdoodles, and at her insistence, we follow the directions exactly. "There's a reason they're there," she tells me in the most patronizing voice imaginable. "So you don't end up with a crime scene."

"It wasn't a crime scene. There was no blood," I grumble.

"A disaster area, then."

We're mixing the eggs into the whipped butter and sugar when Stephen, Lance, Max, and Cliff arrive. Baba explains how it was pure coincidence that Dela found her; she wasn't lost, not really, and after thanking Dela, Stephen exchanges somber looks with Lance and Max over Baba's head. He takes Baba into the living room to try to figure out how she ended up lost.

In the meantime, Lance busies himself chopping vegetables, bacon, and a leftover pork chop. He pulls out a plastic container of leftover rice, and soon, there's a wok full of fragrant yakimeshi and a cooling rack full of snickerdoodles for dessert. Baba has the good manners to thank Lance, and she even praises his cooking. But apart from that she barely looks at him through dinner. We all pretend not to notice. Not long afterward, Baba has gone to take a bath and get ready for bed.

Cliff and Max take kitchen duty while Stephen and Lance go back to the living room and FaceTime with Dad in hushed tones so Baba doesn't overhear, and Dela and I are sent to the store to get more flour and butter.

After walking in silence for a block or so, I ask the question that's been tapping at the window all evening. "So how did you find my grandmother? I know you weren't on your way over to pick up a hammer."

Dela shoves her hands in her pockets and shrugs. "I really was in the neighborhood, kind of. With Arden, actually—there's this restaurant she wanted to go to. But my dad called and told me your grandma was missing and asked if I could help. So, you know. Here I am."

Wow. "But why?"

Dela shrugs again. "I don't know. It was the right thing to do?"

We stop at a corner and wait for the light to turn.

I shiver in the cool night air. It *was* the right thing to do, undeniably. Baba could still be out there if it weren't for Dela.

"But she's—like I know she's my grandmother and everything, and she does have some good qualities. But to you, she's just this homophobic old lady who hired your dad to fix her fence."

"Well. Maybe a little more than that."

"Huh?" Then I remember that connection I noticed between them earlier.

"She folded hundreds of cranes for my mom," says Dela.

"She made tons of meals for us while my mom was sick, and after she died. She taught me how to cook."

It takes a moment for this new version of Baba to sink in. Or rather, the old version of Baba, the one I remember from my childhood. Only better. And this new version of Dela, whose affection for Baba is undeniable, despite the constant barbs that I'm sure she's had to endure about her sexuality. Suddenly I have a different picture of how things with Baba could be. If I want them to be that way. And assuming Baba won't be the type who thinks being queer is okay for some people but not okay for her own family.

The light turns, and we cross. We buy the flour and the butter and walk home without any more conversation. Just before we enter the house, I say, "She doesn't know I'm queer."

Dela nods. "I know."

"She's been so awful. To Stephen and Lance, to you, even. I know it could be worse, but . . ." I can't quite voice my fear.

Dela gives me a long look. I have just enough time to understand that she sees me—she sees it all—before she pulls me into a hug, and the anxiety that's been simmering quietly all summer bubbles over. We sit on the front steps, and I tell her how much I wish Baba could love *all* of me, and how I'm afraid that she'll push me away. And how now I'm dreading watching Baba sink into dementia whether I come out to her or not.

Dela doesn't say anything. Doesn't tell me I'm overthinking it, or blowing things out of proportion, or asking for too much.

She just pulls me to her again, and eventually my thoughts stop their spinning, my breathing slows, and eventually I feel like myself again. I stay where I am for a little longer, just soaking in that safe, calm feeling.

After a moment, Dela says in measured tones, "Tonight may not be the night for a big splashy gay debut."

"Hilarious." I sit up straight again and smile.

"I'm known for my rapier wit."

"Ha."

"And my—what was it? My dark, sour, bitter personality? Sour cherry–infused espresso?"

"That's it."

"Well, if that's what I am, then you're a cream puff."

"What's that supposed to mean?" I say indignantly. It sounds a lot like beige wallpaper, especially given the color of cream puffs. "That I'm bland and vanilla and boring?"

"No! Cream puffs aren't any of those things. Why would you say that?"

"Because . . . whatever, it's something someone said once. It's not important. Anyway, I'm over it, so." I think about my sight-seeing selfies with Willow from earlier: proof that I'm not boring.

"I don't think you are. Over it, I mean."

"I am, too!" I insist. I'm totally over it. Obviously. I've transformed into a brand-new girl, with an amazing life and a gorgeous could-be-my-girlfriend-if-all-goes-well, and I have the photos to prove it.

"You're not." Dela peers through the window into Baba's

house. "They're still busy in there. Let's walk around the block and you can tell me why you think you're boring."

"What are you, my therapist? I don't think I'm boring."

She ignores me and heads back to the sidewalk, where she pauses to look at me over her shoulder. "You coming or what?"

"Ugh. Fine."

The story only takes us one circuit: crush, kiss, balcony, wallpaper. Only this time, with Dela, I don't skip the parts about how out of my league Helena was, and how small I felt when I heard her say what she said. Dela only sees me as someone who makes a mess out of everything, anyway—first impressions, art installations, double dates, and now cookies— so there's no point in hiding anything. I couldn't impress her even if I wanted to.

"But I'm not letting it get me down," I conclude. "I'm using this summer to bounce back and live my best life and all that. See? Look." I show her the Hawk Hill post of me and Willow.

"Uh-huh." Dela barely glances at the photo but is regarding me with an unsettling intensity. I feel myself getting nervous.

"What?"

"Are you telling me you think this picture is proof that you're not boring?"

Is she deliberately not getting this? "Yes. Obviously."

"Because you're, what—in San Francisco? Because you have a girlfriend?"

I sigh. "Yes. I'm in San Francisco in this like, iconic, romantic spot, and I have a girlfriend, and she's . . . well, look at her!

I'm the best version of myself in this photo."

"Are you, though?"

"Well, of course I am! That's the whole point!" How rude.

"Mm-hmm."

"What."

"Nothing."

"*What.* Tell me."

Dela exhales and looks at me, like she's sizing me up. "You're not gonna like it."

"When have I ever liked anything you've said?"

She grins. "Good point. Fine, this is what I think. I think that maybe you're dating Willow because you like *what* she is at least as much as *who* she is."

What? *What?* "Did you—did you just say that I only like her because she's pretty?"

Dela groans. "I told you you wouldn't like it. And no, that's not what I said at all. It's more like . . . that old thing of not knowing if you want to *be* someone or if you want to be *with* them."

"It is *so* not that." Just because I've been experimenting with my look this summer doesn't mean—anyway, how would she know?

"I've seen photos of you from before this summer at your grandma's house, so don't even pretend you've always been into clothes and makeup. You looked fine before, by the way. But it's like you're doing this lifestyle glow-up and Willow's part of the process. You're in love with the idea of her. Or the idea of dating her. Or maybe an idea of yourself."

I have never been so insulted in all my life. "I am not doing a lifestyle glow-up!" Though once I say the words, I realize I might be. But it sounds so shallow when she puts it like that. "I am undergoing a transformation," I say. "I am becoming my best self. I am living my best life."

"And Willow is part of that life."

"Willow is . . ." Ugh. How can I explain? "She's just Willow, okay? And I like her for *who. She. Is.*" I slow it down to make sure Dela gets this very important point, but she just sighs. "It's like . . . like in *Queer Eye* when the person asks someone on a date at the end and, like, makes dinner for them or whatever. Do the guys sit there and go, 'He didn't ask that girl out for who she is!' Or whatever the pronouns are? No! They go, 'That's awesome! He's taking a step toward happiness!'"

"But is he really? Do those people *stay* happier?" asks Dela.

"Yes." This is what I choose to believe.

Dela looks up at the night sky and says, "A wise person once said, 'We are all connected by our aspirations toward happiness—by our wishes on stars.'"

I gape at her. "*I* said that!"

"I know."

"I wrote that about the Tanabata Pavilion. For the museum website."

"Again: I know."

"You read it?" I know, I know. Queen of the Obvious.

Dela doesn't even bother to answer. But she does say, "I

read a bunch of them. They're really good. You made me think about some of those pieces in a whole new way."

"Well, of course they're good," I say in a huff. She thinks she's so smart. I don't care if she likes my work. I'm only blushing because I'm embarrassed that she read it.

Okay, I might be a little bit pleased that she likes it. I've been working hard, and I'd be crushed if she thought it was garbage. It's nice to get some validation from someone whose opinion you respect. On art, that is.

We're back at the house again, standing in the orange glow of the streetlight. I look at the house, and then at Dela. "Ready?"

Dela reaches toward my face and rubs what must be leftover traces of flour—or maybe it's eye makeup—from under my eye, and smiles. "Yep."

For a moment, I think she's misinterpreted, and that she thinks I'm asking if I can kiss her. The very idea kind of short-circuits my brain, and I have a sort of micro-hallucination where we *are* kissing, and it's . . . well, it's ludicrous. Completely preposterous. As if I would ever fall in love with—I mean kiss—anyone so ornery. I blink dazedly as I come to my senses. "Good. 'Cause I'm ready, too. To go inside, that is."

Dela also looks slightly dazed—was that glitch in my circuits that obvious? But I'll never know, because she shakes it off, squares her shoulders, and says, "Okay. Let's go, then."

27

I DIDN'T HEAR FROM WILLOW AT ALL UNTIL THIS morning when I stopped by the gift shop. Not that she owed me a text or anything, obviously. But I couldn't help feeling a little disappointed that she never thought to check in last night to see if Baba was okay.

But she did ask right away when I walked in. She was visibly relieved to hear that Baba was safe and sound, and that Dad had jumped on a red-eye last night and would be staying with Baba for a while. "I was so worried for you! I got a little distracted with Arden—I have to tell you about her, oh my god—but I kept thinking about your grandma. I'm so glad she's okay."

"Yeah, me too." Distracted? With Arden? Oh my god?

I wait for Willow to tell me about the distraction, as

promised, but she's busy logging into the computer and I have to wait.

Finally, the computer makes a satisfied blip, and Willow turns to me. "Okay, are you ready? Arden called me right after I left you at your grandmother's, and she wanted to talk." Willow opens her mouth and eyes wide: *shock!*

I feel my own mouth drop open. This can't be good.

"Mm-hmm," says Willow, presumably responding to the expression on my face. "She was all, 'I feel like we should talk, just to get closure.'" Willow sighs out of . . . frustration? Satisfaction? "She never could leave a fight unfinished. She's all about closure."

"So . . ." A chill starts to creep into my chest. "What happened?"

"Okay. So." Willow tells me what a hard conversation it was, and how they ended up admitting that they missed each other, and the chill spreads.

Then she says they discussed the depth of their connection, how intensely they still loved each other, and how they realized that the toxicity of jealousy was starting to eat away at that love, and—

I can't take it anymore. "Are you saying that Arden wants to get back together? That's great!" I force my features into something that hopefully conveys joy—a big, toothy smile, wide, blinking eyes. "Everything worked out perfectly!"

"Right? I feel like some kind of evil genius whose nefarious plan has come to fruition," she says with a little grin. "Not that it was nefarious. Well"—she pauses to think about it—"it kind of was."

Technically, I feel like saying, *I* am the evil genius, it was *my* nefarious plan, and it's gone hideously awry.

"Do you need us to break up? I mean, you know"—I add air quotes with my fingers—"'break up'?" I consider winking but decide against it.

"No! No, no, not at all! *This*—" Willow gestures between herself and me. "What we have? It's perfect."

Wait, what?

"Arden said she noticed that I seem happy again—just like we talked about, remember? But here's the thing: I realized it's *not* just an act anymore. I *am* happier. You've gotten me to go out, gotten me inspired in my makeup work again . . . you don't even know."

"Oh!" Wow. This is—

"To be honest? Lately? I sometimes think you and I might . . . I mean, maybe if things were different . . ." She trails off and blushes.

You and I would what? Maybe if things were different, what? I want to shout. *Let's do it! Let's make things different!* Instead, I just say, "Oh," and try not to hyperventilate. Maybe I should kiss her. That would do it. Just sweep her into my arms and look tenderly into her eyes, and—

"Whatever. No point going there, right?" (*Go there! Go there!* I will her, but to no avail.) "My point is that seeing me being happy and independent is making her realize what she gave up. Not pathetic, sad, needy me, but the independent, happy me that she fell in love with. And I'm pretty certain she's having second thoughts about leaving me for Dela. And it's all because of you." Willow looks at me, glowing.

All because of me. Arden and Willow are going to get back together after all, and it's all because of me. And my plan. My train-wreck-garbage-fire-disaster of a plan.

I put on a smile and say faintly, "That's perfect! I'm so glad!"

"So, I'm thinking we should do this dating thing just a little longer. It'll be tricky, though. We can't go too far, or she'll give up. And then at exactly the right moment I'll let her know I'm ready to try again—maybe at her birthday party? No, that's too soon. But it *would* be the perfect time to really show her how much I've grown. Wouldn't it be great if she came crawling back to me on her own after that? She wouldn't even have to crawl. If she just came back . . ."

I want to gnash my teeth in frustration. I was so close— *am* so close. It's maddening. I feel like Taylor Swift in her old song about being in love with the boy next door who only has eyes for the short-skirted, high-heeled cheerleader. Or Gilbert Blythe in *Anne of Green Gables* when Anne thinks she's going to marry that tall, dark, handsome guy with the snobby sisters. Why does Willow have to be so obsessed with Arden? Why can't she see that if I'm the one who's making her happy, then I'm the one she should be with?

I give Willow a hug and tell her how incredibly amazing this is, then leave the shop and go back to work. As I set up the next entry on my tablet, I experiment with gnashing my teeth, which, it turns out, is neither as dramatic nor as cathartic as it sounds. And then the strangest thought surfaces. I wish she hadn't said anything about "if things were different." I wish she did want to break up (well, "break up," ugh). I'd still have to suffer the exquisite agony of unrequited love, but at least I'd be free to consider other relationships. Not that there are other relationships to consider. For example, Dela's already dating Arden, so it's not like she'd be a realistic option. Hypothetically. I don't actually want to be with Dela, obviously.

I don't know how much more of this up-and-down I can take. All this scheming isn't as fun as it used to be.

28

I DIDN'T SEE DAD WHEN HE ARRIVED THIS
morning because he went straight to Baba's, so I left my
origami session with Dela early today to have dinner with
him. I felt bad about bailing for the second day in a row,
especially after Dela rescued Baba last night, and I offered to
bring a bunch of origami home with me, but Dela refused. "No
offense," she said, "but I think it's safer if you don't." And she
smiled, just a little.

Dad meets me at the curb, and when I get in the car, he
hands me an envelope, saying, "From Mom." Inside, there's
money and a note that reads, *Buy yourself something beautiful to
wear for the gala!* ♥ *Mom*

"Wow," I say. It's a *lot* of cash.

"Hmm?"

I show Dad. I see his mouth tighten for a split second, but then he smiles and says brightly, "That's nice of her."

"Yeah," I say. "If she wants to buy my compliance, I'm not above taking the money." It slips out before I can stop it, and I feel guilty immediately, which isn't fair. She's the one trying to bribe me into approving her ill-advised life choices, from her purchase of an ugly Släkt twin bed frame (admittedly partly my own fault since I refused to participate in the choice) to her cohabitation with a prematurely balding hipster ten years her junior. I know I'm being judgmental and ageist, and I don't care.

"Nozomi. Be. Nice."

"I'd be nicer if she'd stop doing stuff like this." I wave the envelope at him. "Like it'll make up for her acting all, 'Oh, I'm on a journey of self-discovery!' and expecting me to be okay with it."

"Nozomi," Dad says again sternly. Though I notice he's trying to hide a smile.

"I'm just saying. It's true."

"She loves you."

"Yeah, well. Love isn't always easy," I say. It's one of his favorite things to say, and I'm beginning to understand why.

This time he laughs outright. "That's true."

Dinner conversation at Baba's is breezy and pleasant, probably because we've all agreed not to bring up anything that could upset her. We talk about Max's battle against the bugs in the software he's rewriting, and whether *Glass Cube* is art.

Baba, Max, and I say no; Dad and Stephen say yes. "It's a statement about art," Stephen explains.

"Then call it a statement. Don't call it art," says Max.

"It's both, which is why it's so fascinating."

"Sometimes," says Baba, "an artist has the idea, but no matter how hard he tries, he can't make it. Maybe this is a same thing."

"Artists rarely capture their original visions perfectly—at least, that's what artists say," says Stephen. "But I think *Glass Cube* does it pretty well." He goes off on a rambling lecture about art and perception, and Baba announces that she's bored and starts clearing the table.

After dessert, Dad shows us a couple of boxes of Jiji's old clothes that he found under the bed in his old room. He asks Baba to pick her favorites, and she chooses a cashmere cardigan and a Hawaiian shirt. She tells us about her honeymoon with Jiji in Hawaii, where Jiji bought the shirt, and how they had tried surfing, and she'd gotten up on the first try, but he'd fallen and fallen, and how he'd laughed the whole time. The cardigan was the first fancy gift she'd ever given him, and he'd worn it during his final days at home in hospice care.

"You should save those," I tell her. "I bet Jiji would like that."

She looks confused. "Of course I'm saving," she says, and folds them carefully and puts them back in one of the boxes.

"No, I mean make sure to put them somewhere special so they don't accidentally end up getting donated with the rest of the stuff," I say—and then I realize my mistake.

A brief but intense argument with Dad and Stephen ensues, ending with Baba calling them thieves and stalking out of Dad's room and into hers.

"Nice one, Zomi," says Max. I give him the finger.

"What did she *think* we were going to do with it all? Put it back?" I ask Dad and Stephen. "I can't believe she even held on to all those clothes for as long as she did. It's been, what, ten years since he died?"

Dad sighs. "Try to be kind, Zozo."

"I'm sorry," I say. "I didn't mean for it to come out that way. But it's so frustrating. I don't understand why she refuses to accept the inevitable. She got *lost* yesterday. How much clearer of a sign does she need that she can't go on like this?"

"How would *you* cope in her situation?" Dad asks.

Not for the first time, I try to imagine how it would feel to forget where the silverware goes, or how to get home from the grocery store, and to know that I would forget more and more and there was nothing I could do to stop it. As always, it's terrifying. But now, instead of shuddering and shoving those thoughts away and feeling sorry for Baba, I stick with it. How many times would I have to search for the silverware drawer before I'd finally ask my son to make little signs to help me remember where it was? How many times would I tell myself, "So I got lost this one time. Next time I'll remember how to get home," before I stopped trying to go out alone? What if I forgot that I'd gotten lost the last time?

"Okay," I say. "I get it. But if I knew how much everyone was worried about me—if I knew that my being stubborn was hurting other people—I bet I'd listen."

Stephen smiles sadly. Of course. Baba was willing to hurt Stephen for years so that she wouldn't have to accept that he was gay.

"It's so unfair," I say.

"I know, honey. But I've learned that if she can't accept the truth, then we have to accept *that* truth and work with it. It doesn't mean we give up trying. It just means we do what we can with what we've got. It's just the way love works sometimes."

"Is it, though?" I persist. "I thought love was about accepting *each other*. I thought it was about facing hard facts *together*."

"Are you saying that Baba doesn't really love you? Or me?" asks Stephen.

That's the million-dollar question, isn't it?

"And if you're unwilling to accept Baba the way she is—or Mom the way she is—do you really love them?" says Dad.

My mouth drops open. "That's not fair."

"I know," he says. "Love rarely is."

29

I LOVE THE CONCEPT OF DELA'S TANABATA Pavilion and I know it's going to look beautiful when it's finished, but the fact is, folding a thousand wishes is really tedious. Some days, I look at my tiny pile of cranes and butterflies and feel like I haven't made any progress at all, compared to the towering pile of wishes that Dela has transcribed. I'll finish folding a wish and turn to find that she's added three or sometimes even four more to the stack. It feels like I'm Mickey Mouse in "The Sorcerer's Apprentice."

I have to admit, though, things have improved lately. Dela finished transcribing a few days ago and has been folding cranes and butterflies with me ever since, so production has sped up considerably. In fact, today will be our final day of folding. I can hardly believe it, but I almost feel sorry that it's ending. Dela's as peevish as ever, of course, but ever since the night she rescued Baba, these after-work torture sessions have turned into something kind of . . . dare I say fun?

Don't get me wrong. I'm excited to be done. I've even made plans to go out with Willow this evening—just for coffee, to celebrate the end of this ordeal. She suggested it when I happened to tell her about today being the last day of folding, and I immediately said yes. Am I being pathetic? Maybe. But I need something to make me feel better after hearing about the wild success of Operation Make Arden Wish She Never Left. Plus, *she* asked *me*, and it wasn't for show or anything. And I keep thinking about that unfinished sentence from the morning after Hawk Hill: "If things were different between us . . ." It *has* to mean something.

"Look at this cat one," Dela says, and shows me a wish she's about to fold. It says, *I wish for Houdini to come home.* "It's so sad."

She opens the list on her laptop and points me to an entry where someone has attached two photos. One is a clumsy crayon drawing of a black blob with whiskers, and the other is a sweet-faced little boy holding a black cat.

I picture a four-year-old boy gripping a crayon in his chubby little fist, coloring that blob, his beloved Houdini, and dictating the message to one of his parents. I wonder how long Houdini's been missing, if he's still alive, and if that little boy stares out the window every night, certain that because he put his wish into the wishing website, he'll see Houdini leaping down from a tree or darting from behind a parked car, and trotting up to the front door. I hope that one day Houdini *will* return, but I feel an indescribable sadness because the odds are stacked against both of them.

"He might, though," I insist. "You never know." And despite the odds, this is what I will believe. Houdini the cat might come back. Because you never know.

Dela frowns. "He's probably already been run over by a car."

I gasp. "How can you say that? You'll jinx it if you say things like that! Take it back."

"Seriously?"

"Take it back, Dela. That poor boy is depending on you. You're like the . . . the keeper of his hopes and dreams. You *know* that. You can't just dismiss them because you think the odds are bad. That's not your decision to make."

A long—but not uncomfortable—silence follows while I stare her down. At last, she says grudgingly, "Fine. I take it back about the stupid cat."

"Say, 'This wish is hereby reinstated and restored to its full power. Houdini the cat has not been run over by a car and will return to his family in good health.'"

Dela stares at me in horror. "I'm not saying that."

"Say it."

"No."

"Say it!"

"No! It's completely absurd." But she's laughing, so I know I have her.

I fix her with a ruthless stare. "Say it."

Finally, she caves. "Fine. What do I have to say, again?"

I tell her.

With a sigh so deep I could swim in it, she says, "This wish is hereby reinstated and . . ." She looks at me for help.

"Restored to its full power," I prompt her.

"Restored to its full power," she recites obediently. "Houdini the cat has not been run over by a car and will return to his family."

"In good health."

"In good health," she repeats. She folds her arms and cocks an eyebrow. "Okay?"

"Perfect," I say with smug satisfaction. "You're glad you took it back. I know you are."

Dela juts her chin out defiantly, and slowly, deliberately, turns her back on me—but not before I see her press her lips together to hide a grin.

"Come on," I say. I lean over and nudge her with my shoulder. "Admit it. You're glad."

She nudges me back. "Maybe. A little bit."

She doesn't take her shoulder away, but leans in a little, and I'm just beginning to register the pleasant pressure of her shoulder against mine when she looks at me from under her eyelashes, and a jolt of heat zips through me, along with a vision of what it would be like to kiss her—just like the other night—and I get this heady wave of a feeling that if we stay like this for much longer, I might try to make it happen.

Stop it, Nozomi! What are you doing?

Luckily, Dela seems to realize something's off as well, because she jerks away at the same moment that I do.

It must be all of this pent-up, pushed-down desire I have for Willow—I'm sure it's practically pouring out my ears. It must be clouding my judgment.

I hope Dela didn't see something in my eyes and get the wrong message. That would be the worst. Because what if she decided she liked me back, and broke up with Arden to be with me? That would leave Arden free to return to Willow, and then where would I be?

"Hey, you wanna go out for coffee or something afterward?" Dela says abruptly. "To celebrate being done."

"Ohhh, I'm sorry. I, um. I already have plans with Willow." I don't know why I hesitate to tell her. No, I do. It's because now that I think about it, I *do* want to go out and celebrate with Dela. We've been working together for so many days now, it makes perfect sense. I hope she doesn't feel too bad.

"Oh. Okay, no problem. Just thought I'd ask," she says, and she's very nonchalant and cool about it, so I guess I haven't hurt her feelings. Good. Only you'd think Dela would be a *little* disappointed. I mean, *I* am. Not because of that weird little whatever-it-was that I felt just now with her, of course.

Seriously, though. What *was* that, and where did it come from?

Wait. I think I know. I've been so discouraged about how well Willow and Arden are doing that I've started to give up.

Despite all the pep talks I've been giving myself, despite the fact that I *just* told Dela not to throw dreams away simply because the odds were stacked against them coming true—I'm losing hold of my own dream. I'm starting to give up.

If things were different . . . How much do I want the end of that sentence to happen? Because if I allow myself to get dragged down and distracted, it won't happen for sure.

I can't give up. I promised myself I would never give up. Willow is the one I've wanted since the beginning, right? If I want my dream to come true, I have to stay focused on her. I have to believe I can make this happen.

30

DELA LEFT TEN MINUTES AGO, AFTER HAVING given me a little origami star on which she'd written *thank you*. I thought it was sweet, given our rough start, and I told her that. She laughed, and we had a moment where we almost hugged but didn't, and off she went.

Now I'm in the bathroom, where I stopped to do my makeup for my date with Willow. I've just finished applying mascara the way Willow taught me while we were waiting for the cable car—primer, wait; first coat, wait; second coat—and my lashes look incredible. I'm happily batting my perfect eyelashes at myself and pulling out my lipstick when she calls to cancel.

"I cannot *believe* them," she says. "I was literally walking out the door and they're like, 'Where are you going? You have an appointment with your college counselor in half an hour.'"

"Oh," I say. "That's okay." I look in the mirror at my work. All that effort for nothing. Despite what I told myself not thirty minutes ago, I feel my heart start to sink. I *want* to stay focused and positive, but the universe keeps testing my resolve. It's like every good thing that happens with Willow comes with an unpleasant twist that ruins it. It's like eating brownies with walnuts—if you hate walnuts, which I do. If only she'd cancelled a little earlier. Then I could at least have gone out with Dela.

"No, it's not okay, Nozomi. They keep saying they told me, but I know they didn't. And now I have to bail on you, and that's not fair to you. And I really wanted to see you." She sounds flat and dejected. "I had a present for you and everything." A present? There's a positive thing to focus on. My heart drags itself out of the pit of despair, sprouts a tiny pair of wings, and starts fighting its way upward.

"You can give it to me tomorrow," I say.

"It won't be the same."

"No, but I'll still be so happy," I assure her.

"Okay," she says. I can hear the energy seep back into her voice. "I can't wait for you to see it. Oh, and! To make up for bailing on you tonight, what if you come to my house for a couple hours on Saturday before Arden's birthday party? Does that sound good to you?"

Well, *yeah*. I'll trade a couple of hours in a coffee shop for a couple of hours in Willow's bedroom any day. Another positive.

Though of course, we'd still have to go to Arden's party afterward. Where, presumably, she'll be thinking about Arden and not about me.

"Sweet!" Willow says, then adds, "We're going to have so much fun."

"Mm-hmm." Focus on the positive, Nozomi. She hasn't mentioned making Arden jealous.

Wait, that's odd. That *is* a positive. A real one.

"Seriously, it's like I told you, Nozomi. I've grown so much because of you. I feel like I'm so much more . . . *me*. In fact, I think you might be the best thing that's happened to me all summer." Her voice is soft and sincere.

That's a pretty strong positive, I'd say.

By the time we hang up, I feel like hope has made a comeback, even if I'm still having to construct it out of scraps. But they're pretty good scraps. Enough to convince me that I have a fighting chance. Enough for me to commit myself to my plan one last time.

Okay, Nozomi. Eyes on the prize. Let's do this.

31

"MAX. I WILL EXPLAIN IT TO YOU ONE MORE time," I say slowly, as if to a small child. "Willow gave me this very nice lipstick that she wants me to wear to Arden's party tomorrow night. Which she is going. To put. On. My. Lips. It is *symbolic*. It is *subliminal*. Everyone knows that lipstick equals kissing."

"Everything you just said makes me embarrassed to be sharing DNA with you. And if everyone knows, then it's not subliminal, is it?" Max says as he smushes a pot of hot Rice Krispies treats into a pan. They're the only thing he knows how to bake. Which I guess is one more thing than I know how to bake. If it's even baking.

"Shut up," I say. I refuse to take the bait. He's trying to sabotage my renewed sense of hope, but I won't let him. Not after I've worked so hard to build it back up. "Anyway, you have to take this in context. I told you what she said to me the other day, after Baba got lost."

"Yeah. And may I remind you that she didn't actually finish the sentence? I can't believe we're still having this conversation. What's it going to take for you to wake up to the truth?"

"She didn't have to finish the sentence, Max! Context, remember? Also, body language! I told you what happened on Hawk Hill."

"Okay. Right. Sure."

"There was significant sexual tension, Max."

"Sexual tension?" Max shakes his head. "Uh-uh. That's one of those things that's easy to misinterpret. Maybe you feel it and the other person doesn't. Or maybe you feel it and it's good, and the other person feels it and is like—" He makes a cross with his two forefingers and pretends to cower away from me.

"You weren't there, so you can't judge," I say.

"You know what I *was* there for, though?"

"What?"

"When Dela brought Baba back."

"What does Dela have to do with any of this?"

"Dela showed up for you."

"So?"

"So . . . ?" He gives me a loaded look.

"I'm not interested in Dela, and she's not interested in me. We're both involved with other—" At Max's raised eyebrow, I walk it back. "Dela's involved with another person. And as far as she knows, so am I."

"All I'm saying is, Dela was there. And there was something going on with the two of you."

"There was not."

"And Willow could have stepped up and helped with Baba, like given you some moral support, but she didn't. And I think if she really liked you, she would have."

"She offered to. I told her she didn't have to come."

"And what does that say about *you* and how you really feel about her?"

"I didn't *ask* Dela to help, did I?"

"Fine. Point taken," he concedes. "Maybe the thing with Dela isn't real. But . . ." He shakes his head. "I don't get how you can dismiss Dela just like that"—he snaps his fingers—"and at the same time believe that this thing with Willow is real. It makes zero sense."

I haven't dismissed it just like *that*, I want to tell him. But that's an argument I'd rather not wade into.

"Look, I just— I want to be with Willow, okay? There's nothing wrong with that! Just let me want what I want!"

"Fine. Have it your way," says Max, looking resigned. "But can I give you some advice?"

"What."

"Stop fucking around. Stop pretending you're dating and letting that be enough. If she likes you the way you say she does, she needs to step up and own it. No more of this 'if things were different' bullshit. Tell her that you're into her, and if she's into you back, then make it real. Otherwise, shut it down. Because this fake-dating stuff is manipulative and dishonest, and it's going to bite you in the ass if you don't stop."

I leave Max and his Rice Krispies treats in the kitchen without responding. But my mind is churning. Maybe he's right. If I really want to be with Willow, if I'm really, truly committed, maybe it's time to make a stand.

32

I GO TO MY ROOM TO LOOK UP "LIPSTICK symbolism," which leads me down a rabbit hole about feminism and red as the symbol of both power and sexual promiscuity and questions about whether makeup is a joyful form of self-expression or if it's pandering to the male gaze and the beauty industry. I'm just starting to wonder if wearing makeup to pander to a *female* gaze indirectly supports the patriarchal power structure that has always defined feminine beauty standards when Mom calls.

After some awkward chitchat about my "sweetie," as Mom insists on calling Willow, she says hesitantly, "Do you think you might consider softening your stance on staying with me and Roy? Or your stance on me and Roy generally? I understand how difficult it must be for you, but it would mean so much to me if you could just—"

"No."

"Zomi, come on. Be reasonable."

"Mom, I think it's reasonable to be upset about you moving in with my former English teacher literally weeks after you moved out of the house."

We go a few rounds over whether this is appropriate, whether it matters that she's an adult and I am, in her words, "a child," and I'm just getting to a very important point in my argument about how it's unwise for *anyone* to make a decision like this after only *two freaking months* when she says, "It hasn't been two months, Nozomi, it's been nine!"

That shuts me right up.

"What?" I say, finally. I can't quite believe what I've just heard.

"It hasn't been only two months, okay? Roy and I have been dating for almost nine months now, which is plenty of time for two grown people to decide it's time to move in together."

I'm still trying to catch up. "Nine months? As in, since last November?"

A pause. Then, quietly, "Yes."

As the initial shock begins to subside, the implications of what she's just confessed begin to rise. She lied about when she started dating Mr. Jensen—she was already deep in the relationship when she moved out this spring. Which means . . . "You lied about that lightbulb moment in April. You didn't finally give up trying to make things work—you stopped trying last fall! In fact, you actively made it worse! Does Dad know this, or did you lie to him, too?" I'm so furious with her, I can't sit still. I get up and start pacing around the room.

I hear her sigh before she says, "He knows. And it *was* a lightbulb moment, Zomi. I'd been sneaking around and feeling guilty about my relationship with—"

"Your affair, you mean?" I say snidely.

"My relationship with Roy," she continues as if she hasn't heard me, "and this spring, I realized it was pointless to pretend there was any reason left to stay. I decided it was time to honor what I had with him and let go of what was clearly an unsalvageable marriage with your dad."

"It wasn't unsalvageable until you wrecked it."

"I didn't wreck it, Zomi. It was far beyond saving at that point."

"Dad didn't think so. He told me he wanted to do couples therapy and you refused."

There's a pause before Mom says, "You've got it wrong, Zomi. I tried to make it work. I tried for *years* to get him to go to therapy, and *he* refused. You must have seen how unhappy we were toward the end."

Dad refused to go to therapy? That's . . . new. And really upsetting, if it's true. But I'm too angry to concede any points right now.

Another sigh. "Nozomi, you just can't understand the desperation I felt. I hope you never have to experience it. It's soul-crushing."

That's it. I draw the line at self-pity. Because she ended up with what she wanted, didn't she? I say, "I think I've had enough of this conversation. Goodbye."

I hang up and realize that my heart is racing and my breath is coming in short gasps; I'm filled with an anger so ferocious, I feel like it's going to eat me alive. She lied to me. It was bad enough that she lied about having an affair—that she had an affair in the first place!—but then to pretend that leaving Dad was the honorable thing to do? And spin it as a last, desperate attempt to, what—find true love? I get that she was unhappy with Dad. I get that the magic was gone. But—my phone rings. I let it go to voicemail and then block her number.

"Max!" I rush downstairs to find Max, who has left the kitchen and is practicing shooting pool in the living room. "Did you know that Mom had an affair? With Mr. Jensen. *Before* she moved out."

I expect him to react like I did, with shock and outrage. But his gaze only flicks up briefly from the cue ball before he goes back to it and nods. "Mm-hmm."

"Wh—what? How? Did she tell you? Did Dad?"

"I figured it out on my own. And then I confronted her and she admitted it."

"When?"

"February." He shoots, and a ball drops into a pocket with a *thunk*.

February. Long before Mom moved out and started dating Mr. Jensen—before she told us she was dating Mr. Jensen, that is.

"But you haven't even been home! How did you figure it out from college?"

"I had eyes and a brain," he says before sinking another ball. I want to shove the remaining balls around the pool table and ruin the rest of his game, but I want even more to hear how he figured it out, so I content myself with sneering at him.

"I just kept seeing all these restaurant-food pictures on her Instagram, and barely any of those big group shots of her and her middle-aged lady friends at restaurants. And you know how much she loves a group restaurant shot."

I nod. Way back when we were still going out to dinner as a family, she never failed to corral some poor waiter—or worse, a random patron on their way to the bathroom—into taking a photo of us at the table.

"So I thought, what's she hiding? And I asked her, point-blank, and she told me."

Wow.

"Why didn't you tell me?" I ask.

"She asked me not to."

"*Ever?*"

He shrugs. "You know now, don't you?"

I feel betrayed by everyone. How could Mom have cheated on Dad? And why has Dad been such a doormat about it? (And how dare *he* lie to me, too, about the couples therapy?) And how could Max have kept this to himself and allowed me to skip along like a child for months, completely oblivious to the ugly reality right in front of my face?

"They would have split up eventually anyway," says Max.

"What a comfort."

"Yeah, well. Reality sucks. I told you."

"Ha. And now you know why I prefer living in a dream world."

Only I'm tired of feeling like the universe is playing tricks on me because I've been closing my eyes against the truth. I think about Willow and tomorrow night and my rededication to my plan. If I'm serious about living my life with my eyes open . . .

Except I'm so close. I'm not exactly *ignoring* reality. I *know* it's a long shot. And there's evidence in my favor. *If things were different*, she said. She wanted to come sit with me the night Baba got lost; if I hadn't pushed her away out of pride, maybe things *would* be different now. It's my own fault, really. And I don't care what Max says—that lipstick means something, when you put it together with everything else.

I'm going to trust my instincts just this one last time. If I'm right, then Willow will do something that even Max will accept as proof that she likes me. She'll finish that sentence. She'll kiss me for real. Something.

And if I'm wrong . . . that will be the last trick the universe plays on me.

Please, universe. Let me be right. I really need a win right now.

33

WILLOW'S BEDROOM IS EVEN BIGGER THAN THE
one I have in Stephen's house, with an actual vanity set: table,
mirror, and chair. "Here, sit down. Let's prep your face," she
says as she leads me in, and I don't think I've ever been so glad
to think about makeup—and not just because it's Willow. I've
been chewing myself up inside since Mom called, and it's nice
to think about something as small as making myself pretty for
a party.

I sit down obediently, and she arranges a bewildering and
slightly terrifying phalanx of facial-care and makeup products
on the table. They span a spectrum ranging from neutral grays
and browns to wild colors like teal, dark plum, and bright
orange. I see a dark shade of foundation and wonder if some
of these are for Arden. That's okay. It's okay. So what if she's

kept them? In fact, maybe they're not even just Arden's. Willow probably does makeup for lots of people.

Oh my god, Nozomi. Calm. Down.

Willow pulls up her own chair, selects a few bottles and a box of cotton balls, and proceeds to swipe my face with a series of potions, creams, and powders, declaring, "When I'm finished with you, you're going to look *amaaazing*."

I smile, but the questions immediately begin ricocheting around my brain like ping-pong balls. Does that mean that she sees something in me that others don't? Or does it mean I'm not good enough as I am? Or does it mean nothing? I feel like I have to pay extra-close attention to every word Willow says, every gesture, every glance that might sway things in my direction so I can feel confident about my putting my heart on the line tonight.

She dips a brush in a pot of eyeliner and dabs off the excess. "Okay. Eyes closed."

I close my eyes. "This is going to look so great," she murmurs, and I almost forget to process her tone (focused? romantic?) because this feels so good, and eventually I lose myself entirely to sensations. The cool tip of the brush skimming along my lash line, and the heel of her hand where it rests on my cheek. The silky caress of the blush brush. I have to concentrate on breathing slowly, calmly, so I don't accidentally sigh with pleasure. And when Willow uses her fingertip to dab lip primer on my parted lips, and then again to blend the lipstick—*the* lipstick—it feels so sexy that I can't help smiling.

I'm practically kissing her right now. The lipstick *was* symbolic.

"There!" she proclaims, finally. "What do you think?"

I look in the mirror and gasp. I'm unrecognizable. My skin is flawless. My lips are a plummy pink, and she's done something to my cheeks and my eyes that makes me look like a supermodel. I look glamorous and self-assured. Like a girl Willow would fall in love with. *I'd* fall in love with me right now. "Wow."

"I know, right?" Willow says. She looks positively jubilant. "Wait, hang on." She leans forward and rakes her fingers through my hair, zhuzhing it here, smoothing it there, before she looks into my eyes and smiles. "Beautiful," she breathes. She holds my gaze for a lifetime. Is she admiring me, or is she admiring her work? Is she going to crush me and say something about my mascara or my eyeliner? I look for an answer in her eyes.

I think she's admiring *me*.

I think we're having a moment. A real one.

But then she straightens up and the moment is gone. But *then* she laughs and says, "Maybe I've been chasing after the wrong girl this whole time," and there's a sort of twinkle in her eye and a lightness in her voice, but . . .

She turns away from me and starts on her own makeup, gazing only at her own face in the mirror . . . oh my god. She just said she's been chasing the wrong girl, and I didn't even respond. What is wrong with me? I've been so busy collecting and analyzing all these moments tonight, I've been letting them slip by without *acting* on them.

I watch her as she sponges foundation onto her already

perfect skin with deft, practiced strokes and feel that same thrill I always do. She's so beautiful. So confident and strong. Everything I want in a girlfriend. The question is, have I become everything *she* wants in a girlfriend? Am I as beautiful, confident, and strong as she is?

Wait a sec.

A memory nudges me, pokes at me . . . It's that thing Dela said the night Baba got lost. About me dating Willow for *what* she is as much as *who* she is . . . about being in love with an idea and not a person . . .

That's absurd. First of all, there's nothing wrong with wanting to be the kind of person Willow would fall in love with. Hasn't that been my goal all along? And she just happens to fit into my . . . vision of an ideal . . .

Okay, reset.

Did Willow say that I've helped her be her true self?

Yes, she did. And I *love* that self.

And . . . has she helped me be *my* true self?

Stop. Just stop this right now. Obviously I'm nervous and letting myself get distracted, like before, like when a bride has qualms just before she's about to walk down the aisle, and she wonders if she's made a colossal mistake and maybe she should be marrying someone else. Yes. Yes, that's it exactly. I've spent my entire summer wishing I could be with Willow, and tonight could be the culmination—or the end—of everything I've been working toward. I'm just nervous. That's all.

34

ARDEN IS CELEBRATING HER PASSAGE INTO
legal adulthood in a private room at the DNA Lounge with live
entertainment from her cousin's band. The room is crowded
with a mix of Black, Asian, Latinx, and white kids, but I see her
spot us as soon as we walk in; it's as if she's been waiting for
us—or for Willow, anyway. The expression of dismay on her
face when she sees me and Willow stroll into the venue hand in
hand is fleeting, but it's definitely a thing that happens, and—I
know this is small of me, but—it is profoundly gratifying. I'm
wearing faded jeans, a vintage Violent Femmes T-shirt that
Lance lent me, and a pair of Willow's ankle boots. Add in my
fashion model makeup, and I finally feel a hundred percent
convincing in the role of Willow's girlfriend; finally, I'm not
worried that random passersby will ask each other, "How did

that girl end up with *that* one?" I feel like Cinderella at the ball. I feel like the Beast transformed by Belle's kiss.

"Heyyyy!" Arden says, and envelops first Willow, then me in a fragrant hug. She smells like jasmine and lemon. And she looks stunning. She's wearing a bright orange top in a silky, clingy fabric, and artfully torn jeans and metallic blue ballet flats that give her an effortless everyday-casual-meets-high-fashion look that I could never pull off.

"You look great, Nozomi," she says. "Did Willow do your makeup?"

I smile my biggest, brightest smile, and instead of, "How very passive-aggressive of you," I say, "Thanks! She's amazing, isn't she?" and give Willow a kiss—just on the cheek, but I let it last long enough to make it kind of hot. I hope. We smile at each other for a second, and I see a look that gives me shivers and boosts my confidence. "Happy birthday, Arden," I say, turning back to her. I look around. "Where's Dela?"

I'm just wondering. It makes sense to wonder where her girlfriend is, doesn't it?

"She's over there with the band," says Arden, and nods vaguely in the direction of the back of the room: there's two hapa guys, one tall and lanky, and one in flip-flops; a purple-haired white guy; a Black girl with plaid paper-bag pants . . . and finally, Dela, in overdyed, cuffed jeans and a white button-down shirt. She tosses her bangs out of her eyes, and a rush of butterflies swoops unexpectedly into my chest. I do love a bangs-toss.

"She's so cute, isn't she?" says Arden.

Cute is not exactly the word I would use to describe Dela or her look, but then again, I'm not an Amazonian warrior princess from Themiscyra.

Actually, I remind myself, thanks to Willow and her magic, I am. Or I look like one, anyway. A little bit. I wish Dela would look over; I want to see her face when she sees the new me. Though let's be honest, it's more like the temporary me—I could never replicate this face on my own. Cinderella's dress only lasted until midnight, after all.

Though it was enough to get the attention of the prince.

Who is obviously Willow in this scenario, except that she's a princess. All the pieces are finally falling into place, and I intend to see this through.

Arden's attention shifts to a clutch of friends who want to talk about the guy with the purple hair—does Arden know if he's gay? Or maybe bi? If he's single? Because he is so hot! Will she introduce them? Arden leads them over, and Willow and I go to the bar and order sodas from a surly bartender in a black band T-shirt.

We lean against the side wall and watch the band climb up on the stage. Purple Hair and Flip-Flops pick up guitars; Plaid Pants goes to the keyboard; Tall and Lanky sits behind the drums.

"Hey," Willow says suddenly. "You really meant it just now, didn't you. When you said I was amazing."

"Well, yeah," I say. Did I let too much of my real feelings show? Only—that's good, right? That's what tonight is for. "Why?"

She looks down and smiles. "No reason," she says, but before we can say any more, Arden climbs onstage, stands in front of the mic, and starts addressing the crowd.

What *is* the reason, though? There has to be a reason.

"Hey, everyone! Thanks for coming to my birthday party," says Arden. A cheer goes up from the assembled. "This is Ruse, my cousin Olivia's band." She gestures at the keyboardist. "Before they get going, I want to start the night with an original song for my girlfriend. Where's Dela?"

Purple Hair's fan club cheers and points to Dela, who's still with them. Dela's mouth makes a smile, though her eyes look a little deer-in-the-headlights.

Arden looks at her and says, "This song is inspired by a Langston Hughes poem about loving without regrets. This one's for you, Dela Mayumi Benedict."

The band plays an intro, and she croons,

Out of love, no regrets
So put your trust in me
Out of love, no regrets
I think we're meant to be

We don't know where we'll go
Next year, next week,
or even tomorrow
So let's love with no regrets
'Cause it's the only way I know.

Wow. If a girl like Arden was directing that smoldering gaze at me and singing those words to me, I'd be so happy, I'd be lighting up the room. But Dela's smile looks unsure—which doesn't surprise me, I guess. She's so private, I'm sure she hates all this attention.

"I used to beg her to sing to me from the stage. Beg her," Willow says glumly. But she's not furious, which is what she would have been only a month ago. So glum is an improvement.

"You'll be okay," I say, and after a moment's hesitation, I put my arm around her and give her an encouraging squeeze. "I'd offer to sing to you, but I think that might make you feel worse." Holding my breath, I leave my arm where it is.

Willow responds by laughing, and then threading her arm around me, pulling me close, and leaning her head against mine. "You can't be that bad. And thank you."

I think I might faint. Or float away like a helium balloon. Or both—they'll have to chase down my unconscious body as it drifts out of the club and down the street.

Now seems as good a time as any to say the thing.

Just kidding. I still have to figure out what to say.

Okay. Just one second, and then I'll do it.

Okay, now.

No, wait.

All right. Here we go.

For real this time.

Aghh, just say it, already!

"Hey," I say. "Can I talk to you about something?"

"Sure. What?" Willow says. Is it my imagination, or is she tensing up?

"I know you're not all the way over Arden," I start to say, but I only make it through "I know you're not" before we're slammed by a wall of sound from the stage and the rest of my sentence is swallowed by the opening notes of "May the Odds Be in Your Favor" by Meet Me @ The Altar.

"WHAT WERE YOU SAYING?" she shouts.

"NEVER MIND! I'LL TELL YOU LATER!" I was so close. *So* close.

"OKAY! YOU WANNA DANCE?" Willow nods her head toward the dance floor.

I nod back. I guess dancing with my girlfriend—okay, my *almost*—ugh, fine, my *pretend* girlfriend—is almost as good as laying bare my soul and professing my undying love.

Turns out, though, it *is* pretty good. Ruse is talented, and before long, we're both sweaty from dancing and from the press of bodies around us. Willow's face is flushed and her hair keeps falling over one eye as we dance, and she keeps flipping it back with a toss of her head, as if she knows that's a thing with me. I look around for Dela—and Arden—Dela and *Arden*, but I can't see them. Halfway through a slower song about bad therapy, Willow shouts, "I HAVE TO PEE." I follow her off the floor and wait outside the bathroom.

A few minutes later, she emerges, looking stunning— I think she must have taken the opportunity to refresh her lipstick and clean up her eye makeup, and I regret not having done the same. I must look like a raccoon, what with all the sweating I've been doing.

"Hey, let's go in there." Willow points at a short passageway that leads to another, smaller room that a handwritten sign tells us is RESERVED FOR THE BAND. "They're onstage. They'll never notice," she says, and she pulls me with her. The walls are painted in bold diagonal black and white stripes. There's a table laden with snacks and a case of Kirkland water bottles in the corner. Feeling slightly criminal, I grab one along with Willow and start drinking. As she points out, though, there's no way those guys are going to drink forty bottles of water.

She smiles at me. "I know I've said this like a million times, but you look gorgeous."

"Well, I have this great makeup artist," I say with a grin, and she laughs. Then she stops laughing and her eyes soften. Oh my god. This is the moment. This is when I tell her how I feel.

"So. Um," I say. "That thing I wanted to talk to you about earlier?"

"Uh-huh?" She looks like she's getting ready to listen, then stops herself. "Actually, there's something I want to tell you, too. Do you mind if I go first?"

"Oh! Sure. Go ahead." I suppress a sigh and resign myself to another Willow therapy session. Not that I mind those. But still.

Willow looks at me and laughs nervously. "I'm about to

get into some sensitive territory, so be patient with me, okay?"

I nod, my own nerves suddenly prickling again. She doesn't usually open like this.

"So. I'm not sure if you remember, or if you saw it the same way, but last week, when we were at Hawk Hill? I felt like we might have had a . . . a moment. Or we almost had one."

Oh my god.

"It threw me so hard, the next day I almost told you how I felt. I don't know if you noticed."

When you started to wonder what it would be like if things were different and then didn't say the second part? I'm too excited to speak.

"I've been doing a lot of soul-searching since then. And the thing is, doing the whole fake-dating act to make Arden jealous . . . it was a good idea, and it's been a fun distraction, but the more we've been dating—*fake* dating—the more it's started to feel . . . well, it's been starting to feel real. Just like in the movies." She glances at me briefly, as if to confirm that this is how I feel, too.

Oh. My. God.

Willow takes a sip from her water bottle and says, "But the thing is . . . well, I'm not totally over Arden yet." She gives me a regretful smile. "But you know that."

No. This can't be happening.

And yet it is. I feel like when a cartoon character gets flattened by an anvil that falls out of nowhere. *Clang*, you're dead. Gone. Smashed into a pancake.

"So I can't guarantee that I'll be a hundred percent available to you, like, emotionally. But I'm ready to try to move on. From Arden."

Move on . . . from Arden . . . I almost stagger from the whiplash as the words sink in—I actually feel dizzy. I can't even nod. All I can do is stare at her.

She looks into my eyes and goes on. "And tonight, I just keep looking at you, Nozomi, and it's like, every time I see you, I get this little—" She shivers a little, and I shiver, too—that same shiver I've been getting since Day One.

"And I was kind of hoping you felt the same way about me." She moves a step closer and takes my hand in hers, looking down as our fingers intertwine.

My mind is reeling and my mouth is dry. I've turned into such a quivering, gelatinous mess, I don't know how I'm even standing upright. But I manage to croak, "I did. I mean, I do," in a voice that only sounds a little bit like I'm choking to death on my heart, which seems to have lodged itself in my throat. Because I *do* feel the same way. Obviously.

She lifts her eyes to mine and gives me a small, intensely intimate smile. Then her arms are around my waist, pulling me even closer to her, and my hands slide up her shoulders and around her neck as her lips meet mine, and finally, we kiss for real—a long, sweet, perfect kiss if ever there was one.

Only I can't concentrate. Don't get me wrong. It's amazing: soft, tender, and totally, *totally* hot. Or it should be. It's just—I'm a bit nervous, I think.

It makes no sense. The girl I've been swooning over for weeks is finally in my arms, gazing at me with her perfect eyes, grazing my cheek with her perfectly manicured fingernails, and kissing me again and again with her perfect lips. My fantasy has finally become reality. I should be spinning off into the stars in a whirlwind of kisses and moonbeams, totally lost in this perfect moment . . . but the more we kiss, the more I'm worrying about where to put my hands, and how hard to kiss her, and—weirdly—what Dela will think if she sees us. Which should be nothing, obviously. Because I am Willow's girlfriend, as far as anyone knows. Oh my god, stop! What am I doing? Why am I thinking about . . . Just stop. Think about Willow.

Willow pulls back and looks at me. "Are you okay? Is this okay?" she asks.

Focus, Nozomi, focus. Focus on the moment. Focus on kissing the girl of your dreams!

"Yes! Definitely yes. I just. I'm, um, giddy with joy, that's all."

She laughs. "You're so funny. We don't have to rush into anything official yet if that's freaking you out. But I think this could be really good."

"Me too," I say, and we go back to kissing, which *is* really good. Gradually, I relax and begin to enjoy it. Okay. I *was* just nervous before.

"Uh, is that behavior really appropriate? I think the band and their groupies are the only ones allowed to make out in here," says a voice behind me, and I jump and bang my teeth into Willow's. It's Dela, looking amused.

"Oh. Uh, hi," I say, feeling caught out and guilty, somehow. It makes no sense. Dela must believe that I kiss Willow all the time. So why do I wish she hadn't seen me doing it?

"Come on, Nozomi. Let's go," says Willow, and stalks out without so much as a glance in Dela's direction, leaving me a little dumbfounded. I don't want to go. I feel like I need to tell Dela that the kiss she just saw wasn't real, that it didn't mean anything. Which is absurd. Especially because for the first time all summer, it *was* real. It *did* mean something.

"I don't think she likes me very much," observes Dela. "Though I guess I can't blame her."

Speaking of which. "Where's Arden?" I ask. I know it's her birthday party and everything, but why haven't I seen Dela with her all night?

"Out there somewhere." She takes a long swig of water and says, "Between you and me, I'm not sure we're going to last much longer."

What? A dozen scenarios swirl through my head, mostly involving Arden and Willow getting back together. Which . . . isn't breaking my heart the way it should? A couple of scenarios also involve Dela ending up with me. Faced with those, I discover that the butterflies that were bopping around in my chest earlier have returned. Not only that, but a few have escaped into my head, and I can't think for all the flittering and fluttering going on in there. Me and Dela? The butterflies threaten to lift my entire body off the ground. An understanding begins to take shape inside me, and I know that I have to say something. I have to tell Dela the truth, that Willow and I aren't really dating.

"You know, it's funny you should say that because . . . um. There's something I need to tell you about me and Willow."

"Yeah?" There's something cautious and deliberate about the way she says it, and I'm filled with giddy hope that this is going to turn out well, that I'm making the right choice.

"The thing is, Willow and me—"

"Hey, I've been waiting for you! Are you coming?" It's Willow, looking irritated.

"Oh. Yeah! We were just—we were talking about um, the um . . . the uh . . . ," I stammer.

"The installation," Dela cuts in.

"Yes, that's right. The installation," I repeat. "Work stuff."

"Okay, so are you done?"

"Yep!" I say, my heart falling. "All done."

I take Willow's outstretched hand, and as we go back to the main room, the understanding solidifies and then bursts open and burns through me like lightning.

It's not Willow I'm supposed to be with.

It's Dela.

35

WILLOW AND I SPENT THE REST OF THE PARTY
dancing, kissing some more, and drifting around in a blissful
little bubble before one last tender kiss good night. All my
hopes and dreams and plans for the summer have finally come
to fruition. I should be out of my mind with excitement. But
I'm not.

All that romance, all that perfect happy-ending energy,
everything I always wanted, and I couldn't enjoy it because the
whole time, all I could think about was how to tell Dela that
this wasn't real, and how to break out of this bubble without
breaking Willow's heart. Or if I should. Because what if I do?
Where does that leave me and Dela? And what about Arden?

Also, I can't gloat about it to Max. Winning is meaningless
if you don't want what you've won.

And to top it all off, I woke up this morning to the notifications that I'd been waiting for all summer. Helena's not only liked the photos I posted last night, she's even commented on a couple with flames and heart-eye emojis and even this: **You two look so great together! Wishing you the best.** 🖤 🖤 🖤 🖤 And a DM: **Hey** 😊

It's no fun finally getting a message like that when you've realized that the girl you look so great with is the wrong girl.

Okay, it's a little bit fun. I may have spent some time on the way to brunch with Baba this morning entertaining myself by thinking of mean replies to Helena, like, *So glad I'm with her and not you,* and *Wait, who is this?* But it's an empty kind of fun—the cotton candy kind that you bite into and it's only sweet for a second before it's gone. Anyway, next to my distress about Willow and Dela, my anger at both of my parents, and my worries about brunch, this little victory over Helena hardly matters.

As for brunch: Dad and Stephen ended up buying one of the top spots on Oak Vista's "exclusive wait list," which almost guarantees an apartment opening up within the year. They've been scheming and strategizing for the past couple of days about how to break the news to Baba, quibbling over the details of when, where, who, and how. Today's brunch is the setting they've picked, and Max and I have been roped in, presumably to minimize the risk that Baba will shout at Dad and Stephen when they tell her. As for the how, "You're her favorite," Stephen insisted to Dad this morning on the phone. "You know this is part of the reason you're here, so don't flake on me. She'll take it much better from you."

"I don't know, Zomi," Max says as we enter the restaurant. Baba and Dad have already been seated, and Baba sees us first and waves cheerfully from their table. Max and I look at each other, and he adds, "There's no way this is going to end well. It's not fair to set her up like this."

I wish he wasn't like this. I really want to believe that Dad and Stephen know what they're doing. After all, being at the restaurant with her grandkids *will* ensure that Baba is in a good mood to start off with, and it should help her to stay calm and rational when Dad breaks the news.

We sit down at the green formica-topped table, and for a while, all goes according to plan: friendly greetings; questions about Arden's party, which I do my best to deflect; strange looks from Max, which I do my best to ignore; orders placed; food brought to the table. Baba is happily cutting up her Belgian waffle when Stephen launches the next stage of the plan by talking about an art auction he's been invited to. Then Dad drops the bomb.

He says cheerfully, "Speaking of auctions, great news, Mom! We bid on a top spot on the wait list for Oak Vista last week, and we won!"

Baba puts her fork down and eyes him with suspicion. "Hm?"

"A spot on the exclusive wait list at Oak Vista. That elder care community on the Peninsula. Remember, we took you there the other week? They're in very high demand, so it was really lucky that we were able to get it," Stephen says.

"As soon as a new unit opens up that meets your requirements, you get to move right in," Dad adds. "They'll redecorate the whole apartment for you. You get to choose the carpeting, the wall colors . . . isn't that great?"

Baba, whose eyebrows have been drawing themselves further and further downward as she listens, says, "I have my own house. Why should I pay extra money to keep the apartment there?"

She can't possibly think that's what this news means. Max nudges me under the table. I know he's saying *I told you so*, and I wish he wouldn't. Dad clears his throat and looks at his hands and says, "Ah. Right," and then looks at Stephen, who raises his eyebrows back at him and nods meaningfully. Dad taps his fingers together and tries again. "So. The thing about the exclusive wait list is that they expect you to move in as soon as they notify you that a unit is open. Not instantly, of course, because they have to redecorate. As for the house, you could sell it. Or rent it out."

There's a long, uncomfortable pause before Baba says, "No." Her mouth is set firmly in a stubborn line. "I don't want to."

"Mom," Stephen begins, but Baba shakes her head and says sharply, "Nn-nn." Then she says, "You are my children. You cannot tell me what to do, just like that—*pahn!*" She claps her hands once.

"But Mom, it's really nice there. Remember? There are activities, there are people to help you with anything you need—"

"No!" Baba's voice is sharper now, almost shrill. "I am fine! I want to live in *my* house!"

Dad looks at me and Max, and then at Baba, and says, "Mom, please. The kids," and I know that my role as a tantrum-prevention measure is a good and useful thing, but I suddenly feel like a tool and a traitor. I stare guiltily at my French toast. I don't know how I feel about this operation anymore. Before it felt manipulative, but necessary. Now it just feels manipulative.

But it doesn't matter, because Baba doesn't care. "Kids can hear! You are setting the bad example for them, how to take care of the parents," she says without lowering her volume a single notch. People are starting to stare, and I begin to consider sliding down in the booth and under the table. I wish Baba wouldn't yell.

"Mom!" Stephen mutters. "Please! People are staring!"

"Please calm down, Mom," adds Dad. "You're making a scene."

"*You* are making the scene!" she says inexplicably and with rising hysteria. "You are the failed children. You don't know how to show the love of your family. I have failed you as your mother." She's quivering with emotion. "I quit. Mou, iya." She scoots out of the booth and stalks out of the restaurant.

After exchanging looks with Stephen, Dad gets out of the booth and rushes after Baba. Stephen groans, covers his face with his hands, and leans forward, resting his elbows on the table.

I get how Baba must feel; if anyone knows what it's like to be ambushed with bad news, it's me. On the other hand, how could she not have seen this coming? How could she be so unreasonable when Dad and Stephen are just trying to do what's best for her?

"Well," says Max gloomily. "That was fun."

Dad texts and says he's caught up to Baba and is trying to persuade her to go home, so Stephen gets boxes for the rest of our brunch and drops me and Max off at home before heading over to Baba's. He and Dad return within an hour in the midst of a heated argument, having left Baba in the care of her next-door neighbor.

"I *did* prepare her," Stephen is saying. "We've gone through the attic, sold a bunch of her stuff, taken her on the tour . . . I thought she'd see it coming."

"That wasn't what I meant by preparing her, and you know it. You know she can't take a hint."

They enter the kitchen and don't even see Max and me sitting at the table finishing our brunch with Lance. "I was trying to be gentle!" Stephen says.

"You were being a coward."

"I'm sorry, did *you* tell her you were marrying a man? No,

wait. That was me. Remember what happened after that?" Stephen walks over to Lance and lays a protective hand on his shoulder.

"Hey, love," says Lance quietly, and puts his hand on top of Stephen's.

Dad sighs. "Fine. You're right. You're not a coward. I'm sorry."

"I don't know why I always have to be the one who tells her stuff she doesn't want to hear," says Stephen.

"Hey, I had to tell her about the divorce."

"That was different. You're her favorite. And it was Jennifer's fault."

Huh? "So *Baba* knows Mom cheated on you, too?" I cut in. "Am I the only one who didn't know?" Not to make this all about me, but I feel betrayed all over again, like everyone's made a fool out of me . . . a little like Baba must have felt earlier today, actually.

Dad looks at me blankly. "You . . . how did you . . . ?"

"And while we're on the subject, Mom said that she asked *you* to go to counseling and you refused. Is that true?" The anger I've been holding in since Friday night spills over.

He looks at Max, who shrugs defensively and says, "Mom told her."

Then he looks at Stephen, but Stephen shakes his head and says, "This is between the two of you."

Dad turns to me again and says, "Zo, I never meant for you to—" and then interrupts himself. "This is more than I can handle right now. Can we talk about it later?"

Sure. When it's stuff *I* don't want to talk about, he's Mr. Let's Have a Heart-to-Heart, but when it comes to stuff *he* doesn't want to talk about, he runs for cover.

I glare at him. "When?"

He shuffles his feet uncomfortably and clears his throat. "I don't know, Zozo. I'll be busy taking care of stuff for Baba, so—"

"How about lunch tomorrow? Max can babysit."

"You mean Baba-sit," quips Max, and I roll my eyes.

Backed into a corner like this, Dad has no choice but to agree. "Fine. Okay. Lunch tomorrow."

36

DAD SHOWED UP AT WORK AND BROUGHT ME TO Tartine, the legendary bakery where, uh, legend has it that Steve Jobs tried to cut in line but the staff made him go to the back and wait his turn for a sandwich like a normal person. I can't decide whether I find that refreshingly down-to-earth and egalitarian or snooty and self-important, but anyway, their bread and their Scharffen Berger chocolate croissants are supposedly famous among foodies, and it's been on Dad's San Francisco bucket list for a few years now. Dad gets a ham sandwich: gourmet Spanish ham, organic brie cheese from Marin, locally grown organic arugula, and organic fig confit on their famous sourdough; I get a chocolate croissant.

We get our food to go and walk to the top of the hill at

Mission Dolores Park, where we find a spot on the lawn and Dad fusses with the blanket he's brought with him and asks me if I've got sunscreen on. Finally, we sit down and take in the view. "This is *so* San Francisco, huh?" says Dad. "Exactly what you'd expect." He takes a massive bite out of his sandwich and beams at me, and then at the skyline, munching and making contented little eating noises.

I only have an hour for lunch and we've spent nearly half of it standing in line, so I don't have time to mess around talking about how much I love my croissant, even though it's so flaky and delicious that I bet even Dela would like it. I jump right in. "Did you really refuse to go to counseling when Mom asked you?"

Dad stops mid-chew and looks mournfully at his sandwich, as if it had secretly promised to help him get out of this conversation and suddenly changed its mind. He takes a second, slightly less enthusiastic bite and says after a while, "It's hard to accept that your marriage is in trouble. It's easier to tell yourself that perfectly happy marriages are a fairy tale, and *your* marriage is the reality that everyone lives with."

"So, yes."

He sighs. "Yes."

"Things were bad, and you lied to yourself about it." Just like Baba. Just like yesterday, in fact, when he and Stephen convinced themselves that breaking the bad news to Baba at the restaurant would make things easier.

"In my defense, love is—"

"Never easy," I finish. "I know. But Mom *asked* you and you said no."

He just looks sad. UGH.

"And did you really ask Mom to go to counseling to try to save the marriage, like you told me this spring? Or was that a lie, too?" I ask next.

"No! No, that's true. I *begged* her, Nozomi. But she said it was pointless to pretend there was any reason left to stay."

I remember Mom saying those very same words: *It was pointless to pretend there was any reason left to stay.* And that was why she decided to leave . . . which means . . . "You only asked her to go to counseling *after* she told you she was leaving?" Incredulity makes my voice shrill.

Dad looks tragic. "Sometimes, Zo, it takes a disaster to reveal how bad a situation is. And you know me. I like to make the best of things. I thought that we could go to counseling and fix things. She didn't."

"That's not my point!" I want to throw my croissant at him—but that would be a waste of the best croissant I've ever tasted. "My point is, she's not the bad guy! And you're not the good guy!"

"No. I never said I was."

"But you let me believe it!"

Dad turns his sandwich over in his hands; he looks like he's lost his appetite completely. I know I have. Well, maybe not quite. I take one more cautious bite—for the record, it's still delicious—and wait for him to respond.

"I did," he says. "It was wrong of me. I wanted to believe that I'd done everything I could, and it helped to focus on that part of the story. I'm sorry for misleading you."

This is completely bonkers. How could he have lied to me like that?

"Hey, at least you're less angry at your mom now," he says with a hopeful smile, as if he hadn't just flung my very last crumb of faith in him to a metaphorical flock of faith-devouring Canada geese.

"Nope," I say. "Still pretty furious with her. You're both bad, but she's the one who cheated. And I'm still mad at you for not telling me."

He sighs. "She asked me not to."

"Why? Why would you agree to that?"

"Because what happened was between us. It had nothing to do with you."

"It had everything to do with me! I'm her daughter, Dad. She betrayed our entire family."

"She only left me, Zozo. She didn't leave you."

"I don't care!" I splutter. "She's still a liar and a cheater, and someone should have told me."

"She's also still your mother. I don't want this to poison your relationship with her."

"Well, it has, and she deserves it. And your lies have poisoned my relationship with you." I take a savage bite out of my croissant and chomp on it angrily—partly because of Mom, and partly because Dad's being the good guy again, and what am I supposed to do with that?

The thing is, it's hard to be angry and appreciate a delicious pastry at the same time. Damn. I take a short break from my anger so that I can enjoy my food, and Dad must sense that I've let my guard down, because he chooses this moment to pounce.

"And what good is this knowledge doing you now?"

"What good is—" I'm too confused to keep going. What?

"Are you glad you know the truth?"

"I—" *Am* I glad? No, of course not. But is it better than not knowing? I settle on saying, "If you'd told me when it happened, I wouldn't have felt bad about blaming her for leaving. I wouldn't have felt like such a dupe when Max told me. I would've handled it better."

"Quite frankly, I don't think you are handling it very well right now," he says.

"Being angry at my mother for cheating isn't handling it well?" I ask. "Am I supposed to think it was okay for her to do that? Because she seems to."

"No, you're right, Zozo. Anger is an entirely appropriate response. But I don't want you to cut yourself off from her."

"Why? Why do you care if I have a relationship with her? So you can be the good guy again?"

"Because she's your mother, and I know how much she loves you. That's why. Because you deserve to have a good relationship with her. I know it's hard to get over the damage.

But I also know you love each other enough to have something worth saving."

Something worth saving. Ha. Not likely. But even as I think this, I know it's not true.

I look at him and can't help wondering out loud, "So if you and Mom didn't have something worth saving . . . did you ever love each other?"

Dad looks out over the city for a long time before saying, "I think we did."

"You *think* you did?" Not helpful. Because what I need to know now is, how do you tell the difference between real, lasting love and some other kind of love that's doomed to implode? How do you know when to hope and when to give up?

"I wish I could give you a better answer, Zozo," he says. "If it's any comfort, I'm not sorry I married your mother. I'm just sorry I couldn't love her in the way she needed." He regards his sandwich and seems to decide that it might still be good to eat after all, and takes a bite. "So don't give up on loving people, okay? In the end, it's always worth the risk to follow your heart."

37

FORGET ABOUT DAD'S MANTRA, "LOVE IS NEVER easy." It's so far beyond that. Love is exhausting. Love is painful. Love is diabolically confusing. My life is descending into chaos, and it's all because of love.

Stephen is stressed about the gala and Dad is stressed about Mom, so naturally they've been bickering a lot about Baba, who has been crabby and uncooperative. Max is annoyed with me because Mom keeps asking him to tell me to unblock her and I keep refusing. And then, of course, there's this surreal problem of being in love with my formerly fake girlfriend's ex-girlfriend's real girlfriend.

Compounding that last problem is the fact that I'm not even sure how I feel. Yes, I had that epiphany about Dela the other night, but it's not like the Willow Crush Bus simultaneously came to a screeching halt. I still feel kind of dazed when I'm with her and when I remember that I'm really-for-real dating her. And how can I end things with her so soon after she opened up and told me how much she liked me—and my response was to kiss her all night? I'm sure I would feel like I was in love with Willow, if it weren't for Dela.

Sigh.

Dela's on my mind even now as I'm out with Willow, shopping for a dress to wear to the gala. Willow has cajoled me into going with her to Fillmore Street, which is where she and her mom found *her* gala dress, and I keep thinking that in the unlikely event that Dela would have agreed to help me buy a dress, we'd be done by now and enjoying an ice cream somewhere.

I'm not one of those girls who hates shopping. But when nothing fit at the first store, and Willow rejected everything at the second store, I began to revise my stance. After eleven dresses and three stores, I think I might hate not only shopping, but fancy events, the fashion industry, and capitalism generally. But nothing can stop Willow—not the astronomical prices, not the endless racks of dresses clearly designed for someone much richer and cooler than me, not my flagging enthusiasm or my sagging confidence. At this point, my sole purpose is to make it through the afternoon without screaming. Why am I so hopeless at this?

In my little curtained-off dressing room in store number three, I'm trying on garment number twelve: a cobalt-blue sleeveless, backless, sequined jumpsuit with a plunging neck-line. I twist and turn in front of the mirror. I'm not a bright sparkly colors girl or a plunging neckline girl, but it does look good on me, as long as I stand with my back ramrod straight and don't move my arms. What would Dela think? She'd prob-ably laugh.

"Come out and let me see!" calls Willow from the other side of the curtain, and I step out stiffly, feeling self-conscious and exposed. "What do you think?"

"Oh my god, it's gorgeous!" she exclaims, adding, "Pull your hair up, like an updo." I lift my arms cautiously so as not to shift the fabric and expose a boob, and twist my hair together and hold it up at the back of my head. She gasps. "Oh, Nozomi. Look in the mirror." She takes my shoulders and turns me to face the mirror in my compartment.

"You have to get this," she says as I gaze doubtfully at my reflection—at our reflection. "You look like a goddess—*my* goddess." She slides her arms around my waist and kisses me, then turns back to the mirror. "Mmm. You're perfect."

Mmm . . . if that's how she feels about it . . . I guess I can spend an evening without bending my back, raising my arms, twisting my shoulders, or making any sudden movements. It could be good for my posture.

Which explains how I end up buying a dress that makes me feel like a sexy goddess-mannequin.

It's fine.

It's fine.

Oh, who am I kidding? It's not fine. Not at all.

How do I get myself out of this mess?

Two more days of bickering with Max, stressing about Baba, avoiding Dad, making out with Willow in the gift shop office, and dreaming about Dela, and I'm still—surprise!—stuck. Willow's parents are making her volunteer at a pediatric clinic today, so I have the afternoon free. I wander around the museum with the vague idea that art might somehow help me figure this out.

Max was right. I've been ignoring what's in front of me and chasing after an impossible dream. I've had this image in my head of the perfect girl—beauty queen looks, movie star glamour and charisma, rising star talent—and I've spent my summer—my *life*, really—chasing her, putting her on a pedestal, and trying to make myself worthy of her, all of which is messed up. If I keep going like this, I'll end up like Baba, who thinks she can live alone forever, or like Dad, who only admitted that his marriage was in trouble after Mom had an affair and asked for a divorce. When I'm with Willow, I'm either taking care of her, or I'm pretending to be something I'm not—as if I don't like who I actually am. And I guess I didn't, when I first got to San Francisco. I didn't want to be the girl who Helena rejected and laughed at.

But that *is* who I am. Someone I'm *not*, though, is the girl who Willow thinks she's dating. But that's okay—because I've realized that I don't want to be that girl. She's not real. She's not me. And pretending to be her isn't fair to me or Willow.

What if I got Willow to break up with me? What if I convinced Arden she really *should* try to get Willow back? How could I make that actually happen?

Eventually I end up in the courtyard, where Dela, Cliff, and two Academy of Art students are putting the finishing touches on the Tanabata Pavilion in preparation for the gala this weekend.

I haven't talked much to Dela since Arden's party; I've been extra busy with Willow, and Dela's been extra busy with the final preparations for the gala. She did ask me once what I'd been about to tell her about me and Willow in the break room, but I couldn't tell her the truth, because it wasn't the truth anymore. I had to pretend I'd forgotten. I watch her frowning over a knot she's tying in some thread, and then reaching for a pair of scissors to cut it off the spool, and—*ting*—a solution comes to me.

What if I broke up with Willow?

It's so obvious, I'm ashamed I didn't think of it before. But I see it now. Those complicated schemes are the old me—the one who didn't want to face reality. If I break up with Willow, I'll make her sad. She'll be angry with me, probably. I'll feel awful. But it's the right thing to do.

"Hey," says Dela. "If you've got time to stand there watching us, maybe you could give us a hand."

"Happy to."

I join Dela in tying each wish to a silver silk thread and

hanging them from the bamboo trees in the Tanabata Pavilion. As I work, I'm aware of Dela's every movement. Now she's behind me. Now she's across the courtyard, talking to Cliff. Now she's next to me, stretching on tiptoe to reach a branch over her head. She's rolled her sleeves all the way up, and there's a freckle on the top of her upper arm where it creases into her shoulder that I wish I could kiss. Not that I would ever, of course.

"What?" Dela glances at me over that freckle, and I feel my cheeks flame.

"Nothing!" I say. Dela's gaze intensifies. I look at her arm again. "Sunscreen! Maybe you should put on some sunscreen. So your arms don't burn."

Dela looks up at the sky, which is overcast at best, and back at me. "From the sun?" Her voice is weighted with irony.

"Cloudy days are deceptively dangerous," I protest.

After one more pointed look at the sky, she says with a little grin, "I'll pass. But I appreciate your concern."

Should I ask her if she still thinks she and Arden aren't going to last? Should I tell her I'm planning to break up with Willow? Maybe we could rely on each other for moral support.

But that's just more of the same, isn't it? More plotting and planning. And I don't want my breakup with Willow to be just a part of my grand plan to be with Dela. I have to break up with her whether I know Dela really wants to be with me or not. And, come to think of it, I don't want Dela to break up with Arden for my sake.

No, I do want that. That would be amazing.

But I don't want to be the one who makes it happen. That wouldn't be fair to Dela or to Arden.

I watch her as she ties another butterfly to a branch and gives it a little push. She watches it swinging back and forth. "What are you thinking?" I ask. When she doesn't answer right away, I lean close to her and joke, "Are you making a wish?"

"No." She gives the butterfly another push and her cheeks turn pink.

She *was* making a wish.

I will not make this into a whole new fairy tale. I will not. I'm going to do what I'm going to do, and I'm not going to do it because of some romantic fantasy I make up in my head.

But I really hope her wish was about me.

38

IN THE END, I COULDN'T HANDLE THE LOW, LOW neck and back of my gala jumpsuit (and neither could Dad), so Stephen and Lance gave me a couple of safety pins and found a short friend who was willing to lend me a tuxedo jacket. And Willow couldn't do my hair and makeup since Mrs. Hsu booked salon appointments for their own glamorizing process, so I've been left to my own devices on that front. But I think I've done a pretty good job, and the end result is that I love how I look.

I spin around, turn my back to the mirror and look over my shoulder at myself, then face the mirror again and do a couple of the red carpet poses that Willow taught me. And I know I promised myself no more fantasies, but tonight is special, so I allow myself to have just one. I imagine myself standing all made up and gorgeous in the soft glow of the fairy lights amid the butterflies and cranes of the Tanabata Pavilion. Dela will enter the courtyard, and when she sees me, she'll say something like, "Wow," under her breath, and I'll say, "What?" and she'll say, "You," and I'll tuck a lock of hair behind my ear and say, "Me?" all bashful and shy, and she'll say, "You look beautiful." And then Max clears his throat and yanks me back to the present, and I realize with a jolt that I'm smiling and waving coyly at Dela (which is to say, myself) in the mirror.

"Hiiii," he says, imitating my wave.

"Get out!" I throw a shoe at him, but he ducks and runs, and it sails past him into the hallway.

Anyway. Back to the fantasy:

We'll approach each other slowly. And with the lights sparkling around us, and music from the party playing faintly in the background, we'll each take a final step forward, we'll hesitate for a tantalizing moment . . . and then we'll share our first kiss, sweet and soft as a whisper, and everything else will fall away, and it will all be romantic and swoony and beautiful and perfect.

But in order for any of this to happen, Dela has to break up with Arden. And I have to leave that up to Dela, which I hate. The old me is still begging to be allowed to *make* it happen—I can think of three ways right now—but I won't let her. Because not only do I want Dela to come to me on her own, but nothing I've planned has turned out the way I thought it would, anyway.

Speaking of things not turning out the way I planned them, there is the tiny problem of me not having broken up with Willow yet. I've asked her twice to go out after work, fully intending to tell her—but both times, she started talking about how excited she was about the gala and how much fun we were going to have as a real couple, and I couldn't summon the courage to tell her that I didn't actually *want* to be a real couple. And I can't break up with her tonight, at the gala—that's practically like breaking up with someone at the prom.

"Hey, anger management." Max appears in the doorway once more. "Hurry up. We're all waiting for you downstairs," he says, and mimics my wave again before ducking my other shoe and disappearing.

I collect my dignity and my shoes, and hurry downstairs to a chorus of oohs and ahhs, which helps my mood a little. Dad and Baba are here to see us off, and Dad gets all misty-eyed. "Look at my baby," he keeps saying, and Lance keeps saying, "Don't infantilize her," and Dad keeps replying, "Yeah, yeah," and then saying it again. Baba, to my shock, not only doesn't snap at Lance for correcting her son, but agrees with him. "You are so grown-up," she says to me. "So sophisticate. Not a baby anymore." Of course, she ruins it by recalling the time Stephen and Dad went to prom and how they were so handsome and their dates (both girls) were so pretty and sophisticated, just like me. Maybe it's a sneak attack on Lance and Stephen, or maybe it's just a fond memory that she doesn't feel she has to filter. Or maybe she can't filter it anymore.

Ha. Leave it to Baba to remind me that I can hope and dream and look for silver linings all I want, but I can't escape real life. So, fine. I had my fantasy, and now I will face every part of this evening—painful, joyful, whatever it might be—exactly as it is.

39

WILLOW FLIES TOWARD ME ACROSS THE ATRIUM, breathtaking in an emerald-green, diaphanous dress, a tasteful rhinestone tiara set in her flowing black locks, and shimmering eye makeup that makes her look like a real fairy princess. I experience a ghostly flicker of regret. She is unquestionably the most beautiful girl I've ever met. But beyond her, just as she wraps me in a hug, I see Dela. She's wearing skinny black pants, a bolero jacket, and funky patent leather loafers, and she's upped her makeup game with a smoky eye that makes me melt. Suddenly, the girl in my arms feels the way she looks— impossible, magical, a romantic fairy-tale illusion—and all I want to do is let her go so that I can embrace the real-life girl across the room.

"What happened? Why are you wearing that jacket?"

Willow steps back and surveys me from top to bottom. "You're hiding the best part of the outfit!"

"Oh, I . . ." I rehearsed saying, *It just wasn't me* earlier this evening, but it turns into, "My dad made me wear this," as I pluck at the jacket. Crap. Come on, Nozomi. Girl up.

"It's okay," Willow says with a reassuring smile. "You still look great."

"And you look like a princess!" I say. Best to keep the focus on her.

"Oh, you're sweet. You don't think the eyes are too much, though?" Willow glances down and plucks at the gauzy layers of her dress before lifting her eyes to look intently at me. She turns her head from side to side, the better to give me all the angles. Her eyes are lined in dark green, with a streak of gold shadow under her lower lashes and sparkly green and gold shadow on her eyelids—it's a slightly toned-down version of her Titania look from *A Midsummer Night's Dream*.

"It's perfect," I say, and it's true. On anyone else it would look like a costume, but on Willow, it's spellbinding.

Arden enters the atrium with an elegant older Black couple who I guess are her parents. She's just as glamorous as Willow, in a cream-colored gown dotted with dozens of blue appliquéd butterflies. Her hair has been straightened and pulled into a sleek updo and arranged into gleaming black rosettes on top, encircled with blue and white bejeweled butterfly combs. It looks like she's moving in her own personal cloud of magical winged creatures.

Willow murmurs, "Wow."

"She looks good," I say.

"Yeah."

Is that longing I hear in her voice? Regret? I cross my fingers. Please let her be having second thoughts about me. Please let her be wondering if she should try one more time to get back together with Arden.

"Hey! We should get our picture taken before the line gets too long," Willow says, the light and energy back in her voice. She grabs my hand and pulls me to the Instagram booth, and we pose for a series of photos before Mrs. Hsu finds us and suggests in a strained voice that we get to work.

For the first part of the evening, each of us has to do a shift at our daytime jobs: Willow works the gift shop. Max and I hand out pamphlets of some of the blurbs I've written and take guests on tours of the museum. Dela is working at the Tanabata Pavilion. Willow and I exchange a few careful kisses (nobody wants to risk messing up their lipstick this early in the evening), before she drifts off to her post at the gift shop, mouthing *Later,* and giving me a look that would have set Past Me's insides on fire with longing, but which, now, only makes me a bit wistful. She won't like breaking up, but I know that she'll be happier with someone else in the end.

I check my watch. I still have twenty minutes before my first tour, and I want to get in a wish at the Tanabata Pavilion while it's still quiet.

The installation is open but still empty when I arrive.

Good. I stop at the Wishing Table at the entrance to the courtyard, where stacks of delicate origami/wishing paper and ceramic cups full of pens sit at intervals on one side of a long table. After writing their wishes down, guests will hand them to one of five Wish Administrators on the other side who will fold each one into a crane or a butterfly, and hand it back. I pause to write something on a wishing paper and fold it into a crane myself.

I wander through the courtyard, which is suffused with the light of hundreds of tiny LEDs. The origami forms float among them, suspended from the bamboo branches; it really looks like a magical bamboo grove filled with stars, birds, and butterflies. The paper wishes flutter and rustle against each other, and everything is hushed and quiet, the way it should be, so that the wishes can be heard. I know I should exchange my crane for one of the wishes suspended here, but I keep it in my hand and climb the spiral staircase to the roof of the pavilion at the center.

I emerge onto the rooftop platform and pause, surprised, under one of the glass lanterns that punctuate the railing around the deck. Dela is sitting in an Administrator's chair in the opposite corner, lighting the wishing fire in a high rimmed glass bowl. The fire casts a warm glow on her face, which is serious and pensive. She's never looked more beautiful to me. She looks up, and while she doesn't stop and gasp the way she did in my daydream, she does look happy to see me.

"You have a wish to send up?" She nods at the one in my hand.

I look down at it and turn it over in my hands and realize that now I have to give it to her, and I panic. I didn't think this through. She wasn't supposed to be here. What if this whole thing with Dela is just another story I've made up, just another fantasy I've woven out of nothing, to replace the one I let go? Suddenly I'm seized by the absolute conviction that Dela will unfold my wish, read it, and look at me with the same derision that I heard in Helena's voice this spring.

I tighten my grip on my wish and croak, "No, I just picked up some paper and folded it out of habit." I listen to myself in dismay. I meant it to be a joke about all the folding we've done, but it comes out sounding like the lie that it is.

Dela's eyebrow twitches, and she holds out her hand. "Give it to me," she says. "I'm not going to look at it."

"No, really, it's blank. It doesn't say anything," I insist, and hide it behind my back, which I realize too late is about as incriminating as it gets.

"You're lying." She walks over and I crumple it up in my fist and try to decide whether it makes more sense to throw it off the roof or push past her and throw it into the flames.

She reaches her hand out again, and when I don't produce the wish, she sighs and says, "Here." She steps aside and points to the fire. "Do it yourself. Go ahead."

I take a step forward, but then I remember what I promised

myself earlier. Didn't I swear to face every part of tonight—even the painful stuff—exactly as it was? I did.

"You should see it," I say, and reluctantly I hold out my hand and close my eyes.

I feel her take the wish from my hand, hear the paper crinkle as she uncrumples it and unfolds it. There's a moment of unbearable silence, and I picture what she's seeing in front of her. I drew a heart with our names in it, the way you do in elementary school:

Nozomi
+
Dela

"Nozomi plus Dela," she reads. It's so childish. I don't know what I was thinking. I squeeze my eyes shut tighter, aware that I'm trying, ridiculously, to make myself disappear.

There's the soft hiss and crackle of the wish catching fire, and a flash so bright I can sense it even with my eyes closed, and the smell of smoke. And then, unexpectedly, the light pressure of her hand on my arm. I open my eyes in surprise. What I want more than anything is for her to pull me toward her, to see her brown eyes sparkle before I close my eyes again and feel her lips on mine . . . No. Stop. Even though literally every molecule in my body is straining toward her, she's still with Arden, and she thinks I'm with Willow. Which I am. Right. She's probably just going to apologize and say—

"Arden and I broke up."

I blink at her. "You what?"

"We broke up. A few minutes ago."

"Oh" is all I say, but in my head, it's mayhem. Why tonight? Whose idea was it? What did they say to each other? And I know this is exactly the path I just told myself I wouldn't go down, but . . . does this have anything to do with me?

Oblivious to my internal frenzy, Dela continues. "I wasn't planning to. But she started talking about all these plans she had for us as a couple, and I couldn't handle it. I told her it was too much for me, and she accused me of not trying hard enough. And I said why should I, because she's obviously still into Willow. Like at her birthday party? I know she sang that song to me and all, but she couldn't keep her eyes off you and Willow. Well. Off Willow, anyway."

"Oh," I say again. "And then what happened?"

"We yelled at each other for another minute. But then she admitted I was right. And then we broke up. So . . . yeah."

"And why, um." I swallow. I have to ask. "Why are you telling me this right now?"

"Come on, Nozomi. You have to know."

Her hand reaches toward mine, and our fingers catch for a moment before she lets go. I feel as if my insides have turned into pure light, that it must be pouring out of my very skin.

It's happening. I can hardly believe it. My fantasy is actually coming to life, and for once, I'm not making any of it up. Right? It's not the result of some elaborate scheme I've concocted, it's not all in my head . . . Dela decided this all on her own. It's perfect.

We're standing so close to each other that I can feel the heat coming off her body, so close that I think I can even feel the air around us and between us pulsing with the rhythm of her heart, or mine, or our two hearts combined. And then, just as I lean forward to kiss her, I hear a voice.

"Nozomi?"

Willow is standing at the top of the stairs, her lustrous green gown shimmering in the fairy lights, her face like stone.

40

I JERK AWAY, QUELLING THE URGE TO SHOUT, "It's not what it looks like!" because, of course, this is *exactly* what it looks like, and for some reason this strikes me as so funny that I have to fight back a very strong impulse to laugh.

Dela says quietly, "I think I'll leave you two to figure this out," and starts to walk across the deck, but she's waylaid by Willow, who has moved forward and planted herself directly in Dela's path.

"No, I don't think you should go anywhere. This is the second girl you've stolen from me, and I think you should stay here and deal with the consequences."

Dela's shoulders stiffen. "I didn't *steal* anyone from you. Arden chose me. And Nozomi—"

"And you!" Willow turns on me. "Cheating on me! How

could you? At least Arden had the courtesy to break up with me before she hooked up with someone else."

"I—but it wasn't—I thought . . ." I don't have an excuse, so I go on the offensive. "You only started dating me to make Arden jealous!"

"That was *pretend*! And it was *your* idea in the beginning, as I recall. I started dating you—actually *for real* dating you—because I liked you!"

"What the hell are you two talking about?" Dela interrupts.

"Nothing!" I yelp. "Nothing. It's not impor—"

But Willow says with an exasperated sigh, "Nozomi and I had this plan to fool everyone into thinking we were together."

"I really don't think we need to—" I try again, but Dela silences me with a glare.

"You were pretending that you were together?" she prompts Willow with mock politeness. Dread closes its icy fingers around my heart and lungs.

"It started as a joke because everyone went nuts over this one photo we posted, and then . . . um . . ." Willow slows down, since, I guess, this part isn't really flattering to her, either.

"You wanted Arden to get jealous and go back to you," Dela says, having figured it out herself. "Nice."

I feel like I'm trapped in a leaky barrel, plunging through boulder-studded rapids toward a giant waterfall. I have to do something. I have to get myself out of this nightmare before—

"Oh, hi, Arden," says Dela, her cheery voice practically

bleeding irony. "Welcome to the party. Did *you* know about their little plan to break us up?"

Aaaanndd over the waterfall I go.

Willow whirls around as Arden rises slowly from the staircase like some kind of avenging angel. "No, Dela, I did not," she says. "But I do now." She gives me and Willow a look so deadly, I'm surprised we don't burst into flames on the spot.

"Nooo! No! No, no, no!" I hear myself shout, and even I wince a little at the shrillness in my voice. "You've got it all wrong! You weren't supposed to break up! That was *not* the plan." Not *my* plan, anyway. Willow gives me a slightly wild-eyed look but doesn't say anything, so I plow ahead. "I mean, yes. *Willow's* plan was to get you two to break up. But in *my* plan, you *weren't* supposed to break up. *My* plan was supposed to end up with you two staying together and Willow falling in love with me!"

All three girls are staring at me with their mouths open.

Oh. Crap.

This is not good.

Dela is the first to speak. "Let me get this straight. Your plan was for Willow to catch feelings for you, but now you're interested in me. Which can only mean that she didn't fall for you, because if she had, you'd be with her." Her expression shifts as she talks, as if she's seeing a picture come gradually into focus. "So you're hooking up with me to make yourself feel better because the girl you *really* want isn't into you." She looks at me and I can see the pain blooming in her eyes. "I'm your consolation prize. I'm your rebound hookup."

"No, that's not it at all!" I protest. "She *did* catch feelings for me. But I've realized that *you're* the one I want to be with. So you're not a consolation prize. I was offered the grand prize trophy, but I chose you instead! And . . . that didn't come out the way I meant it," I finish feebly, when I see the expressions on everyone's faces.

"Hang on." Arden looks at me and then at Dela, her brow furrowed. "Are you saying you're into her?" She points at me. "Because that seems like pretty important information. Funny you didn't mention it when we were talking earlier."

"They were practically having sex up here," says Willow.

"We were not!" says Dela hotly. "We weren't even kissing!"

"Whatever. You might as well have been," says Willow. To me, she asks, "Is this for real? Are you breaking up with me right now?" Despite the scorn in her voice, she looks genuinely hurt, and remorse courses through me.

"No, no! I would never! I mean, um." I falter, looking at Dela, who crosses her arms and cocks an eyebrow. "Not right now."

"Why not?" The pain is now threaded with bitterness. "Because I'm your *grand prize trophy*?"

"Well, I mean. That's a good thing, isn't it?" I mumble, and honestly, I don't know why she's *quite* so upset about that part. What's wrong with being wanted?

"I'm not a prize to be won," says Willow in dignified tones.

"And what about me?" Arden demands. She looks at me and says, "Did you consider my feelings for even a *second*? You say you didn't want me and Dela to break up, but that was only so you could get what you wanted. And now that you want something else, you're okay with getting Dela to break up with—"

"*We* broke up because of *your* feelings for *Willow*," Dela interjects.

"And *your* feelings for *Nozomi* had nothing to do with it? Right." Arden scoffs.

"Wait—you broke up?" Willow says to Arden. "Because of . . ." She places her hand on her chest.

"Yes," says Dela.

Arden glares at Dela and says, "Partly."

Then it hits me. If I can get everyone to see what they've *gained* out of this, instead of what they've lost, maybe I can reverse some of the damage.

"You know, this really isn't so bad," I say. Dela, Willow, and Arden look at me, united for the moment in disbelief. "Just hear me out, okay? This is all just a huge misunderstanding. It's . . . it's kind of comical, actually." I attempt a lighthearted laugh. None of them laugh with me. That's okay. Keep going. "I had such a crush on you, Willow, and I didn't think someone like you would ever consider dating someone like me, so when that first photo got all those comments—pretending to be together seemed like a good way to put the idea in your head. It always works out in books and movies, right? Only

I've realized—and I think you know this, too—we're not right for each other. But Dela and I are. And Dela and Arden broke up with each other because"—Arden laser-eyes me—"*partly* because," I amend myself hastily, "Arden still has feelings for you. And you're not over Arden. You told me that." Here, Arden looks at Willow, who blushes. "So . . . what if you two got back together? That's what you want, isn't it? And—and Dela and I can be together, which is what *we* want. See? It all works out. Everyone gets what they want, everyone's happy. It's like a real-life rom-com!"

My voice has taken on a slightly hysterical pitch. But it really *is* the perfect romantic comedy plot. The heroine's best-laid plans go awry, but in the end, everyone ends up in love and all's well that ends well. I know, I *know* I said I wasn't going to do this anymore, but I'm *right* this time.

Please let me be right.

Arden is staring at Willow, and Willow is looking at me with slightly less hostility than before. Yes! Please let her have heard my point. Please let her feelings for Arden win the day. Please let me not have screwed everything up.

"Is that true?" Willow asks Arden. "Do you still . . . ?"

Arden looks down and says, "Yes," so softly I barely hear her.

"And you're . . . not . . . with Dela anymore?" Willow asks. She looks at me and Dela and adds pointedly, "I don't want to sabotage anyone's relationship."

"Let's not forget that your whole plan was to sabotage me

and Arden in the first place," says Dela with equal pointedness.

"We broke up like half an hour ago," Arden confirms.

"Hm." Willow draws herself up to her full height and looks at me. "Well, I'm glad we never got serious. You and I are over."

I nod meekly.

Then she says to Arden, "I'm leaving if you want to come with me."

Arden looks at me and Dela like we're a pair of bugs she'd like to squash. "I don't see any reason to stay," she says, and she and Willow turn and glide to the staircase. I hear their heels clacking down the stairs; I look down and see them sweeping through the bamboo grove like the majestic fairy queens that they are, with their skirts sparkling and swirling behind them. And with a tiny pang of regret, I watch Willow as she follows Arden through the door and disappears into the museum. My dream of being her girlfriend really is over now.

Which leaves me and Dela and a thousand paper wishes.

I turn to Dela hopefully. "So. It's just us, then. That's what we both wanted, right?"

But Dela says, "No, Nozomi. This is not what I wanted. I mean, it's not—" She runs her fingers through her hair and looks at me sadly. "I'm not sure I want that anymore. You lied to me, you manipulated me and Arden—and Willow. You set up this whole scheme without ever thinking about how anyone else would feel."

"I did, though," I protest. "I did think about how you would feel! And Arden. And Willow. I thought about it a lot!" This was all *about* everyone's feelings. I built my entire *plan* around people's feelings!

"If you call trying to engineer our breakup—"

"YOU WEREN'T SUPPOSED TO BREAK UP!" I shout. "How much clearer can I make this? You and Arden breaking up was *Willow's* plan! In *my* plan, you were supposed to stay together! It was supposed to be a happy ending for everyone. And it still can be—it's just different from what we expected. Better than expected! I only wanted everyone to be happy! Why isn't that good enough?"

"Because you *lied*," she shouts back. And then she hurls my words back at me: "How much clearer can I make this?"

"It's not like I concocted some evil, twisted plot to break people's hearts. It wasn't mean-spirited lying. It was just fake dating," I mutter. "People do it all the time in rom-coms."

"Life! Isn't! A rom-com! What part of that do you not understand?" says Dela. "Real life isn't a story starring you and your feelings and whatever feelings you *make up* for other people. It involves other people, and other people's real feelings, and you don't get to control any of that. When you make up your little stories to control people's feelings, you end up hurting them. They start to hope for things, instead of preparing for the biggest loss of their lives. It's the worst feeling in the world to be betrayed like that, Nozomi. And if you don't like it, if you can't accept that you've hurt people, then too bad for you."

It takes me a second to get it. I look at her, still wounded and grieving and still fighting ghosts. Of course that's where her mind went. She couldn't help it.

But that's not where we are. *This* situation is about Dela, me, Arden, and Willow, and yes, it's horrible and painful and awkward, but it's not fair to try to make me feel even more guilty because she's still mad at her mom. I didn't lie about *dying*.

It occurs to me that maybe I'm not the only one stuck in a story I'm telling myself. And that maybe that's what she needs to hear. I remember what she said that first time we really talked, about not protecting her feelings. Well. Okay, then. Let's do this.

"No, Dela, it's too bad for you," I say. "Because you've given up. It sucks what happened to your mom, and I get why you feel betrayed. But you're letting it poison the rest of your life. You won't let anything good or hopeful come in. You're a pessimist and a cynic and you see yourself as this, like, victim of this terrible tragic story, and yeah, it's sad, but you don't have to make everything revolve around it. Stop wallowing in your tragedy and stop taking it out on everyone else and start living your life!"

Which is the meanest thing I've ever said to anyone, and I immediately regret every word of it, but she turns and storms off before I can apologize, and I'm left alone on the roof with the wishing fire flickering merrily away in its glass bowl.

The rest of the evening feels like an out-of-body experience. I watch myself as I walk back into the museum and take up my post at the bottom of the ramp to the second floor. I look on as I smile and lead gala guests around the museum and encourage them to look at a glass cube as art that changes depending on where it is, and where you stand when you look at it. Most people buy it, or at least pretend to; one guest just guffaws and thanks me for the best BS explanation of contemporary artwork he's heard in a long time. "That's all modern art is, if you ask me," he says, lowering his voice. "Bullshit masquerading as high culture." He looks down at his tuxedo, and then at all the fancy people in their fancy clothes, and adds, "That pretty much sums up all of us here—myself included!" and wanders off in search of a champagne refill, laughing uproariously at his own joke.

41

IT'S THREE O'CLOCK IN THE AFTERNOON AND I'm still in my room with the shades drawn when Max taps on my door and says, "Hey. Stephen and Lance want to know if you're alive in there."

I groan and pull the covers over my head.

"Okay, so that's a yes," he says. I hear him open the door. "Would this have anything to do with the drama from the gala?"

"No." How does he know? My weeping may have been tragic and pitiful last night, but I know it was silent. And I can't imagine that anyone would have told him what happened.

"Really? Because Stephen and I went looking for Willow to investigate reports that the shop was unstaffed, and we found her with Arden in that little back office."

This shocks me into peeking my head out. "What . . . were they . . . ?" Wow, that was fast. You'd think she'd have waited a *little* longer before flinging herself into Arden's arms.

"They were just talking, if that's what you're asking," says Max drily. "Anyway, Willow said you knew."

"Oh." Okay.

"So did you?"

"Yeah."

"And . . . is that why you're in here shunning the daylight?" Ughh. "No. Not exactly."

"Then what the hell is going on? Whose life did you screw with this time?"

Which reminds me of just what a huge, unfixable mess I've made, and the weeping starts again. I pull my covers back over my head, and Max says, "Hey, I was just kidding! I was kidding, Zo, I'm sorry!"

"Go away," I say.

I feel his hand on my back. "I'm sorry. Really." And then he sighs and says, "I'll listen if you want to talk."

"You're gonna laugh. You'll say *I told you so.*"

"I promise I won't," he says. "Just tell me."

So I do, because I'm the world's biggest sucker when he's nice to me. By the time I'm finished, his face is buried in his hands and he's muttering unintelligibly to himself.

"Don't. Say it," I snap as he takes a breath to speak.

"I wasn't going to," he says irritably. "But I will say that you better tell Dad and Stephen about all of this because Dad is seriously considering texting Mrs. Hsu about how she needs to talk to her daughter about respecting relationship boundaries."

"What!? Why didn't you tell me that to begin with?" There's very little Max could have said that would have gotten me out of bed quite as fast as this.

I send him out and get dressed. He was right about how this would come to bite me in the ass. Dad in don't-you-mess-with-my-offspring mode is not a pretty sight, and I would be mortified if he got into it with Mrs. Hsu.

And Dela was right, too. I did see myself as the heroine of my own movie, where no one had their own stories outside of how those stories affected mine. This thing with Dad is just another example of how my plans—and now, their collapse—have affected other people in ways I never thought about, because I was so focused on myself and what I wanted.

Thirty minutes later, Max has gone to Baba's house to Baba-sit, and Dad, Stephen, Lance, and I are sitting around the kitchen table with beers (them) and a bottle of small-batch ginger ale (me). They look at me expectantly. It's excruciating, but I tell them everything, all the way up until a couple of hours ago.

"Honey, I'm sorry." Lance reaches across the table and gives my hand a sympathetic squeeze.

"Am I a terrible person?"

"You're a teenager," says Dad, thus winning the award for

Least Comforting Thing to Say to Me Right Now.

"It's hard to remember that pursuing your own happiness can hurt other people. Especially when there's nothing wrong with the thing you want," says Stephen. "I'm just sad that things are so hard between you and Dela."

"Me too," I say miserably. "What do I do now?"

"Have you tried apologizing?" asks Lance.

"She won't talk to me. She told me to leave her alone."

"Sweetheart." The look on Dad's face, the empathy in his voice, nearly makes me cry.

"And did you?" asks Stephen.

"First I told her that I wasn't going to give up that easy, and that I was going to text her every day until we talked."

All three men wince. "Oh, honey," says Lance. "She blocked you, didn't she." A bell dings and he goes to the counter to punch down a mound of bread dough that's been rising in a covered bowl.

"I thought that it would show her how much I cared and how much I wanted to work things out."

"Of course you did," Dad says. "My little engine that could." He reaches out and smooths my hair, and that makes me feel a little better. "It's exactly what I would have done," he adds, which makes me feel a little worse. Have I really sunk to his level?

"What if I wrote her a letter? I could apologize and explain everything."

"No!" Lance jumps in. "The biggest mistake you can make is to keep trying to contact her right now."

"But I can't give up! I want to apologize! I want to work things out!" How can that be bad?

"What's more important right now, honey? Her need for space and time to be angry and hurt? Or your need to explain yourself and win her back?" he says.

"My needs, obviously."

"Zozo," Stephen and Dad say simultaneously.

"Fine, I get it, I get it," I grumble. "I was just kidding."

Stephen gives me a half smile, his eyes gentle. "I know it's hard. But this is the best way to show her that you care about her."

"I don't get why she wouldn't want to at least *hear* my side, though." I can't let this go, for some reason. "It would be much easier to leave her alone if I had a chance to say something first."

Dad raises his eyebrows at me as he takes a swig of beer. He puts the bottle down and says, "That's what your mom said when you blocked her."

"That's hardly the same thing. I didn't cheat on my husband and lie to my kids about it. Mom made that choice. And except for me not talking to her, which I'd like to point out is a *consequence* of said choice, she's *happy* with the way things turned out."

Dad says mildly, "I'm just saying."

"It's *different*," I explode.

"She has regrets, though. A lot."

"She should."

Dad gives me that same sad half smile that Stephen did. "Loving someone the way they need to be loved is hard. People can be really bad at it," he says. "All we can do is keep trying."

42

DELA ISN'T THE ONLY ONE I NEED TO APOLOGIZE to. So a week later, I text Willow and ask if she and Arden will come to lunch with me.

I take them to this cute little café that I pass every day on the way to the museum. I've always wondered what it was like, and now seems like as good a time as any to try it out. But the interior smells like dirty dishrags, the pastries are stale, and the "rich hot cocoa" that they advertise in the window is the kind that comes spitting out of one of those cafeteria machines. Quite the apt metaphor for my life right now, I must say.

Still, it's nice to be with Willow and Arden without having to put on a performance, or take care of Willow, or worry about whether this place is cool enough for them. And it's nice to take a sip of this watery hot chocolate and not stress about my lipstick coming off. (I've gone back to a makeup-free lifestyle, and that extra half hour of sleep every morning is heaven.) It's also nice—beyond nice; it's a huge relief—that no one bites my head off once I lay everything out and apologize.

"But why did you feel like you needed that whole elaborate game plan?" Willow says once I've finished. "You understand it's not the fake dating part that makes those relationships work, right? It's the spending time together part that's important."

"I know. But to be fair, you didn't *really* start to be interested in me until you did my makeup and lent me clothes, and I started looking more like . . . well, like you and Arden."

Willow and Arden glance at each other, clearly confused. "What's that supposed to mean?" says Willow indignantly.

"You're both so gorgeous and put together. Your hair, your makeup, your clothes . . . you're so, like, sure of yourselves. You stand out. People like me are just part of the background to people like you."

Willow shakes her head. "That's so not true."

I think it is. But arguing won't help, and I'm about to let it go when Arden surprises me by agreeing with me.

"No, I get it," she says to Willow. "Everyone judges based on appearances. Even if they don't mean to. Plenty of people would ignore me or dismiss me or worse if I didn't dress nice—not that dressing up always works. I'm not even sure *you* would have seen me as someone you wanted to date if I didn't dress up."

Wait. Is she implying what I think she's implying?

Arden says with an ironically lifted eyebrow, as if she's read my mind, "Because I'm Black."

Willow's face is a portrait of distress. "Are you . . . but . . . do you really think if you didn't dress up or wear makeup that I wouldn't date you . . . because you're Black?"

"Oh, I think you would have fallen for my charms eventually." Arden smiles coquettishly at Willow. "And trust me, if I thought you couldn't handle me being Black, I wouldn't be here. But . . ." She hesitates. "I also think the way I dress and act helped you get over, like, an initial hurdle. I'm not saying all this gorgeousness isn't really me." She spreads her fingers and gestures playfully at herself with another smile. "But it helps you see me as someone who's more like you than not. I'm just saying that Nozomi has a point about appearance and first impressions."

"But—but we're past that, right? I was the one who wanted a deeper connection. You were the one who wouldn't let me in."

Arden stirs her iced latte with a wilting paper straw, looking uncharacteristically off-balance. She takes a sip and stirs some more, peering into her glass, out the window, anywhere but at Willow. "You have this way of setting expectations," she says finally. "I feel like you see me in this one context, through this one lens, and you're always saying I'm your dream girl, and how perfect our relationship is. . . . Maybe I was afraid of how things might change if you saw anything that didn't fit with your picture of me."

Willow looks stunned. "But I . . . did I really make it that hard for you to trust me?"

Arden shrugs. "You didn't mean to."

They look at each other, then away. I look at my fingers and wonder if I should excuse myself.

"I don't want perfect," says Willow in a trembling voice. "I know I say that, but all I really want is you. The way you are. No illusions. No acting. Just you."

Her eyes are sparkling with tears. Arden nods and whispers, "Okay," and blinks away her own tears. Heck, *my* eyes are welling up. Willow takes Arden's hands, and the two of them smile and sniffle and gaze into each other's eyes like I'm not even there.

I guess it's time for me to go. Quietly, I pay the bill and leave them to their blissful reconciliation.

I'm so happy for them. Everyone deserves a beautiful romance with a happy ending, and I don't even feel the slightest hint of envy or bitterness that things turned out so well for Willow and Arden, and so rotten for me. Not even one little tiny twinge.

Okay, maybe one. Or two.

43

WE HAD DINNER AT BABA'S HOUSE TONIGHT, and she taught me and Max how to make gyōza. We ate a million of them, and Dad invited me and Max to stay and watch *Love Actually* after she had gone to bed. "For old times' sake," he said, but I know better.

"Why didn't you do something?" I ask when the movie is over. "Why did you just sit there and let Mom do whatever she wanted and not fight for her?"

Dad sips his coffee and smiles at Max, who is snoring softly. Then he watches the credits roll for a while. Finally, he says, "This is going to be hard for you to hear, Zozo, because it's the exact opposite of what Mom and I have always encouraged you to believe. But sometimes love isn't enough. My love wasn't, anyway. Not the way I was doing it or feeling it. Mom gave up on me, and I had to give up on us."

It reminds me of Dela (everything reminds me of Dela). "But that's just lying down and letting things happen," I protest. "What happened to 'never give up on love'? What happened to 'we have to keep trying'?"

"Sometimes you have to give up," says Dad, but before I can get too furious, he adds, "on a *relationship*. Just because one balloon gets away doesn't mean you have to let go of the entire bunch. I gave up on staying married to Mom, on rebuilding what we had—if we had anything at all. But I haven't given up on love."

"But I don't want to give up on Dela. I know I can do better. I want to keep trying."

"So keep trying."

"But what if she gives up on me? I was so awful to her."

"Then you've lost one balloon," he says. "You've learned something about how to keep the rest of your balloons. Watch your balloon until it disappears, and then when it does, enjoy all the balloons you have left. If you don't have any left, go looking for more. The great thing is that you'll never run out of them if you look carefully enough. They're everywhere."

It is about the corniest, sappiest, Daddest thing I think I've ever heard.

I check the clock on my laptop. I hate this. I don't know why I'm doing it.

No, that's not true. I do know. Because I'm not sure if Dad

is a zen superhero, or if he's pretending to be one, or if he's just a pushover, but there's a chance that he's right. Maybe Mom deserves a chance to explain herself. And if she's had the patience to wait for me, maybe I can summon the patience to listen to her. Maybe a person can be angry and hurt and still be willing to listen to the person who hurt them. And okay, maybe there's a little bit of magical thinking going on here: if I listen to Mom, then maybe Dela will listen to me. I know it's not logical. But I can't help hoping.

I keep telling myself that Mom's transgression was exponentially bigger and more hurtful than mine. Of course, Mom didn't also tell me that I was pathetic because I wasn't over my mother's death—though I guess she could only say that to me if she were speaking from beyond the grave. But the point remains. She didn't screw up and then say something cruel, ignorant, and completely unnecessary on top of it.

A notification flashes: Mom wants to hang out.

All right. I will be patient. I will be openhearted. I will treat her the way I want to be treated.

I open the chat window and—oh dear god. Mom was always a little on the artsy, boho side of the fashion spectrum, but over the past few weeks, her look has evolved from Kind of Artsy-Boho to Aggressively Artsy-Boho. It is not good.

She's wearing a white top that looks like it's been made out of a couple of napkins and some string, accessorized with a chunky turquoise necklace around her neck and a paisley scarf around her head. It's a miracle that I don't burn to ashes from embarrassment right here and now.

"Hey, baby!" Mom says, and I can tell she's trying to make her voice sunny and cheerful.

"What are you wearing?" is my response, which is not an ideal way to open a dialogue with your estranged mother (or is it me who's estranged?). But someone needs to tell her the truth about her choices, both fashion-related and otherwise.

The smile on her face wavers just a bit, but she rescues it and it stiffens and stabilizes. "It's a new top I bought on Etsy," she says. "Do you like it?"

"No. It's totally inappropriate."

She immediately gets defensive. "I can wear whatever I want, Nozomi. I refuse to be defined by oppressive social norms around what's considered to be appropriate attire for women my age."

"You look like you're having a midlife crisis. Is that what Mr. Jensen is? Or are you his midlife crisis? Oh no, wait—he's too young for one of those."

She flinches as if I've slapped her, and looks away, pressing her lips together like she might cry. I wait, furious, horrified, and ashamed. I've been despicable to her sometimes—I remember when I was twelve or thirteen, I used to scream, "I hate you! You're the worst mom ever!" at her with shocking regularity—but I've never done anything that made her cry. Only I shouldn't have to feel bad about being rude. *She's* the monster. She's the cheater and the liar.

When Mom turns back to me, her cheery mask has

dropped, and she just looks exhausted. Though she's not crying, which is a relief, because I really would have felt monstrous
if I'd made her cry.

"I love him, Nozomi. And he loves me."

Ugh. I roll my eyes, hard. I know Dad wanted me to listen,
but I don't think I can handle a sappy love story starring Mom
and Mr. Jensen.

Mom takes the hint and tries a different tack. "You need to
understand, baby, your father and me, our marriage—it was
on its last legs. It was dying. *I* was dying."

"Dying," I repeat. The word echoes painfully in the back
of my mind as I think about Dela's mom, who actually died.

"Nozomi, staying together was making both Dad and me
into terrible, unhappy people, and he refused to acknowledge
it. And I'm sorry if this offends you, but what Roy and I have
is real. I'm trying to set an example for you and Max—for you,
especially, as a woman—not to settle for anything less than the
love you deserve."

"Are you *kidding* me?" I can't believe that she thinks
she's being some kind of feminist *role model* for me. "I would
have been fine if you'd gotten divorced and that was it. And
I would've hated it, but I would have understood if you fell in
love with Mr. Jensen and waited till after you left Dad. But you
didn't. You. Had. An. Affair. You keep talking about it like it
was okay, and it's not. I don't care how much you love Mr. Jensen, or how doomed your marriage was. Dad loved you. Maybe
not the way you needed him to, but he loved you. And you

betrayed him. You *must* know it was wrong, or you wouldn't have kept it hidden from me."

Three times, Mom opens her mouth as if she's going to argue, and then closes it. All I know is if she tries to feed me another excuse, I'm shutting the laptop. But finally, she sighs and says, "You're right, Zozo. It was wrong. I shouldn't have cheated on your father."

"No," I say, "You shouldn't have."

She plays with the fringe on her outrageous paisley scarf for a while and I let her. I hope she feels really uncomfortable. Eventually she says to the fringe, "I think I was so caught up in the story—my love story—that I minimized, in my mind, how much it might hurt you. I guess I thought you'd understand, since you're such a romantic. Love conquers all, right?" She looks up and smiles hopefully at me.

I shake my head and her face falls.

"I know I hurt him, Nozomi. And I'm sorry. I'm sorry for hurting you and Max as well. I hope you can forgive me one day."

"I'm still too mad to say," I tell her, and she nods.

"I understand."

And that's that.

It could have been worse, I guess. I'm still boiling with anger, but I'm surprised by how much has drained away—by how much of it wasn't about the affair itself, but about Mom pretending it was okay because L♥VE. At least she finally admitted that what she did was wrong. That feels like a step forward for both of us.

Because what Mom just said about love conquering all? It's what I've always believed. Like Dad said, it's what he and Mom have always taught me. It's so strange. I never thought I'd say that true love isn't the most important thing, that sometimes you have to wait and sort out the rest of your life. And yet, here we are.

44

DAD AND STEPHEN HAVE AN APPOINTMENT
with a dementia care specialist to help them figure out how to
handle the Baba situation, and I've been assigned to keep Baba
company. Stephen said that the specialist had already warned
him that we'd have to prepare for some big changes, which
makes me sad, especially for Baba. It feels like giving up hope,
like admitting defeat, and she hates losing. But maybe being
able to see what's coming, even if it's not pretty, is better than
holding hands and stumbling around in the dark, which feels
like its own kind of hopelessness. And anyway, we can still
hold hands.

Remembering how much she loves to tell stories about
herself, I ask to look at her old photo albums again, and it's not
long before we're sitting at her kitchen table with a pile of them

in front of us. But it turns out I don't even need them. She tells me the story of how she and Jiji ditched her classmates on the field trip to Kyōto, followed by the story of Nana-chan's bus ride, the jump rope champion story, and the near-drowning story, all nearly identical, word for word, to the versions she's told me before.

I try for a new story. I pick out her wedding album and open it. The first two photos are on facing pages: in one, she's wearing a vermilion kimono decorated with golden cranes, bright green pine needles, and white and gold chrysanthemums, with sleeves that reach almost to the ground. Silver fringes and tiny silk flowers dangle from lacquer combs tucked into a traditional shimada-style wig. Her face is powdered white and her mouth has been reshaped by precisely applied scarlet beni, but you can still see those mischievous eyebrows and the stubborn lines of her mouth. Jiji stands next to her in a black kimono and pinstriped hakama, over which he's wearing a black haori embellished with his family crest. On the opposite page, they're dressed in Western wedding clothes; a tuxedo for Jiji, and a short-sleeved white gown with a narrow skirt and an empire waist, and dainty white gloves for Baba.

"Tell me about your wedding, Baba. It looks like it was pretty fancy."

"Ha! Pictures are fancy but the wedding was not," she says. "I borrowed the kimono and wig and we paid extra for the pictures, but we couldn't afford the fancy wedding. We were married in the hotel, with only twenty guests."

Baba returns her attention to the album, turning the pages slowly, past more studio photos of her and Jiji to photos of the hotel, of her sister and her friends all clad in bright, formal furisode, of her and Jiji cutting the wedding cake, and of her dancing with her father, Yoshi-Jiichan. "*Your* mother and father took the dancing lessons before their wedding," she tells me. I've heard this one before, too, and I almost say the next line along with her: "What waste of money."

"Did they do a good job, at least?" I ask.

She snorts. "How should I know? They did all the steps, though." She gazes out the window absently, remembering Dad and Mom's first dance, I suppose. Then she says without looking at me, "I didn't go to Stephen's wedding."

Now, this one is new. I sit up straighter and prompt her. "Why not?"

"I was angry at him. I had the small wedding, your parents had more informal outdoor wedding, and I wanted Stephen to have a big church wedding with the beautiful bride, like my friends' children had. But it's so strange, to see groom and groom. It's a show-off to other people. I couldn't invite my friends from Japan. It was too embarrassing. So I was angry and sad because I had lost a hope and a dream. I thought, if he loves me, he can do a right thing." She pauses here for a breath, which she holds for a moment before releasing it. "It was a mistake. Perhaps my biggest mistake."

I've never heard her admit she's wrong about anything. I feel my pulse start to quicken.

"When did you change your mind and start being okay with—"

She holds up her hand and shakes her head. "I'm not okay with. Gay is not a natural thing."

I feel like she's slapped me with that outstretched hand. "But you—"

"I don't agree with the gay marriage. I don't approve gay. But I accept it because I love Stephen. I accept Lance. Even I love Lance, because Stephen loves him."

This is not what I was hoping for.

She purses her lips in a little frown. "At first, he said I could be in his life if I would love Lance and be okay with the gay marriage. But I told him I shouldn't have to force to change my views just to talk to my son. I was too angry at him for making a condition for me. Then later I said I would accept, but he said that accept was not enough. Back and forth. I had to grow, and he had to grow. It took a long time because our family is stubborn. We don't like to compromise our ideals."

She flips the page and starts off on another story: the time she secretly taught herself to drive her father's car. But I'm still stuck in the past few moments. It took Baba *five years* to compromise her ideals and accept her son back into her life. All that time, all that heartache, and she hasn't really changed her mind. Will she ever?

I may never have the relationship that I want with Baba. I feel pretty sure now that if I come out to her, she'll still love me and want to have some kind of relationship with me. And maybe it'll feel good to be open and honest with her. But I'll always have to know that deep in her heart she doesn't approve of who I am. Her relationship with Stephen is proof of that. And me coming out will probably upset her and cause all kinds of family stress that none of us needs right now. Can I justify pushing her to change and grow for my sake when she's already overwhelmed by the way her life is changing?

Or can I let go of my need for her to change? Can I let go of my dream of having a picture-perfect relationship with her?

I don't want to. But I think I can. I think I have to. I don't have to stop trying to change her mind. But if Baba can't love me the way I want her to right now, maybe I have to learn to accept her love in the only way she can give it to me.

45

NOW THAT THE TANABATA PAVILION IS UP AND
running and fully staffed by volunteers, and the gala is over,
Dela has stopped coming to the museum. So at least I don't
have to see her avoiding me. The obvious drawback to this,
of course, is that I never get to see her at all, and I'm left to
the hellscape of my imagination. Most of the time I imagine
her with some new girl who's smarter and more talented and
better dressed than me, who looks like a supermodel, and who
doesn't do anything rash or mean or insensitive. It takes every
last atom of my (limited) self-control not to pop into the gift
shop every other day to ask Willow if Arden has heard from
Dela, and if Dela is seeing anyone new. The cold dread I feel
when I imagine that the answer is yes is another deterrent.

I've been trying to let go of so much: my dream of being

part of an impeccably styled, A-list romantic comedy couple; my need for Baba to be strong and sharp and willing to change; my illusion that Dad really worked to save his marriage; my fury at Mom for cheating. I'm trying to face the messiness of my life and not run away from it, and to focus on loving quietly and patiently, with empathy. It's been feeling more and more possible, but I still struggle.

I wish the universe would just let me hang on to one small thing, just this one little relationship with Dela—but it's been a couple of weeks with no word from her, and I'm resigning myself to letting go of her, too. It's really hard.

Max is tapping away at his laptop and I'm on my way out of the staff room to do some Digital Archive Interning one morning when he calls to me.

"Hey. I heard one of the Tanabata Pavilion volunteers is out sick today. And Dela's subbing in."

Dela? I freeze.

He clears his throat and says with a mischievous grin, "If you hurry, I bet you can get the other volunteer to give you their shift."

Why does he have to be so mean? "Shut up, Max. I learned my lesson, okay? Reality, good. Escapist rom-com plans, bad. You don't have to rub it in."

"No!" Max's eyes go wide. "I didn't mean it that way. I meant for real. Listen, I know I give you a hard time about all your romantic bullshit, but . . . life is less fun when you're not reaching for something big. I don't like seeing you all sad and defeated. And I think you deserve a chance to apologize, at least. And maybe if you're lucky . . ." He shrugs.

I stare at him. "Wait—are you suggesting that I take an emotional risk without any guarantee that it'll pay off? Are you perhaps implying that a little optimism might be a good thing?" I almost smile at this.

"Best-case scenario, you get back together. Worst-case—and this is more likely, if you ask me—you apologize and she tells you to fuck off."

"So there's a best-case scenario now? And it's a happy ending? Who are you, and what have you done with my brother?"

"Did you not hear me say the worst-case scenario is the most likely?"

"But the best-case—"

"Shut up and go to the courtyard."

There she is, in her usual jeans and T-shirt; her jacket is hanging on the back of her chair. I freeze. What do I do? I can't go in and sit down next to her. But I can't exactly quit and walk out.

I could, though. I could pretend to be sick. I could pretend to sprain my ankle and have to be taken to the hospital. I could pat my pockets and go, "Oh! My phone!" and run out like I'm just going to fetch it, and then never come back. Dela probably wouldn't care, anyway. In fact, she's probably hoping I'll do just that. She's probably hoping I'll—

Sigh.

I can't leave.

Deeper sigh.

It would be cowardly.

I'm taking a breath and getting ready for an even deeper sigh when someone taps me on the shoulder and says, "Um, excuse me. Are you going in?"

It's one of the Academy of Art students, looking very artsy with multiple facial piercings and electric-yellow hair. I step aside and let them pass, and then, because I am not a coward, I walk into the courtyard after them.

Dela greets Yellow Hair with a polite smile, which fades when she sees me.

"Um. I think I'm supposed to sit here with you for this shift," I say.

"Welp. Have a seat, then."

We sit at the Wishing Table in agonizing silence for ages, during which Dela doodles on one of the wishing papers and I watch her out of the corner of my eye and wish I were anywhere else. I can't even escape into my phone, because we're supposed to be playing a role, like actors.

It's torture.

I try to call up all the imaginary conversations I've had with her over the past weeks, but the only opening lines I can remember are terrible:

Hey, how've you been?

I can't stop thinking about you.

Ahoy there, matey! (This was if I saw her at the Pirate Supply Store on Valencia, where I went with Stephen last week.

Though I would not have said *Ahoy there, matey!* in real life. In my imagination, though, Dela thought it was hilarious.)

Out of sheer desperate need for something to do, I start doodling on my own piece of wishing paper. I hope she doesn't think I'm copying her.

I go through a couple of sheets of scribbles and curlicues, and then as my mind drifts, I find myself drawing a horse—the only thing I've ever practiced drawing. It's appalling—vaguely equine at best, only distinguishable from any other quadruped by virtue of its mane and tail. On a whim, I add a horn on its forehead, and immediately regret it. Now it's a vaguely horse-shaped creature wearing a party hat.

I'm about to crumple it up when I have another idea. Carefully, I draw a speech bubble over my ~~party horse~~ unicorn and write in my fanciest script *You are a rare and magical creature and I'm sorry I was such a monster.* Only I run out of room, so I have to write *such a monster* in a microscopic scribble. I probably should have just stuck with *I'm sorry*, but it's too late now. It'll be too hard to draw another horse. Unicorn. Unidentifiable four-legged beast.

Before I can change my mind, I fold it into a crane, and push it over to Dela—just as she drops her own origami crane in front of me. We look at the cranes, and then at each other. This has to be magic. I don't dare speak; I hardly dare to even breathe. I pick up the crane that Dela has given me, and unfold it carefully, keeping an eye on Dela so we open our papers at the same time.

I undo the final fold and my heart leaps. It's a horse—or the suggestion of a horse, just a few strokes drawn with a swift, sure hand. Along one of the lines that represents the mane, written in tiny block lettering, are the words *I'm ready to listen.* I turn my head to look at her and see her squinting at the last line of my message. "It says, 'such a monster,'" I tell her. "You are a rare and magical creature, and I'm sorry I was such a monster."

Her mouth is a line, but it's turned up at the corners. She faces me and turns my picture toward me, and I can see the laughter in her eyes. "You weren't kidding about not being able to draw horses," she says.

"It's a unicorn," I say a little defensively. "And I can't help it if I suck at—"

"I like it." She allows her mouth to open into a full smile, and my heart feels like it might burst—from joy, from relief, from hope. She likes my drawing. That has to be a good sign.

There's no time to say more, though, because a field trip of campers comes in, and then another one, and we're busy folding wishes until our shift finally ends at lunchtime and Dela gets up and stretches one of those velvet theater ropes across the brass posts on either side of the wish-writing table. The other Administrators stroll out, chatting and checking their phones.

"Can you two lock up for lunch?" says the yellow-haired art student, and Dela nods. And then we're alone.

Dela takes my paper out of her pocket. She reads it again, and then looks at me expectantly. "So?"

"I'm sorry. For a couple of things. Number one, I said some really shitty, ignorant things about your mom, and about you, and I'm sorry. You should be allowed to feel sad or angry or however you feel for as long as you need to. And I understand if you hate me and you don't want to see me ever again."

Dela nods silently and I feel my heart pounding in my head. All the hope I felt a moment ago starts to drain away. She liked my drawing, I tell myself. She smiled at me and told me she liked my drawing.

"It's not fair to ask me to be happy and positive right now," she says finally.

"I know. I'm sorry."

"Not everyone can be as upbeat as you all the time, even under normal circumstances."

"I know that, too." I hesitate, then add, "But I'm not sorry about that part."

Dela smiles wryly. "That's fair. And maybe I could lighten up a little. I'm working on it."

I move on to the second part of my apology. "Also, I'm sorry I lied to you about Willow. I'm sorry I set up that whole scheme in the first place. I wanted to remake myself out here, like, take on this new identity—and I got carried away, I guess. I treated you—I treated everybody—like just another part of my plan. But you were the best part. The only real part. I'm sorry I treated you that way. I'm sorry I hurt you."

"Why, though? Why would you even need to remake yourself?"

I tell her what I've figured out about myself—about how dreaming up and focusing on my plans for a perfect summer was so much easier for me than slogging through the painful realities I was facing. How Willow seemed so perfect, so far above the messiness of my life with her beauty and poise and talent—and how it felt like winning her heart would help me rise above my parents' failures, and Baba's, and my own.

"Anyway, I don't want that anymore. I don't want some perfect fantasy that I made up in my head. I want something real, with a real person."

"I may be real, but I'm a mess."

"So am I. But I'm trying to be better. And anyway, life is messy. So." I take a breath and say, "Do you think you might ever want to start over and try again? For real? With me?"

This is the part where we kiss. Where we stand nose to nose, arms around each other, our lips almost touching but not quite. The part where, for a moment, for an eternity, we float in that liminal space between fantasy and reality, where I feel her chest expand as she breathes in, and I see her eyes flutter closed as her lips part in a tiny smile, and then I don't see anything else because my own eyes are closed and we're kissing, and it's exactly like in all the movies and books, just like I've hoped and dreamed it would be.

Ha. I wish. But that's not what happens.

What happens is Dela sighs. A big, long sigh. She says, "I'm not going to be the bright, sunny girlfriend of your dreams."

"You like lemon meringue pie. You can't be all bad."

"I don't want to be a sucker."

"You won't be a sucker. You'll be someone who believes in something good."

She takes my hand in both of hers and turns the palm up, then back over. "You're leaving at the end of the summer."

"We'll make it work. We'll talk all the time. Maybe I can fly out and visit."

"You won't lie to me and tell me things are fine, and then bail? Long-distance relationships are hard. I don't want to fall in love and then get burned."

I choose my words carefully, for once. "I guess you're right. I can't promise anything." I think for a moment, then add, "Life doesn't always turn out the way we want it to, and love doesn't always conquer all. You know that better than I do. But you can acknowledge that things are bad, and still find a way through. And maybe sometimes that means you stop loving each other, or maybe you have to find a new way to love each other. I know that. So, okay. It'll be hard, but I'm still hopeful. I want us to be together and I'm choosing to believe that it's worth trying. Because I'm really, truly, head over heels for you."

I feel a little light-headed, and I can't quite believe myself—I really laid it out there. Panting slightly, heart racing, I watch Dela's face for a reaction.

"Wow," she says. "That was quite a speech."

"I meant it," I say.

"I believe you," she says, and smiles.

Okay, now. Now is when we kiss, for real.

Author's Note

In *Love & Other Natural Disasters*, I wanted to explore (among other things) the complexities, contradictions, and limitations of love, which means that some of the characters end up making tough compromises in order to maintain loving relationships. I think it's important to remember, however, that everyone has to make decisions according to their individual situations, that love can be deeper and more forgiving than we might expect, and that people can change and surprise us in all kinds of wonderful ways. Whatever compromises you make— or don't make—in your life, my wish for you is that you end up surrounded by people who can give you exactly the kind of love you need.

xoxo

Misa Sugiura

Acknowledgments

During the process of writing and revising this book, I discovered that romantic comedies feel light and effortless because their authors (at least this one) toil mightily and with lots of help to make them so. Hopefully, I've pulled it off—and if I have, you may give credit to the following people:

I owe so much to my agent, Leigh Feldman, for her faith in my abilities and her staunch, savvy, tireless support of my writing, both as my advocate and as my adviser. I am beyond lucky to have her in my corner.

If you found yourself swooning or laughing or nodding in agreement as you read, it's thanks to Stephanie Stein's patient, good-humored, and insightful guidance from the (not very romantic or very comic) first draft all the way to the gorgeous book you are holding in your hands.

Speaking of which, you would not be reading or listening to this book if not for the work of all the talented people who put the finishing touches on it, gave it its physical shape and form, and sent it into the world: Stephanie was ably assisted by the indispensable Louisa Currigan; copyeditors Christine Corcoran Cox and Alexandra Rakaczki smoothed out the bumps in my grammar and usage (all remaining errors are mine); Alison Klapthor designed the sweetest cover ever; artist Hannah Good brought their ideas beautifully to life (follow her on Instagram @hannagoodart); and my publicist, Aubrey Churchward, and HarperTeen's fantastic production (Erin Wallace and Kristen Eckhardt), marketing (Lisa Calcasola and Audrey Diestelkamp), conference and convention coordinators (Lindsey Karl and Stephanie Macy), and school and library mavens (Patti Rosati, Katie Dutton, and Mimi Rankin) spread the word about this book and made sure it got onto bookstore and library shelves, both real and virtual.

I am extremely fortunate to have been able to work with authenticity readers C. B. Lee, Camryn Garrett, Zia Stephen, and Kyra Miller, whose counsel on sensitivity and authenticity issues helped deepen the characters, sharpen the dialogue, add texture to the settings, and even improve the plot of this book. Any inaccurate or insensitive representations are on me.

Many thanks to Traci Chee, Gordon Jack, Kelly Loy Gilbert, Lisa Moore Ramée, and Sonya Mukherjee, the brilliant YA authors who read early drafts and helped me get unstuck when my characters went on strike. (Do yourself a favor and read all their wonderful books.) Many more thanks go to my monthly writing group, Viji Chary, Sandra Feder, Alicia Grunow, Louise Henriksen, and Rebecca Isaacson, who convened over Zoom to provide feedback on key scenes.

I had help from lots of talented teens this time around. Audrey Mueller and Ava, Millie, and Addy Kopp gave me smart, valuable notes during my first round of revisions; Grant McKenzie, Hunter Johnson, and Tai Hofmeister of the real (and perfectly named) band Ruse generously agreed to appear on the page at Arden's birthday party. See their website (www.ruseofficial.com) to learn more about them and their music.

My sons helped me with teen diction and reminded me whenever I shouted, "I hate this!" that I say that in the middle of every book I write. They teach me daily how to love deeply and live authentically even when it's hard.

My husband, Tad, loves me for who I am even when I'm crabby and difficult and refuse to admit that I'm wrong. He is my rom-com hero and proof that true love really is possible.

Don't miss . . .

"Fresh, funny, authentically messy, and sweetly romantic."
—KELLY LOY GILBERT, Morris Award finalist for *Conviction*

It's Not
Like It's
a Secret

Misa Sugiura

1

"SANA, CHOTTO . . . HANASHI GA ARUN-YA-KEDO."

Uh-oh.

Something big is about to go down.

It's Sunday afternoon and we're almost ready to leave the beach at Lake Michigan, where I've begged Mom to take me for my birthday. It's just the two of us because Dad is away on business—he's always away on business—and I'm crouched at the edge of the water, collecting sea glass. I've decided I'm not leaving the beach until I've found sixteen pieces, one for each year. Sweet sixteen and never been kissed, but at least I'll have a handful of magic in my pocket. Sixteen surprises. Sixteen secret treasures I've found in the sand.

And now this: *hanashi ga arun'*.

Mom never asks if I want to "chat" unless she's actually

gearing up for a Serious Discussion. She walks over and stands next to me, but I'm too anxious to look up, so I continue picking through the sand as possible Serious Discussion Topics scroll through my head:

She's pregnant.

She has cancer.

She's making me go to Japan for the summer.

"It's about Dad," she says.

Dad's leaving us.

He's dying.

He—

"Dad got a new job with start-up company in California."

—what?

"It's the company called GoBotX," she says. "They make the robots for hospital surgery."

I don't care what the company makes.

"Did you say *California*?"

When I say Serious Discussion, I suppose I should really say Big Announcement Followed by Brief and Unhelpful Q&A Before Mom Closes Topic:

"How long have you known?"

"Dad applied last month. He signed contract today."

"Why didn't you tell me earlier?"

"No need."

"What do you mean, no need?"

She shrugs. "No need. Not your decision."

"But that's not fair!"

"'Fair' doesn't matter."

"But—"

"Complaining doesn't do any good."

"Are we all moving? When?"

"Dad will go in two weeks, at end of May. He will find a house to live, and we will go at end of June."

She doesn't know the answers to the rest of my questions: Where will we live, where will I go to school, what am I supposed to do all summer all by myself. Then she says, "No more questions. It is decided, so nothing we can do. Clean the sand off your feet before we get in the car."

We don't talk on the way home. Mom's not the type to apologize or ask questions like, "How does that make you feel?" My own unanswered questions swim in circles around the silence like giant schools of fish, chased by the most important question of all—the only one I can't ask.

When we get home, I go to my room to finish some homework. But before I start, I take out a lacquer box that Mom and Dad bought for me when we visited Japan seven years ago. It's a deep, rich orange red, and it has three cherry blossoms painted on it in real gold. Inside, I keep my pearl earrings, a picture of me with my best friend, Trish Campbell, when we were six, all the sea glass I've collected from trips to Lake Michigan, and a slip of paper with a phone number on it.

I pour in my new sea glass, take out the piece of paper, and stare at the numbers. They start with a San Francisco area code. Could this be the real reason we're moving?

The paper is small and narrow, almost like something I might pull out of a fortune cookie. Like if I turn it over, I'll find my fortune—my family's fortune—on the other side: Yes, these numbers are important. No, these numbers are meaningless. But of course the back of the paper is as blank as ever. I bury the phone number under the other things, put the box away, and lie down on my bed to think.

A few minutes later, Mom comes in and frowns when she sees me lying on my bed, staring at the ceiling. Mom is the most practical person I know. She doesn't sugarcoat things, and she doesn't look for a bright side. Which is okay right now, because a fake spiel about exciting new experiences, great weather, and new friends would just piss me off.

"I am sorry that you have to leave your friends," she says, not looking one bit sorry, "but the pouting doesn't make your life better. It just prevents you from doing your homeworks."

Then again, it probably wouldn't kill her to show a *little* sympathy. Also, she's totally off base about what's upsetting me. But since correcting her is out of the question, I just turn and face the wall.

"Jibun no koto bakkari kangaen'no yame-nasai. Chanto henji shina-sai."

I don't think I'm being selfish. But since "AAAGGGGH-HHH! I'M NOT BEING SELFISH!" is probably not the "proper reply" she's looking for, I just say, "I'm not pouting. I'm think-ing."

"There is nothing to think about. If you want to think, you

can think of being grateful for a father who works so hard to get the good job."

"It's not that I'm not grateful—"

"Ever since he was teenager," she continues, "Dad dreamed of working for the Silicon Valley start-up. That's why he came to United States."

"But what about me? Don't *my* dreams count?" Okay, maybe now I'm being a little selfish. Especially since the truth is that I don't actually have what might be called dreams. What I have are more like hopes: Straight As. A love life. A crowd of real friends to hang out with. But it's also true that if I did have dreams, they wouldn't count anyway. Not to Mom.

"You are too young for the dream," she says. (See?)

I want to remind her that she just said Dad's start-up job was a teenage dream. But she has a conveniently short memory about things she's just said that contradict other things she's just said, so instead, I switch tracks. "What about *your* dreams?"

"My dream is not important."

"Ugh. Come on, Mom."

She crosses her arms. "My dream is to make the good family. I can do that in Wisconsin or California."

"Mom, why do you say stuff like that? Like, 'Oh, our lives are just going to change forever, no big deal.' It *is* a big deal! It's a *huge* deal!" I can hear myself getting screechy, but I can't help it. Dad changes our lives around without consulting anyone—well, without consulting me—and Mom just . . . lets it happen.

It would make anyone screechy.

"Shikkari shinasai," she snaps.

But I don't know if I'll ever be able to do that: gather myself into a tight little bundle with everything in its place—shikkari—like she wants. I put my head under my pillow.

She's quiet for so long that I begin to wonder if she's left the room. When I peek out from under the pillow, she's waiting for me, her face softer, even a little sad. "Gaman shinasai," she says, and walks away. *Gaman*. Endure. Bear it without complaining.

Her life's motto and my life's bane.

2

I'M UNDER ORDERS TO PACK ALL OF MY belongings into boxes labeled KEEP and THROW AWAY by the end of the week. Which is harder than you'd think, because who knew I had so much stuff? I'm drowning in a sea of books, old papers, and odds and ends that I've spent over a decade smushing into the corners of my closet, cramming into the back of my desk drawers, and piling on the edges of my bookshelf.

It started off easily enough:

My lacquer box: KEEP

Four Super Balls from who knows where or when: THROW AWAY

Collection of poems by Emily Dickinson, my favorite poet: KEEP

Assorted elementary school certificates: Perfect Atten-
dance, Fourth Grade Math Olympiad Participant, etc.: THROW
AWAY

But now it's getting tricky, because some of the things I've
dug out have some messy feelings attached to them, and I'd
rather not go there right now.

Don't think. Just sort. The wedding picture that I found
in the attic last year and that Mom refuses to display because
it's "showing off." KEEP. The Hogwarts robe that I loved so
much, I wore it two Halloweens in a row. I'd meant to be
Hermione but everyone said I was (who else?) Cho Chang.
THROW AWAY. A cheap plastic vase left over from my thir-
teenth birthday party, which three girls skipped to go to the
movies instead. THROW AWAY.

Don't think.

As I toss the vase into the THROW AWAY box, a scrap of
fabric flutters out: a swim team ribbon that I found in the Glen
Lake Country Club parking lot when I was seven. Hmm. Now
that's a feeling I can do something about.

All the best families in Glen Lake belong to the Glen Lake
Country Club, which has a historic redbrick clubhouse, a lush
green golf course, and a lily-white membership. Back in grade
school, when Trish and I spent more time together, she used
to bring me with her to the club all the time during summer
vacation for barbecues and lazy afternoons at the pool. But in
high school, she became suddenly, dazzlingly popular. The
boys and queen bees started swarming, her Instagram filled

up with likes and pictures of people who barely acknowledged me in the halls, and our country club days became a thing of the past.

Don't get me wrong. It's not like she's been mean, or anything. Days might go by without her texting me, but she always answers my texts right away. She's usually too busy to hang out with me, but she's always apologetic. And even though it's painful to sit on the edges of her crowd at lunch, listening to stories about parties I haven't been invited to, it's not like anyone's ever asked me to leave the table.

When we used to see more of each other, Trish was always after me to "open up" and "spill everything." Which, whatever, she's an oversharer. For example, she texted me seconds after Toby Benton, her first boyfriend, put his hand up her shirt in eighth grade. (OMG I just let Toby touch my boob!! Under my shirt!! 🫣 🔥 🔥 🔥)

But whenever I thought about telling her anything important, I froze. Even now, when people talk at lunch about who wants to hook up with who, or who hopes their dad gets custody on the weekends because he's totally cool about drinking at the house—I feel relieved that no one's especially interested in me or my life. I don't want anyone poking around and freaking out about what's wrong with my family, what's wrong with me. Like what if I'd answered honestly the first time Trish asked me at the beginning of freshman year, "Sana, who do *you* like?"

"Well actually, Trish, I think I might have a crush on *you*."

Nope. Forget it. Not happening. I'm not even a hundred percent sure it's true, and life is already complicated enough.

But now . . . things have changed. I mean, we leave in three weeks, and I might never see her again. So I'm going to ask her to bring me to the first Glen Lake Country Club barbecue of the summer, for old times' sake. I've got nothing to lose, right? We'll get drunk together for the first and probably last time—I've never been drunk before—and maybe . . . maybe if all goes well, she'll get nostalgic, we'll bond again, and . . . and . . . something good will happen. I don't want to think too hard about what, exactly. But something good.

On Friday, I find Trish in the parking lot after school, sitting with her boyfriend, Daniel, on the hood of his car. Daniel is a big-shot football player, with a face like your favorite love song and a body like fireworks on the Fourth of July; sadly, though, he doesn't have the brains or a personality to match. His biggest claim to fame is that he got a Mustang for his sixteenth birthday—and one week and a six-pack of Milwaukee's Best later, he drove it into a tree and his dad gave him *another Mustang.*

When I ask Trish about the barbecue, it turns out she's already going with Daniel, but she seems excited to have me come, too.

"Oooooh!" she says. "We. Are going. To get. So. Wasted. Together. It'll be so much fun! And Daniel can drive us back to my house afterward." She snuggles up to him. "Right, honey?"

"Sorry, babe, but Drew and Brad are back from college and they're bringing a bottle of Jägermeister tomorrow night." As he says this, a couple of football bros walk by. "Did you hear that?" he shouts at them. "Jäger shots!" The three of them high-five each other and howl together like a pack of teenage werewolves, and for the millionth time, I wonder what Trish sees in him. Beyond the obvious, I mean.

When Daniel sees that Trish—thank goodness—is unmoved, he whines, "Come on, make someone else drive."

Trish rolls her eyes at me. Then she wraps herself around Daniel and says, "I'll make it worth your while," and whispers something to him. She starts nibbling his ear and kissing his neck, and pretty soon they're making out right in front of me, and I have to look away or I'll vomit. If she's using her womanly wiles to get her way, he seems to be falling for it—though from the sound of it she's having as much fun as he is.

But at least he seems to have agreed to drive.

Trish and Daniel arrive to collect me and my overnight bag at six o'clock on Saturday. I've persuaded Mom to let me go by reminding her of all the times I used to tag along with Trish's family to the club when I was younger. "Her parents will be there the whole time," I said, which is true.

The plan is to begin sneaking vodka from flasks during dinner, while the adults are too busy getting drunk themselves to care. Then we'll go to the golf course to finish up. I can hardly wait. All I ever hear about is how much fun it is to get drunk, and I am so ready to try it out and be part of Trish's life again, even if it's just for one night.

We arrive at dusk, and pretty soon Trish and I are on the patio with barbecue on our plates and orange juice (and vodka—shh!) in our cups, surrounded by a hive of popular girls. Minutes into my first drink, my face starts to feel warm, and Trish says, "Sana, are you okay?"

"What?"

"Your face is, like, turning red. Like you have a sunburn."

I rush to the bathroom to check the mirror. I'm flushed and my eyes look puffy, as if I'm having an allergic reaction. I'm about to start trying to remember what I've eaten when I take another look in the mirror and recognize someone: Mom. I look just like Mom when she has a glass of wine with dinner. Dad, too, come to think of it.

I realize it's the alcohol, and I don't dare take another sip. Plus my head is starting to throb, and I have a feeling it will get worse the more I drink. Great. Leave it to my parents to make it genetically impossible for me to fit in—as if my hair and eyes weren't enough to make me stand out in a crowd of white kids, now I can't even get drunk with everyone.

Trish makes sympathetic cooing sounds when I tell her I can't drink, but then something catches her eye, and she squeals. "Ooh, Sana, look—there's Mark Schiller! He told me when we got here that he thinks you look hot! I bet he's look-ing for you! Come on, let's go dance!"

She grabs my hand and drags me to the dance floor,

collecting members of the hive on the way. In a couple of minutes, the guys wander over as well. Trish vanishes for a moment, then reappears. And suddenly, despite my genetically enforced sobriety, I'm feeling pretty good. Pretty great, actually. I mean, look at me. Here I am dancing, surrounded by the cream of the social crop with Trish by my side and ignoring Daniel for once.

Then it gets even better. The first notes of that old Beach Boys version of "California Girls" start to play, and Trish shouts, "I requested this for you, California girl!" She gives me a hug while the entire hive shrieks, "Sanaaaa!" over the music, and now I feel positively giddy. I wonder if just that little bit of vodka and orange juice was enough to get me drunk, after all.

The Beach Boys begin cataloging the different girls in the United States—the hip East Coast girls and the Southern girls with sexy accents, and when they get to Midwest farmers' daughters, we all raise our arms and scream our Midwestern hearts out. We scream for good old-fashioned Midwestern values and hospitality, for prairies and cornfields, for the Heartland. *No matter what,* I vow, *I will always be a Midwesterner.* Things are pretty good here, really.